A FORTUNATE ACCIDENT

The Amagi Series, #2

S. J. PAJONAS

Onigiri Press

© 2022, S. J. Pajonas (Stephanie J. Pajonas). All rights reserved.

Cover design by Najla Qamber Designs.

This is a work of fiction. Names, characters, businesses, places, events, and incidents are either the products of the author's imagination or used in a fictitious manner. Any resemblances to actual persons, living or dead, or actual events is purely coincidental.

❦ Created with Vellum

A FORTUNATE ACCIDENT

1

THE BONFIRE CRACKLES AND SPARKS, throwing hot embers into the sand surrounding the fire pit. The heat dances off my skin, warming only the front of my body. I take a deep breath of crisp autumn air laced with smoke and exhale it all out.

"Ah, I love campfires. Reminds me of far-school." I pull my knees up and rest my arms and head on top. I glance at Saif sitting next to me and remember another campfire we sat around many years ago. Just the fact that he's here with me is such a surprise. I expected him to leave, to be gone from the madness of my family and me.

He smiles and lifts his mug of mulled wine. I tap my mug against his, and we drink. Ah, Vivian makes the best mulled wine.

"Your cousin throws quite the fall festival party," he says, snaking his arm over my shoulder and pulling me to him. I try not to blush at the public display of intimacy, but the fire is hot, and my cheeks are already flush. Besides, I'm not modest. Just unused to this. "I haven't been to one of these in years."

We both smile at the laughter that erupts on the other side of the fire from Vivian's relationship network and extended

1

family. Little Ilaria sleeps in a carrier on Mat's back, and he lightly bounces to keep her quiet. His hands flash with USL. I wish I knew USL. I can only fingerspell, and Mat is too fast for me.

Everyone is here tonight. There are six identical bonfires across the property. All the workers and staff enjoy the night with their families. A few years ago, Vivian couldn't hold this festival party because she had lost the farm. Then she couldn't hold the event because they were too far in debt. Now, things are looking up.

I shrug. "I've never been to one." I press my lips together as I look around. "Seems like it's a good time."

Saif pulls away from me. "This is your family."

I laugh. "It is, indeed. Still, I have never attended a fall festival." I look away from him. "You know why."

Because every time I asked to go, Dominic grounded me and sent me to bed without dinner, or, my favorite, shamed me into submission. Eventually, it was easier not to ask. I sip more mulled wine.

"Did the dads keep you from this, too?"

Saif is still learning about the depths of my childhood abandonment. I don't think he really believed me at first, but it's beginning to sink in.

I jerk my head at Vivian. "Ask Vivian. Go ahead."

She obviously hears her name because she spots me and dances around the fire to us. I snicker at her swaying hips and silly arm pumping. She's a dork, and I adore her. Especially since she's made a home for me here.

"Ask me what?" She plops down next to us.

"Have I ever been to a fall festival party here?" I ask.

Saif says, "Please don't say no."

"This?" Vivian waves her hand in the air at the party atmosphere. "No. Sorry. Skylar has never come. I invited her every year, but... you know." She shrugs, and Saif nods. I drink even more mulled wine. "I just wish I had realized what was going on back then. Maybe..." Her voice dies. "Anyway, it's nice that Ana could attend too."

We all lean forward to look at Ana, sitting in a camping chair and talking to Lia a little farther away from the fire than everyone else.

"Thanks for inviting her." I nod to Vivian before dropping my eyes to the fire. She didn't have to invite Ana. Hell, I have serious guilt about being here myself after everything we've gone through in the last two weeks. But I'm trying to let people forgive me. I'm deciding to let people in. I don't deserve the kindness though.

I try to relax into Saif's side, let him hold me, or just be the wall I lean against. But my body is stiff, remembering all the times I stayed on the family ship as a kid instead of doing the things I wanted, longed to do.

"She's welcome here any time." Vivian reaches over and squeezes my knee. "I hope your room isn't too small. It used to be a closet."

I shrug. "It's bigger than the room I grew up in."

Vivian pulls her lips in and presses them closed.

"I know, I know," I tell her, trying to stop the onslaught of questions. We should probably talk more about it, but now is not the time.

"Hey, I have a great idea." Vivian's eyes are bright with mischief. "Your birthday is coming up soon. Let's have a party."

All the heat I had banked up sitting in front of the fire zips away.

My birthday?

"Ah, no," I say, clearing my throat. "That's okay. I'm sure I'll be knee-deep in mud and fucking terrified for my life in the jungles of Rio."

Saif's eyes widen, and he inhales. "I *love* birthdays. Love them." He nods at Vivian. "Yes, let's do it."

3

I open my mouth, ready to launch into all the reasons I don't want a birthday party, when Ana is suddenly standing over us. With the brightness of the fire and the darkness of the surrounding areas, I didn't see her get up.

"Mom's here. With Dom," she says.

"What?" I spill my mulled wine on the ground as I stand up. "Where?"

Ana points, and there, two bonfires away, Mom is stalking across the lawn with Dom in her wake.

"Fuck," I breathe out. I close my eyes. "Could I not get one party without her bullshit?" I set my mug aside. "I guess that's too much to ask."

My chest tightens as I gauge her mood. Like a fine wine left out in the sun for twenty days, Mom's expression is sour. Her mouth is pinched, and her eyebrows have a permanent trough between them. Hauling trash for two weeks aged her by ten years.

I wish I could say I was sorry about it.

"I'll go deal with her," Vivian says, grasping and squeezing my arm.

"Stop," I tell her. I can see Vivian's network across the fire, and Gus and Jinzo have caught on to the tense situation without us having to say anything. "I'll deal with it. It's my problem."

"It's *our* problem," she insists. "I'm the one that cut off the gravy train two days ago. I'm surprised it's taken her this long to get here."

I sigh and try to pull myself together before Mom is in front of me. Vivian had said she was moving to cut Mom off from the family funds, but I didn't think it would be something that affected me. I figured she would take the blow, understand instinctively why it happened, and then slink off into the stars.

No such luck.

"Skylar, Vivian," Mom says, arriving in front of us. I

glimpse movement from across the fire and find Vivian's network moving in our direction. Saif stands by my side. Lia and Carlos are back in the shadows. "Thanks for inviting us to the party."

My eyes flash to Vivian, but she shakes her head. We did not invite her.

"Can I speak to you both in private?" she asks.

"Mom," I start with a huff and a sigh, "I didn't know you'd be here, or I would have prepared Saif ahead of time."

"Who?" she asks, her voice touched with annoyance.

I glance at Saif, and his face is the picture of grace with the hint of a practiced grin. I hope he's not offended by Mom and her low-key bitchiness.

I school my voice and tell it to stay steady. "Mom, this is my... boyfriend" — I force the word out of my mouth — "Saif Bhaat. Saif, my mom, Fusako Kawabata."

Saif holds out his hand to shake Mom's, but Mom stares at him with an open mouth.

"You have a *boyfriend*? Since when?"

I close my eyes against the anger in her voice. I knew 'boyfriend' was the wrong word to use as soon as it left my mouth. Not because I don't want Saif to be my boyfriend. I sound like a damned teenager, but I want a committed relationship, even if I try to run from it.

It's just that I should have known Mom would latch onto any label as a way to question and badger me.

"She doesn't have boyfriends," Dom pipes up from behind. "She flies and fucks. Don't listen to her."

Saif's hand drops. My body heats another hundred degrees, and not from the fire.

"Hey, now," Jinzo says, stepping in front of Dom. "Don't speak to Skylar that way."

Dom steps into Jinzo's personal space, and my heart races.

"Who the fuck do you think you're talking to?" Dom asks,

5

staring down at Jinzo. Jinzo is not the tallest of Vivian's men, but he's her number one for a reason.

"I'm talking to a dead man if you keep this up," Jinzo replies.

Tingles wash down my back, and fear sucks away all the heat I had built up. I will never forgive myself if something happens to Vivian's network.

This was such a great night, and now...

"Whoa, whoa, whoa." I warn, holding up my hands. I huff a laugh and pull a smile from thin air. "Guys, this is unnecessary. Put your dicks away."

Mom rolls her eyes and scoffs at me. "Skylar, language."

"Oh shit," Saif mumbles.

But no, I will not take the bait here. I should tell my mother that no one gets to police my language anymore, not even her, but this situation is already tense. I reach over and squeeze Saif's arm.

"It's fine. I'm going to take Mom to the house for a chat."

I'm prepared to tell him he doesn't have to come with me because that's what Saif does. He inserts himself in pretty much everything I do. I'm slowly getting used to it.

But he nods.

"I'll save your seat by the fire."

I let go of a held breath and shake out my shoulders.

"Mom, let's talk in the house." Dom turns to join us. "You're not invited, Dom," I say to him as we walk past.

"I go where your mother goes," he replies.

Of course, he thinks that, but I'm not having any of it. I stop in my tracks, Mom by my side.

"No. You don't. I just told you to stay here, and that's where you'll stay. You're not in charge."

Behind seething Dom, Vivian lifts her chin.

"Skylar's right." She steps forward next to Dom. "This is my house and my land. Skylar will go with her mother by herself to the house."

Dom's jaw works back and forth before I see the resignation in his eyes. He can't throw his weight around here, and I am not going fucking anywhere with someone who threatened to kill me only a week ago.

Turning my back on him, I sweep my arm out at the lantern-lit path to the house.

"Let's go, Mom."

2

Our walk across the lawn is quiet. My neck is so tense I can't look at Mom as we enter the house. I sigh at the warm, dry air, the bright lights, and the sound of the farm caterers in the kitchen. There are still plenty more hours to go, full of food and fun.

If only.

"Let's go to the office," I say, leading Mom down the hall and around the corner to Vivian's office. I shut the door behind us and cross the room to the side table of liquor Mat set up in here.

"Whisky?" I ask, holding up a glass.

"No." Her tone is dry and bitter.

I glance at the glass in my hand. Hmmm. What would deaden the eventual pain of this meeting? Getting really sauced. I pour three fingers' worth of whisky and add a splash of water.

"Fine." I lift the glass and smile. "All mine."

Mom stands rigid in the middle of the room, so I take the chair opposite Vivian's desk and sit.

"How's the Mikasa? Although, I suppose, if Takemo Diaz kept his word, you should be off trash hauling duty now."

"Skylar." She nods her head, her blunt bob cut swaying around her chin. "Do you want to explain to me what's going on? Because throwing a fit and cutting me off from the family funds was not how you were raised."

"Throwing a fit? You still think of me as a toddler, don't you?" I swirl the whisky in my glass and watch it coat the sides. "I guess I shouldn't be surprised since that was the last time you were my mother."

My comeback hangs in the air between us. I lock eyes with Mom, and I don't let go. She leans in and sits down in the chair across from me.

"That's harsh, don't you think?" Her voice is so sharp it could separate time and space. "I gave birth to you, taught you how to run the cockpit, kept you fed and clothed."

"And that's pretty much it, right?"

She huffs through her nose. "Well, once we learned you were failing every class you were ever in and fighting constantly with your dad and Dominic, I decided it wasn't worth the effort to spend more time with you."

My breath halts in my lungs hearing this admission from Mom. I nod slowly, taking the statement in and picking it apart in my brain. I aced every class, every test I ever took, so this is another lie. To her, I was a failure and trouble and not worthy of her attention. She had given up on me before I had ever gotten anywhere.

Failure.

Trouble.

Unworthy.

I've heard those words a lot in my lifetime.

I open my throat and slam the whisky, letting it burn all the way down to my stomach.

"Yet, you still trained me to be a pilot." I set the glass on Vivian's desk. "And you must have seen my grades there. They were perfect."

Mom shrugs. "I couldn't let you go without having something, but even now, I see it was a mistake."

She turns her head to the side, revealing her profile. I catch my breath at the memories of her back when she loved me, back when she cared. Her face would loom above me — I was small then — and I would always reach out for her cheeks, rest my head against her chest, inhale her clean scent, and let the warmth of her body seep into my bones.

I sniff up, pushing the memories away. No.

I reach into my gut for the fire that always burns there.

"Mom, we need to come to an understanding," I say, sitting forward. "You've been led astray by what Dominic has told you for years."

"Ha!" she bursts out.

I close my eyes, grit my teeth, and take a deep breath through my nose.

"See?" she says, pointing at me. "Look at you. You never could control your temper. You fought with Ana constantly as a child. Don't try to deny it. She came to me crying more times than I can count."

Okay, yeah, when I was six and raising my younger sisters, I was mean as fuck. I know I was. I was a terrible mother to them. I never hit them or anything. But my words were cruel because I was afraid of being beaten by Dom. When Ana or Jukia stepped out of line, it was my fault.

It was always my fault.

"She's in rough shape now because of you. And don't even deny all the times you hit Dominic, too. I saw the bruises."

I inhale a sharp breath. What's this now?

Oh my God, the lies go on and on.

I can almost feel Dom's spirit over my shoulder, smiling and nodding his head, proud of this web of falsehoods he's concocted over the years. He created a whole other reality, a different timeline from what I lived in.

"I never laid a hand on Dominic. But he did hit me plenty of times as a kid until I could defend myself."

"Oh, come on, Skylar. That man is a teddy bear. There's no way he ever laid a hand on you."

"You think?" I ask.

"I know," she responds, poking herself in the chest. "You don't think I checked the video logs?"

Sweat beads on my upper lip, and blood leaves my head.

What the hell happened to my childhood? Am I insane? Did I imagine everything that happened to me? They all say I was a terrible, no-good person. They believe I'm an idiot and an abuser.

I lick my bottom lip and glance at the empty tumbler on the desk.

What if I am?

"I saw it all," Mom says, standing up. "You would yell and scream and come at Dom with your fists up. I couldn't believe it. Don't you remember our sit-down chats where I asked you to be nicer to him? You always said you would, and then you always broke your promise to me."

I open my mouth to fire back about how Dom would take me to the utility closet where there were no cameras and throw me against the shelves, always careful not to do enough harm that someone could tell what happened.

Mom shakes her head. "You should be ashamed." She sighs and rubs her face with both hands, a gesture I've seen Vivian do when she's at the end of her rope.

"And it looks like you've lied to Vivian and the rest of the family about how you were cut off and sent packing by an ungrateful mother and her abusive network. I thought you had returned to me for forgiveness and that by fighting for the business, you were going to join us and be a part of our family for real."

Tears spring to her eyes, and my gut fills with dread.

"But no. You sabotaged even that by joining forces with Takemo Diaz and making a mockery of our family."

"I did not 'join forces' with him. I did everything I could to get the business back."

"Yeah, well, you certainly did a bang-up job there."

Anger grows in my chest. She's so ungrateful. "I got you out of trash duty. Takemo kept his word, didn't he?"

Her face twists in confusion. "He did. Dominic said he made a deal with Diaz to relieve me of that route. I may be off trash duty, but I'm still out there flying for that bastard."

So, Dominic is going to take credit for that too?

Mom shakes her head and tears fly. I have never seen my mom cry before, and this... this reason for the tears breaks my heart and enrages me at the same time.

I sigh. "I honestly cannot tell if you're sad or you're trying to manipulate me, too."

"For fucks' sake, Skylar." She groans and throws her hands up, letting them crash down on her hips. "You are impossible."

I swallow and consider my options here. They won't believe me. No matter what I say, it will always be my fault.

I have no options.

"Fine. You want to do it this way? You want to end this publicly?" Mom's voice climbs another notch.

I hold out my hands, begging her to slow down. "What do you mean?"

I feel like I'm only getting half the conversation here. There's subtext and innuendo I don't understand.

She huffs an exasperated breath. "I read your last message to me. How you want me to choose between you and the rest of the family?"

My whole body cools. What the fuck is she talking about? I never sent a message. I did compose a vidmessage a while ago, before the Bridge tournament, but I never sent it. It's just sitting in my queue.

"I never sent a message, Mom. What's going on here?" I stand up and look around, but I don't know what I hope to find in Vivian's office. Maybe someone standing behind her desk who'll jump up and scream, 'Surprise!,' and tell me this is some horrible joke?

"You're going to deny that, too?"

"Oh my God, I'm going to be sick," I mumble as my head whirls. "Do you still have the message? Show it to me."

I wait while Mom considers me. Her eyes bore through my head, and her chest heaves for a few breaths before she tips over her wristlet, gestures a few times, and my wristlet pings with an incoming message request.

It's text. It's not video, at least not the one I recorded and never sent. This message has my encrypted signature on it, though. Whoever did this is super slick. There are even trace-route notes that lead to Carlos's Estrela system we use on the Amagi.

The message is a sick joke that makes my stomach churn. I issue a very similar ultimatum to what I had put in my vidmessage, but the subtext is twisted. My eyes scan down.

"How could you sell the business out from under me when you knew I needed it? I was going to take it and finally make it more than you ever could have."

Yikes. I know Mom. She would not have taken this well. She always had pride in how successful her business was before the trouble our family went through.

"I didn't send this, Mom." My voice is strangled through my constricted throat.

"Of course you did," she snaps back. "I had it checked out by three different security specialists."

"*I didn't send this, Mom,*" I repeat, stressing every word.

"It's too late to cover this up, Skylar." She clears her throat and raises her shoulders. "We're taking you to court in Sakata City. I am stripping you of your inheritance, and I'm repossessing the Amagi. Giving it to you and Vivian was one of my worst mistakes. All I've done since is regret the head trip it gave you. We're going to take away your status and your name, too. I'm handing everything left down to Jukia. Ana wants no part of the business, and I understand that after the rough life she led with you as her older sister."

My mouth drops open. This is going from zero to nuclear wasteland in a blink. What the fuck happened?

Oh, wait. I know that already. Dominic.

I jump up from my chair with my hands splayed out in front of me. "Mom, wait. Wait." I press my lips together and think. Think! What can I say to make this better? Where can I start?

Thankfully, she stops in her tracks and looks at me.

"This is all... This is backwards. Dominic abused *me*, abused the other dads. He took everything away from me, bit by bit, until I had almost nothing left but my pilot's license and the Amagi. He even took you." My voice cracks, and tears fill my eyes. "You were supposed to be my mom. You were supposed to look after us..."

Mom's cheeks redden. She points her finger at me. "Don't you dare. My God!" She lifts her face to the ceiling. "The depths of your lies are insane, Skylar." She shakes her head.

Her stony expression stops me cold. Whatever she's been told, it's concrete in her head. She couldn't see the truth, even if it was right in front of her.

Throughout my life, I have read countless tales of this sort of thing happening, mostly in fiction. Someone is fed enough lies through their lifetime, and they can no longer tell what's the truth. Dominic tried to do this to me. I spent my entire life hearing how I was worthless, a horrible human being, a terrible sister, an undesirable daughter. But I never believed his bullshit. I tolerated it because I had to.

Mom, though... It looks like she bought all the lies.

Good job, Dominic.

This can't be happening. I'm doubting my own sanity here, but I blink my eyes and breathe, and everything is still real.

Mom slips past me into the hall, and I take a moment to gather myself and follow her out.

"Mom, please listen to me. I'm not lying. I love you. I love our family. I've only ever wanted to follow in your footsteps. Please don't do this. Please listen to me."

A sob bursts from my lips as she slams through the front door and onto the porch.

Vivian and her mother, Aunt Mayumi, are standing on the front walk, their arms folded across their chests to hold in the heat. Their heads snap to us as Mom storms down the steps.

"Fusako, what's going on?" Mayumi asks, reaching out for her sister. Mom sidesteps her.

"I can't believe you're letting her stay here," she snaps at Mayumi.

"Skylar?" she asks, and Mom nods. "Of course she can stay here." Her eyebrows draw together in confusion. "Vivian and Skylar have been best friends for years."

Vivian takes one look at my tear-stained face, and her expression hardens.

"What's going on?" Vivian demands.

"You've cut me off," Mom says, pointing at Vivian. "And so now, I'm cutting Skylar off. I've had it with all of you. You want to play with me? Make me regret selling off my business because I wouldn't give it to my wreck of a first-daughter? Well, here you go. I'll see you in court."

Mom turns and stalks off, and I don't go after her.

She's gone. Lost to the lies of Dominic.

"Court? What's she talking about?" Mayumi asks.

I wrap my arms around myself, trying to ward off the chill of the night. I miss the campfire already, but Saif is back there, and once again, I'm too embarrassed, too chicken to tell him what's happened. At least not yet. He wants me to be open and trusting, and I'm willing to try. But, shit. I need to really think about this first.

I need a game plan.

I need some space.

I shake my head at Vivian and Mayumi and turn to walk off.

"Sky?" Vivian asks, running after me.

"Don't," I snap at her, turning around to wave her off. "Just leave me alone for a bit."

She stops and nods.

I walk off into the property along the road that leads to the back fields where no one will be. Fuck this world. Fuck this life. And most of all, fuck this bullshit. The lies. The deceit.

Everyone wants to push Skylar to her breaking point?

Go ahead, and fucking try it.

3

I don't sleep. I walk and sit outside all evening until dawn colors the edge of the sky with deep purples and scorched oranges. I don't know what I'm going to do, but I have to do *something*. I can't ignore this situation anymore. When I check with my gut, there's only one thing it's saying to me.

I have to fight this. Dominic and the dads walked all over me for my entire childhood. I can't let them get away with this. It would be easier to lie down and have them take everything from me. But I won't. I can't.

Not if I'm going to save my very soul.

Because my soul is at stake here. A court case will be a public affair, and Dominic would love it if he could sully my name and make me pay for... well, existing. I can't let the Duo Systems think this story of my life is true. No one will ever work with me again if they do.

I have a super keen memory, and it has never failed me before. I *remember* everything that happened to me. But their narrative is so different from mine. Was I wrong? Was it all my fault? My memories are so clear, but they could be wrong.

My memories could be wrong.

I slip into the house before dawn, and no one is up, not even early riser Ilaria. I'm quiet in my bedroom as Saif sleeps in the bed. My heart aches as I watch his chest rise and fall. We're just getting to know each other, and my drama keeps getting in the way. I still need to connect with him, get to know him, and have him get to know me, but I can't do that while I'm constantly fighting these battles.

I grab new clothes, shower in the downstairs bathroom, and leave to catch a train to the other side of Sakata City. It's the beginning of rush hour, so commuters and those with early classes at school crowd the train. I get a seat for the second half of the trip and stare out the window, letting my brain turn over my options as the train winds through the southern suburbs of Sakata City.

My brain hurts from all the thinking, so I switch over to my messages for the last ten minutes of the trip. Sigh. Takemo Diaz is at the top of my message queue.

His handsome yet infuriating face sits right in front of me. *"Hey, Skylar. I just wanted to confirm that I pulled your mother off trash hauling a few days ago. She was pretty belligerent and annoyed, despite the easier line of duty."*

He laughs, and I huff a breath through my nose.

"Now I know where you get it from. So, you still owe me an explanation of how you pulled off that win at the Bridge tournament. Don't think I've forgotten. I plan to pry it out of you if I can. Maybe we'll run into each other at the job site sometime soon. Though not too soon. I'm just getting over the last time we spent time together. You really pack a punch, Skylar."

He winks, and the message ends.

What an asshole.

I turn off my Estrela access as the train makes it out to the western towns. My stop is Katano, a sleepy little speck of a place, filled with quaint houses and small farms.

I take a deep breath before I announce my presence at

Dad's house. It's been a while since I was last here, and I'm not sure of his sleeping habits. He was always an early bird, so I hope that hasn't changed.

"Skylar," he says, opening the door with wide eyes. "What are you doing here so early?"

I inhale and catch the scent of cinnamon and cloves. Dad's been baking. The tea towel tucked into his pants pocket and a light dusting of flour across his sweater affirm the suspicion.

"Ana just got home three hours ago. She's dead asleep." He steps to the side and admits me to the front entryway.

"I never went to bed, so I won't stay long."

His eyebrows climb. "You must be tired. Can I get you some coffee?"

"Please."

I follow him into his kitchen and nod at the apple pie cooling on the counter. Dad's cat, Cleo, meows and undulates in and out of my legs, hoping for a treat. I pick her up and pet her until those wonderful purrs come from her chest. She's the sweetest cat, and I love weaving my fingers through her long fur and burying my face in her coat. I set her down once Dad hands me the coffee cup. Ah, coffee. Pure life, right here.

"Thanks," I mumble, turning and sitting down on the couch.

Dad sits across from me in his recliner. Looking at him, I'm struck by how much he's aged in the last few years. His dark wavy hair has more silver strands than I remember, and a set of crow's feet frame his light brown eyes.

"So, you've probably heard about what happened last night?"

His mouth pinches. "No. I wasn't up yet when Ana came home. Why? Was there a problem at the fall festival?"

"Mom hasn't spoken to you?" I ask, probing deeper into his personal life than I have ever before. Yes, our usual conversations are hopelessly shallow and vague. I sip my coffee and wait.

He hesitates for a long moment before sighing. "Skylar, I haven't spoken directly to your mother in two years."

"What?" I pull back. "How is that possible? You were both at my graduation party."

He shrugs and shakes his head. "Dom handles the correspondence now. Your mother didn't speak to me at your party. Not one word."

I set the coffee aside. "What happened?"

"Skylar," he pleads, his voice weary. "Let's not get into it."

"No," I say forcefully. "No. We are going to talk about this. I don't care how embarrassing it is for you. My whole life is at stake now."

"What do you mean?"

I wave his concern away. "We'll get to that in a minute. Spill it."

He spreads out his hands. "Once we gave you the Amagi, I told your mother I didn't want to take part in the family anymore because I didn't like the way Dominic treated everyone."

"And she didn't believe Dom was anything but kind," I say, filling in the blank.

He shakes his head. "She loves him the most of us all. She then told me how horrible you were. Swears she saw video footage of *you* being abusive. That you came after Dominic, and you treated Ana and Jukia terribly." He worries his hands together, and I hold down the rising anger in my gut. "I didn't know how to convince her, so I didn't try." He shrugs again.

I could launch into a tirade right now about how he was my father and he was supposed to protect me. But I'm stuck on the truth of my memories.

"So, it really was Dominic, and it wasn't me?" This question shrinks me back to a scared little kid again.

"It wasn't *you*, Skylar. I mean, I didn't see everything, but you were a good kid, or at least tried to be."

I breathe out a long, slow breath and close my eyes. The statement is ambiguous, but I'll take it.

The lack of sleep has made me both bone-tired and jittery. I pick up my coffee and gulp it down.

"Okay." I breathe in and out again. "Okay. Well, if you think it wasn't me, and I'm certain it wasn't me, then we should be able to convince a judge it wasn't me."

"A judge?" Dad pulls back, his eyes wide.

"Mom's taking me to court here. She's stripping me of my name and inheritance." I grumble, "Not that there's much left after what she did. And she wants the Amagi back."

"What?" Dad's skin whitens by several shades.

"Yeah. So, what I'm going to do is hire an excellent lawyer, and then you, Ana, Miguel, Juan, and me, we're all going to go before the judge, and —"

Dad pops up from his seat. "No. No, I will not go to court."

My heart races. "Why not? You just said —"

"I know what I said." His voice rises in anger. "And telling you you're not crazy is one thing. Going to court to tell them what happened? No. No. We will just ride it out and hope Dom doesn't come for us."

I stand up to face him. "I can't do that." I throw my hand out to the side. "I have a life to lead. I'm not living some cushy retirement, baking pies and painting landscapes. I'm trying to build my network and a new business. If Mom strips me of everything, no one will touch me. I'll lose it all."

He lifts his chin. "So, lose it all, Skylar. You're strong. You'll handle it."

"Are you fucking kidding me?" My voice has climbed to a shout.

"Shhh, you'll wake up Ana," he says, pushing his hands down and trying to placate me.

"No, no, no. *You* will go to court with me and tell them what happened."

"I'll do no such thing. Do you think this apartment is free? They'll cut me off, and then Ana and I will be on the street."

Fury builds in me so hot that my eyeballs simmer.

"Oh, this is about money? It's not about helping your daughter? Fine. I'll fucking pay for the place then."

He scoffs. "You? With what job?"

Now is the time for me to tell him about the completely dangerous and utterly reckless job I signed on to do for India Dellis on Rio. I should tell him about the credits I'll earn and how this will start me on the path to my own financial independence if I don't die in the jungles.

But I'm stuck on the fact that he won't lift a finger to help me. His life has been pretty easy, and he's got it good. He has no incentive to step out of line.

"What if I sweeten the deal, Dad?"

His mouth drops open.

"I'll pay for this place and regular vacations to Laguna for you and Ana. Is that what you want? Will that be enough for you to help me?" The anger in my voice is unmistakable.

"Skylar, this is not something you can bribe me to do."

"Why the fuck not?" I'm so loud I'm sure the neighbors can hear me. "They are bribing you to keep quiet about something you *know* was wrong. Why can't I bribe you to do the right thing?"

Ana appears in the doorway, yawning. We both turn away from each other to look at her. "What's going on out here? Why are you yelling at each other?"

Dad turns back to me. "I can't help you, Skylar. No one can know about this, about what happened. You think you're the only one with a reputation at stake? I'll be ostracized by everyone if they find out." He points at the floor. "So, do your duty, First Daughter, and take one for the team. Bury it. Settle it out of court. Do whatever you need to do to make it go away."

I gasp for breath. Take one for the team? As if I haven't already given my whole fucking life for this? I take one step away from him, and my chest aches like I've been stabbed. I press my hand to my heart and imagine a sword there. They wish this situation would go away. That *I* would just go away. Not exist.

"Dad," Ana gasps. "If Sky needs help, we should help her."

"No," he says, swiping down with his hand. "It's too risky."

There it is. Risky. Nothing about Dad is risky. He is vanilla ice cream. He is plain white bread. He is a ratty old blanket. He is apple pie.

Apple pie.

"Fine. Don't help me then." I point at him, directing my anger through the tip of my finger. "But when this is done, don't come crawling back to me."

I pivot on my heel, stalk across the living room, grab the apple pie from the counter, and prop it against my hip. Thankfully, it's already cool enough to handle.

"This is mine now. Payment for you being a shitty father."

His face... Oh God, his face is priceless. Equal parts shock and anger. He probably got up at five to make this pie, rolled out the crust by hand, and picked the apples himself. Baking is his favorite thing, and I won't let him have it. Not if he won't help me.

When I reach the door, I turn around. "And when I'm in court, I'm going to roast you. You had your chance to make this right. Now, you can't go back."

I slam the door on my way out.

4

"Why are you arriving home with an apple pie?" Vivian asks, drinking her coffee with Jinzo and Ken at the kitchen table.

I slide the pie plate onto the counter and sigh. "I carried this pie on two trains, and pretty much every person who saw it hates me now, so enjoy it. It's good hangover food."

Vivian smacks her lips and runs her hand through her messy hair. "I think Ilaria is the only person in the house not hungover." She stands up and joins me at the counter. "Where did you go?"

"Dad's. This is his." I wave to the pie.

"Aw, he made this for us? That's so nice." She leans past me to look at Jinzo and Ken. "Want a piece?"

"Yes," they both say at once.

"He didn't make it for us," I correct her. "I stole it as payment. Cut me a slice, will you? I had to smell it all the way home, and now I'm starving."

With a cup of coffee and a slice of pie, I sit at the table with a sigh. What I should do is slip into bed next to Saif upstairs, curl into a ball, and await the heavy rain of shit that's about to

24

fall on me. I am two days away from starting my new life as a plant tester on Rio, and my own mother, the very person who gave birth to me, wants to disown me.

My body, sensing I'm in a safe place, breaks down, and tears roll down my cheeks as I spear forkfuls of pie and shove them into my mouth.

My fucking father and his gorgeous, absolutely delicious apple pies.

"I wish this was awful," I say, laughing through my tears.

Ken sips on his coffee and eyes me warily. "Rough night, Sky?"

Vivian slides into the chair next to me. "Are you ready to tell us what happened? Why your mother was here?"

"I don't want to." Can I stall until the end of time?

Stall, Skylar. It can't be the end of the world if time stands still.

I need more time.

"But you're going to," Vivian says, reaching under the table and squeezing my knee.

"Fine. But it sounds insane the more I think about it."

I close my eyes and remember the conversation with Mom word for word before I recite it back to them. By the time I'm done, Gus and Ilaria have joined us and Mat stands in the doorway.

Jinzo's expression is like concrete. "She wants the Amagi back?" He rubs his face. "Of course she does, after all the hard work we put into it."

"This is pure, vindictive bullshit." Vivian's voice is coated in awe. "Who does this?"

Mat's hands move, painting out his words with USL. "Where's Saif?" I'm glad I understand basic signs.

"I think he's still in bed? He was there when I left."

Mat disappears around the corner, and I sigh and deflate. "I don't want to tell Saif." I turn my watery eyes to Vivian, and my lower lip shakes. Her eyes widen. "Will you do it?"

After the last two weeks, I cannot look at him as he learns of a new way my family is screwing me over. We have a great connection, and I believe he'll be good for me in many ways, but it's still early days. And this added stress will not go over well with his family.

Vivian places her hand on my arm, nods, and leaves the table.

I lean over my empty plate, put my elbows on the table, and rest my head in my hands.

"I don't know what to do," I say, peering into the expanse of crust crumbs on my plate. "I can't let them take the Amagi. It is the only thing I have left that's mine. That I *earned* from the years of being their servant." I sniff up and grab a napkin from the center of the table so I can blow my nose.

Ken and Jinzo glance at each other.

"We'll look into it, Skylar," Ken says. "I think the deed to the ship is yours, but I can't be certain without opening up the records." He sips his coffee and grimaces. "Perhaps after I get rid of this pounding headache."

Gus sits down and hands Ilaria to Jinzo. "We have to remember that we're all a team, working together. Your mother is acting like a lone wolf with only Dominic to back her up, right? Your father isn't getting involved?"

I shake my head. "I don't know about Miguel, though. And I think Juan will stay out of it as well."

Gus nods. "That's the pattern with abusive situations. Eventually, everyone will leave them, and they'll be left with nothing but their lies."

I stare down at my hands clasped together. "But... But what if it's true?"

"What's true?" Jinzo asks.

"What if it's true that I'm the one to blame for all of this?"

"Skylar," Ken says, his head tilting to the side.

"No, no. Hear me out. My memory has always been the best. I remember everything." I close my eyes. "Too much." I push out a long, shaky breath. "What if... What if my memory is so good because I made up my own memories? What if everything they're saying is true?"

Everyone is silent, just staring at me.

I slam my hand down on the table. Ken jumps and winces. "Something has to be wrong. I must be wrong. My own father is wishy-washy on the subject and won't back me up."

"That means nothing," Gus says.

"It will mean a lot in court," I stress.

A throat clears, and Saif stands in the doorway with Mat by his side and Vivian behind him.

"You never came to bed last night." He yawns and stuffs his hand in his pajama pants pocket. My icy heart melts a little, seeing his gorgeous hair, messy and wild. "You must be exhausted."

He's right. My eyes are made of paste, my throat is scratchy, and my heartbeat pounds in my ear, fueled by pure caffeine and not through any energy of my own.

"A little." My voice is caught in my throat. It aches to be free, to confide in Saif, to hum in ecstasy, to mumble my fears into the sheets at night.

"Why don't you come to bed and sleep, and we'll deal with this later?" He holds out a hand. "Nothing more is going to happen today. You should rest."

Gus jerks his chin at me. "Go on. If you're having trouble sleeping, let me know, and I'll bring you something."

Putting a nurse in her network was one of the best decisions Vivian ever made.

I nod to him as I pick up my plate. Moving slowly across the room, I bus the plate and my coffee cup to the sink. My first instinct is to grab the kitchen towel and start cleaning, but Vivian pipes up from the back.

"Don't clean up, Sky. Just go to bed."

She knows I will clean the kitchen until I drop dead, but she doesn't know why. She doesn't know about the countless nights I spent scrubbing the Mikasa's galley kitchen until it was so clean you could have surgery on the counters. If Dom found even a speck of dirt, I would pay for it in meals. I was so skinny until I learned all the divots and creases of the kitchen so well I could scour them in my sleep.

My hand shakes as I push the kitchen towel back on the counter and take a step away.

There. I don't need to clean. Someone else will do it. Someone who isn't me.

I keep my head low as I exit the kitchen, past Saif and Mat, and walk up the stairs to my room. Saif is behind me, his soft footfalls keeping pace with mine.

"Do you want to get cleaned up or showered?" he asks as we pass the bathroom we share with Ken.

"No. I showered this morning before I went to Dad's. I snuck in and grabbed clothes. You didn't budge."

Saif chuckles. "I sleep like the dead. Sorry. If I had known —"

"It's fine," I say, opening the door to my room. Yes, it used to be a storage closet, it's true. Vivian wasn't lying. The room is absent a window and has one overhead light. We pushed a double bed against the far wall, and only a few centimeters worth of space is available on one side to get in and out. My clothes sit on open shelves, and one of Vivian's cats, Pepper, is curled up between stacks of sweaters and shirts, snoozing away. I drop my bag next to the shelves and push it under with my foot. The door closes behind us.

"Do you want to talk about it?" Saif's voice is quiet as I pull off my pants and toss them onto a shelf. "Vivian's explanation was a little... vague."

I yawn as I unclasp my bra and pull it out through my sleeves. Normally, I would enjoy this free time to have sex with Saif, but I'm too drained to give it a go, and it would be teasing him if I got fully undressed. I draw back the covers on the bed and climb in.

"I don't know if there's anything more to say." I wrap the covers up and over my shoulder as I curl into a ball on my side. "My family is suing me. They want their ship back. I'm a horrible person who abused my brothers and sisters, even Dominic, for years, and I don't deserve any happiness." I yawn again. "The usual."

I crack my eyes open before I fall asleep, and Saif is staring into the middle distance, not at any one thing. I've seen this look before. Shock, incomprehensible shock.

"Do you think you did?" he asks, and for the first time since we started dating, doubt fills his expression.

I close my eyes again and try not to cry.

"I don't know," I mumble, and I hate myself for it. 'I don't know' is not something I often say when it comes to my own behavior or memories. I like to own what I've done and do better next time. "Do you want to come to bed?" I ask, my voice low, barely above a whisper.

"No... No, that's okay. You rest." He leans over and grabs clothes from his bag. "I'll shower and head into the city. I want to make sure we have food and provisions for our trip to Rio, and I have a birthday present to pick up." His smile brightens, but my chest fills with dread, and I sit up.

"No birthday presents," I say sternly. When he opens his mouth to protest, I repeat, "No birthday presents. No birthday parties. No mentioning of my birthday ever. Understand?"

I hate that I even have to say it, but it looks like Vivian got into his head last night. She loves to throw a party for anything.

"Skylar, just... just let me do this for you," he pleads.

"No." I lie back down. "I haven't celebrated my birthday in over twenty years, and we will not start now."

I pull the covers over my head, and I fall asleep moments later.

5

I WAS eight years old the last time I tried to celebrate a birthday. I think it's important to note that I did not have a sixth or seventh birthday celebration either. But for this birthday, it just so happened Mom was home on the Mikasa, and therefore the dads were forced to actually do something. This was before Juan came aboard, and Ana was only five, Jukia only three.

Now, as an adult, I completely understand why some people don't do birthdays at all. They may think it's dumb or silly, or it may be a religious thing, or they may not have the credits to do anything. The reason doesn't matter because it's personal. But for me, I had only books as my friends, and I had read a million and one stories about awesome birthdays. I had seen my older brothers have awesome birthdays. An awesome birthday was what I wanted.

Can you blame a girl?

No, most people would not. Most families fawn over their children and their holidays. My older brothers Oliver and Raphael got plenty of birthday presents and parties. *They* had friends because they could go wherever they wanted to. Our tutor spoiled them just as much as the dads did. Me, though? I was never spoiled. I went nowhere. I owned nothing that did not also belong to my younger sisters.

So, on my eighth birthday, I dreamed of how the day would go with Mom home. I had asked for a small party with games, cake, and ice cream, and this intricate puzzle set I saw on the duonet. It wasn't a lot, and I figured it was enough to be a worthy celebration. Mom would love the cake, and she loved puzzles too. I thought we could do them together.

Mom was around less and less, and I missed her more and more. When she was home, I noticed that I had less to do around the ship, and my life was less stressful. Miguel, Dominic, or my dad would do things they expected me to do, like taking care of Ana or Jukia or cleaning the kitchen. I wasn't cooking then yet. That was still another two years away. On this birthday with Mom home, I figured I may get the day off from all the drudgery of life, so I dressed in one of the last nice dresses I ever had and skipped out to the living area, feeling happy for once.

When I rounded the corner into the family room, though, my good mood vanished in a flash.

My older brother, Raphael, stood with tears in his eyes, his face red and swollen with sadness, talking to Dominic.

"But she doesn't deserve a birthday party!" His lower lip quivered, and Dominic set a hand on his shoulder. "You ground Skylar all the time for not doing her work. You told us only the good kids get presents and parties."

I backed away from the door before they could see me. My little eight-year-old body wanted to fly forward and knock Raphael over for being so mean. Yeah, they grounded me all the time, but for stupid shit like walking down the hall too loudly or not writing my assignments neatly or breathing wrong.

"I know what I said," Dominic replied. "And I meant it. You boys, you and Oliver, are the future of this family. Maybe even

Jukia too. And you all deserve the world. Skylar gets a party and presents today, but it means nothing. I promise."

"I don't believe you. Mom won't stop talking about she's 'first-daughter this' and 'first-daughter that.' What about us?" Raphael's voice pitched high and squeaked.

"You will grow up to have whatever you want. Today, though, we have to do this."

"No. I hate it. I hate you and Mom and Skylar."

I was frozen in my spot and didn't react quickly enough to move when he came barreling around the corner. Raphael ran right into me, and he used his momentum to shove me out of his path. I hit the wall with a thunk and lost my breath for a moment.

"Stay out of the way, you spoiled brat!" he yelled before pounding off down the hall.

I still look back on this moment as the turning point for my relationships with my older brothers. They pretended for years to get along with me in front of the adults. There were only a few times, like this one, where they let go of the act to whine or get mad about not being the center of attention. They probably complained about me behind my back for years, and I had no idea.

"Skylar, get in here," Dom's voice echoed out of the family room. My knees locked up, and my heart pounded in my chest. My heartbeat rang in my ears. I was afraid to move, afraid to breathe, afraid to do anything. Dominic had proven to me repeatedly that when he called, I'd better come, or I would regret it.

I turned the corner with my chin up. It was my birthday, and I would not let these people get me down.

He sighed when he saw me. "I thought we got rid of that dress. It doesn't fit you."

I pulled at the sleeves, wishing they were longer like they had been two years ago when Mom gave me the dress.

"I like it. It fits just fine," I said. I wanted to cross the room to the kitchen and get a snack, but Dominic held me prisoner with his locked gaze.

"Go get changed and bring me the dress." His tone of voice was final. "We'll give the dress to Jukia when she's old enough to wear it."

But something inside of me snapped. He was constantly taking my possessions away from me, determined for me to have no joy, no light in my life. And I loved that dress. It was one of the last things I owned that was fun and pretty.

"No. The dress is mine. It's my birthday, and I want to wear it today."

My brain panicked, and my body shook with fear and rage. I tried never to speak back to Dom. He was the ruler of the whole damned family, and I was always his first target whenever he got angry.

He took one step forward. "Just because it's your birthday, Missy, doesn't mean you can talk back to me. We don't tolerate that kind of behavior around here."

"Where's Mom?" I asked, looking up at him. "She said she'd be here."

"She's delayed, and don't change the subject." Dominic looked over his shoulder just as my dad came into the room. He had a smile on his face and a wrapped present in his hand. But his mood cooled as Dominic rounded on him. "Your disobedient daughter is giving me a hard time about changing out of this dress that's too small for her. Do I need to ground her again for not following directions?"

My father's shoulders dropped. "Dom, come on. It's her birthday. Fusako will be here soon to celebrate."

"Are you going to give me a problem, too?" The threat in Dominic's voice was crystal clear.

I saw my father's Adam's apple bob from across the room. "It's her birthday," he stressed. "Give her a break."

Nope. Dominic drew in a long breath and let it all go, and I knew I was in trouble.

Dominic's eyes skated over the room, and he stalked past me, getting close enough so I could feel the rush of his steps. He took the boxed cake that Miguel had picked up on Sonoma the previous day, opened it, and tipped the cake out. Everything moved in slow motion, and I slapped my hand over my mouth to stop a strangled scream. The cake tumbled, end over end, and hit the floor, the icing plopping with a wet squish and the rest of the cake collapsing around it.

"Oh no," Dom said, his tone flatter than the cake on the floor. "Looks like we won't be celebrating at all. Sorry. I don't know how that happened."

I... I couldn't speak. I stood there and thought about how I would kill Dominic if the chance ever presented itself. I was eight years old and already comprehending the concept of murder, what it would take to commit it, hide the body, and then fake innocence for the rest of my life. I wanted him dead, deader than space.

But he was strong and almost a meter taller than me. The balance of power was tipped to his side, and there was nothing I could do about it.

I summoned up strength, crossed the room to the cake, reached down, and grabbed a handful for myself. I knew how clean the kitchen was because I cleaned it myself almost every day. I opened my mouth and stuffed it full of cake, looking Dominic in the eye the whole time.

"Mmmm," I said, chewing and swallowing before grabbing another handful. "It's delicious, and it's all for me."

Dom's face darkened from pale beige to crimson red in a blink. "You like eating trash off the floor?" he asked. Scooping icing into his hand, he turned and smashed it into the front of my dress.

"Hey!" I yelled at him. I grabbed a handful of icing and

threw it at him. It landed on his face and in his hair. Nice shot, Skylar.

His face was the picture of rage, twisted and pinched. I had never done anything like that ever. Sure, I had fought him with words, but I never tried to resist him physically. He was just too big, and I was small, undernourished, and scared out of my mind he would send me out of the airlock when I least expected it.

Dom lunged over the destroyed cake and grabbed me by my hair. It was blinding pain, like nothing I had ever felt before, and I immediately started sobbing.

"No! Stop!" I cried. "Daddy!"

Dominic whipped me around, and my father stood there in shock.

"Hey! That's uncalled for," Dad said, stepping forward. "Let her go."

"I'll do whatever I fucking well please, and you know it," he growled, and pushing past Dad, he jerked me down the hall by my hair, my scalp screaming with pain.

I sobbed through the ship. Each door we passed opened and produced another kid, either in shock or smirking. Oliver, shock. Raphael, smirk. Ana and Jukia, shock. Though I think Jukia was just too young to understand anything.

"Fusako!" Dom called out as we approached her room. He let go of my hair just in time, and my hands flew to my head to try to deaden the pain.

Mom's door zipped open, and her cheerful face vanished. She was dressed for a party in a skirt, a pressed shirt with a vintage scarf, and cute little black flats. I remember the outfit well. That vintage scarf was bright red and orange, and I always knew my mom was dressed for success when she wore it.

But she faced a mess now, and her upright posture and bright face both sank in disappointment.

"Your first daughter ruined her own birthday by throwing her cake on the floor," Dom said, jerking my shoulder.

"Skylar," Mom admonished me. "How could you? On your own birthday!"

"I didn't," I protested. Tears soaked my lips, and I had cake all over me. "*He* threw it on the floor."

"Why would I do such a thing?" Dom asked, pulling back with a gasp.

Honestly, he could have won awards for his portrayal of the put-upon father figure. Mom certainly believed him.

"Why would he do that, Skylar?" Mom asked, her hands on her hips.

"Because he hates me!" I shot back.

"I *love* you, Skylar," Dom said, shock coating every syllable. "And this is the way you treat me?" He pointed to himself. "She threw cake at me."

Mom huffed. "Sky, is this true?"

Uh oh. I *had* thrown the cake at him, and Mom could always tell when I was lying. This was before I learned to cover over every emotion I had, back before I held my thoughts and feelings in check like I cased them in cement.

"Yes. I did. *After* he threw my birthday cake on the floor."

"Okay, I've had enough," Mom said, throwing her hands out to the side. "No more birthdays for you, young lady. Not with this kind of attitude." She tipped her head back, sighed, and stared at the ceiling for two long breaths.

"All the lying, all the disobedient behavior? I've had enough of it." She came forward and stood over me, and this time, I wasn't sad about the cake and my birthday. I was sad I had let her down. She pinched the fabric of my sleeve. "We're going to be even more strict with you now, and I'm putting Dominic in charge of your upbringing. You'll do better with him keeping a firm hand on you." She looked past me to my dad in the doorway. "I'm sorry, Julian. It needs to be done. A Kawabata daughter can't behave like this." She stared down at me. "How do you expect to run our business and lead our family someday if you continue to behave like this? These are the acts of a spoiled child, not a first daughter. You should be ashamed of yourself."

All the fight melted right out of me. I loved my mom more than anything, and hearing her say that about me? I was crushed, absolutely. I had spent the last three years learning to read and do math and passing tests with the highest possible score to prove to her I was smart enough for the job. I was eight, and I was already doing long division and reading far above my school level. I was also single-handedly raising Ana and Jukia to be just like me. Smart and capable. No one else had done that.

I had.

I thought that's what a good obedient first daughter *should* do.

(I didn't know any better.)

"I'm sorry," I said, my voice cracking. "I'm sorry, Mom."

She nodded. "Go to your room. No dinner and no dessert. And take off this ridiculous dress. It's two sizes too small for you. Julian, buy her some more appropriate clothing, please." She let go of me, stepped away, and frowned at the icing on her fingers. "And I got dressed up and everything," she whispered.

"I'll take care of it," Dom said, his hand heavy on my shoulder. "And the videos will be in your inbox later."

Mom waved this away. "Let's have dinner soon. I don't want the food to go to waste."

"Of course, my love."

Dom always trotted out the words of affection when he was close to getting his way.

This would have been an excellent time to knee him in the balls or run away, but I let him direct me to my room and lock me in there for two days. No food. Only the water I got from my bathroom.

I looked at myself in my bathroom mirror and promised myself I would never celebrate my birthday again. My birthday was dead, gone, buried deep in the dirt of my life. I would never feel that moment of happiness for just being born ever again. I blinked and saw myself as a powerful adult, chin up, no feelings, doing what she wanted. I willed the fabrication into existence. I would be so strong. No one would dare touch me again like Dom had.

My punishment continued for some time after. Later that week, he moved me to a new bedroom, the smallest one on the ship without its own bathroom. And everything went downhill from there.

But I remained strong.

And no one was ever going to push me around like that again.

6

THE VIDEOS WOULD BE in her inbox.
The videos. Her inbox.
What did Dom mean when he said that?
I arrive at the Amagi an hour before we're set to leave, so I can settle in and prepare for the journey to Rio. I have two duffel bags full of survival gear and a giant piece of baggage on my shoulders from dealing with Mom's betrayal and the upcoming legal action. I figure, if I'm in the jungles of Rio, she can't serve me with a summons, right? Might as well jump into this new career with both feet.

But the memories of my last birthday just over two decades ago bounce around in my head. Dominic knew ahead of time what he was willing to do to take total authority of the family and me. That's the only excuse I can think of to explain why he crossed the family room to my cake and destroyed it so quickly. With Mom at home, he wormed his way into the caretaker role by proving, in person, that I was out of control.

He planned that, didn't he?

I drag my duffel bags to my room and drop them on the

floor. My wristlet buzzes with a message from Saif. *"I'm on my way. Be there soon. I have dinner."*

I text him back, *"Great. I can't wait to see you!"*

And it's true. My entire life may be fucked up, but at least things with Saif are going well enough. I haven't pushed him away, though my instincts tell me to keep him at a distance so he can't hurt me and I can't hurt him. I'm learning to trust that he's a man of his word, and he wants to be around. Each new time we're given peaceful moments together, I enjoy his quiet and helpful nature. It's not bad at all.

I'm sure it's all going to crumble around me soon enough.

Instead of relaxing in my room, I cross the hall to Carlos's den of technology. As usual, he has some kind of pop music playing, and a bowl of popcorn sits next to all of his keyboards. He tosses a popped kernel into the air and catches it in his mouth.

"Nice," I say, sliding in. "You've got skills."

"Thanks, boss." He pushes the popcorn bowl to me, so I grab a few. "Just got here?" He tips back and looks out at the hall. "I didn't hear you come in."

"Because I'm like a ninja. Quiet as a mouse."

"Ha! Nothing could be further from the truth. Usually, your boots announce you way before anyone sees you."

"Good to know." I poke him in the shoulder and sit down next to him. "So, I have a favor to ask."

"A favor? What kind of favor?" Carlos turns away from whatever he's working on and places the bowl on his knees so we can both reach it.

I lick the salt from my lips and consider again how deep I want others in my shitty life. Things were much easier when I was the lone pilot, and Carlos was a sulky teen.

But Carlos has been with me for a long time, and involving him is the right thing to do.

I explain the lawsuit from my mother and the possible loss of the Amagi, and his jaw drops.

"Skylar, what the fuck? Why would your family do this?" he whispers.

"It's a long story. I mean, I've mentioned a few times how my childhood was a little rough" — he raises his eyebrows — "but I've never gone into the details. Right now, I need *you* to go into the details."

He sets the bowl of popcorn aside and gives me his full attention. "Okay, shoot. What do you need?"

"Well, first of all, I want you to break into the family's Hecate system."

He waves his hand and blows air between his lips. "Did. Done. Like five years ago."

"Really?" I pull away. "You've never said anything."

"A good hacker never kisses and tells." He points his finger guns at me, and I laugh. "I hacked in almost immediately after meeting your family. I set myself up as a superuser, and I scrub the logs regularly to hide my presence."

"What do you do in there?" It never occurred to me that Carlos already had access to everything.

"Nothing really," he says, shrugging. "I honestly haven't even checked the system in a while. I was making sure Dominic was using encryption and taking care of the backups." Carlos shakes his head. "He's a terrible systems administrator. Sloppy as hell. But he gets the job done, I suppose."

My heartbeat races as I consider that Dominic has been destroying the evidence over the years, and maybe even Carlos can't find it. I try to imagine telling Carlos about what happened to me without going into too many details. But each time I picture the scene in my head, I break into a sweat. Carlos may be my friend, but he's also my employee.

Do I really want to burden him with this?

I may not want to, but I have to.

"Carlos," I say, reaching out to lay my hand on his knee, "Dominic abused me, psychologically and physically, for years." I drop my head and gather strength to look him in the eyes. When I lift my head, Carlos is frozen. "I'm betting there's evidence in the family's databases and archives to back this up. We had cameras in several places on the ship, and I remember... I remember a time when he said he would give video files to my mom. Footage of my bad behavior."

"*Your* bad behavior?" he asks, his voice caught in his throat.

"Lies," I say, sitting back. "Dominic always instigated things and then turned it around to be my fault. If he was delivering evidence of *my* 'unacceptable behavior' to Mom, then he altered the videos somehow."

It's the only other explanation. Well, besides that I'm crazy, and my memory is poor. Because I know I'm not crazy. Ana and everyone else saw how Dominic treated me. They may not want to back me up right now, but they witnessed it.

Carlos nods slowly. "I see. Yeah. With a little help from some friends, Dominic could make the videos look like you were the bad party, not him. Hmmm." His eyes focus far off, heading down the hacker rabbit hole he loves so much. "There's a remote backup facility he's been using on Laguna to store the family's historical data. I checked it too at some point, and there were files there pre-dating your birth." He shrugs again. "I'm not sure how neat or sloppy his data retention policies are, though. The data has been lifted and shifted more than once because Dominic found cheaper storage a few times in the last ten years."

I smile at Carlos. "You know a lot more about this than I figured you would."

He inhales through his nose and brings his attention to the present. "You're my family, Sky. I just wanted to make sure these people were being careful." He frowns. "Abused? Really?" When I nod, he shakes his head. "I'll never understand some people. Kids are our greatest treasure. You're an amazing person. I'm... I'm sorry I didn't know this."

My heartbeat slows, and my chest lightens with pride for this young, capable man. He'll make a great father someday. And he just called me his family.

Tears prickle the backs of my eyes, and I need to glance away from him again. He's not just an employee or friend. He's family.

I clear my throat and soften my tone.

"Look, you didn't know because I didn't tell anyone. And only a few people know about this now. But I need to warn you that you may see some things that disturb you once you start digging. Please just remember that I'm here and alive, and I need revenge." I tighten my hand in a fist. "Be careful. Back up everything you find. Get every video and message verified by someone you trust, someone who can testify in court. No incident is too small, okay? If Dominic looked at me wrong, I want the footage. Got it?"

He nods. "Got it, boss. No problem. I'll get you everything you need."

I sigh as a new message lands in my priority inbox. What now? Oh, look. It's a message from some law firm, someone named Chase Montes, Esquire. A quick scan of the letter makes my insides boil with rage. They want me to stay on Ossun while we all resolve the question of the legal owner of the Amagi.

How about hell no?

Because hell no. I'll go wherever I want to.

Carlos's eyes flicker to the ship-wide monitors. "Looks like Saif is here."

I glance up at the screen and see Saif approaching the ship via the spaceport gangway. Good. I swipe the lawyer's message away and put it out of my mind for now.

"I'm going to go take care of Saif," I say, pointing at the monitor. "And I know you and Lia spend a lot of time together, but please don't say anything to her yet. I'm going to talk to her tonight after we're through the jump ring."

"Understood, Captain." He salutes, and I breathe a sigh of relief.

With Carlos on the case, I may just have a chance.

* * *

THE AIRLOCK DOOR OPENS, AND SAIF SHUFFLES THROUGH with two suitcases and a bag of carryout food.

"Hey, let me help." I lunge forward to grab the bag of food. A whiff of spices passes my nose, and my stomach grumbles. "Oh wow. What did you get?"

I eye his giant bags as he drops them inside the ship. He carried that through the spaceport? Looking at the time on my Estrela ocular implant, we're only five minutes away from leaving. He was cutting it close.

"That," he says, sweeping towards me and wrapping his arm around my waist. I squeak as he leans me back. "That is several curries, heaps of rice, and plenty of hot naan bread. You won't regret it."

I work to shed the anxiety that covers my body as he holds me close. Being held by men is not a simple thing for me. Besides the quick roll in the hay, men have shown me little affection in my life. Just look at Dominic and my father.

Saif smiles as he leans in slowly to kiss me. I may not be getting used to being held, but I am used to the kissing. That was an easier hangup to get over. I let his lips draw me in, consume me. Mmmm, he's an fantastic kisser. He shows me I'm the only thing he's thinking of as his lips meld with mine. He nips at my lower lip as he pulls away.

"Maybe I should just have you for dinner," he whispers.

I laugh as I try to bring my body temperature down a few degrees. "I'm pretty sure I'm calorie-free."

"Oh no. You are definitely akin to a giant hot fudge sundae. Decadent and indulgent at the same time."

"You know all the right things to say." I would love to take a hot fudge sundae and eat it off his gorgeous body.

His lips quirk into a sardonic grin as he grabs his giant bags.

"What's with all the baggage? Are you bringing gifts home to your family? You know, I heard they can afford to go back and forth between the major planets without delay."

"Ha, ha. Yes, but this is not a bag of gifts. It's more survival gear for Rio. I want to be prepared for the jungles too."

My good mood cools swiftly. "Wait." I place my hand on his arm. "You're not going into the jungles with me. You're staying in your nice, clean, dry, safe family home."

"Skylar, I told you that I go where you go. I wasn't joking around." His face flattens. "You thought I was joking?"

I cross my arms over my chest and drum my fingers.

"I... I thought you were exaggerating, yes."

I try to imagine hiking through the jungles of Rio with Saif. Saif, who is usually dressed to impress with his thick wild hair and actual jewelry that's worth more than my ship.

"Nope. Not exaggerating. If you're going into the jungles, I'm going too. Besides, I'm your ticket to getting in past the blockades."

"You are? Since when?" No one tells me anything.

"Since I called up India Dellis yesterday and told her that one of the Bhaat gemstone mines is coming up on its annual inspection, and I heard it's close to her newest base."

I open my mouth, and nothing comes out but a laugh. "Are you fucking with me?"

"Nope!" His smile is infectious, and I smile back. "It's one-hundred percent true."

I point at him. "But you're leaving something out."

He shrugs. "Well, maybe India Dellis actually contacted *me* and suggested it, but those details aren't important."

"Saif," I say, sighing and shaking my head, "this is a bad idea. Your family will kill you, then they'll kill me too while they're at it."

"Are you calling my family murderers?" he asks, mock seriously.

"If the shoe fits." I look down at my feet and the old trusty sneakers I wore today. They weren't my usual boots, so Carlos didn't hear me coming. Maybe being silent and sneaky is better than brazen and loud. I've always been loud outside of my family because they kept me so meek and obedient at home.

"Hey, Cinderella, try not to worry so much."

I draw in a quick breath at the Cinderella reference. Am I?

I probably am.

"I'm worried about a lot right now." I sigh as I run my fingers through my hair. "Some lawyer is trying to get me to stay on Ossun, so I don't fly away with the Amagi and not come back."

Saif's face turns into a frown. "That sounds serious. Maybe we should stay?"

I wave my hand. "No. This ship is mine. I'll go where I please with it."

"Skylar," he says, his voice severe. "You don't want to make the lawsuit worse. We should stay."

"We're going," I say to him. We lock eyes, and I swear he's trying to make me blink first. But I'm not budging. I will not listen to some two-bit lawyers who think they know me and my ship.

Not happening. I'm going to Rio whether they like it or not.

"Skylar." Marcelo's voice knocks me out of my stare down with Saif. Damn. I blinked first. He rushes across the cargo bay to me, and his face is clouded with concern. "Uh, we're about to have company."

I sweep out my hand to Saif. "Yeah, Saif is already on board, and the gangway is retracting in a minute."

Pounding comes from the airlock door, so I turn from Marcelo to narrow my eyes at it. Everyone who's supposed to be here is here already. Lia's in her room. Nisrine is in the engine room. I left Carlos in his den, and Marcelo stands behind me.

"Captain, I beg your pardon," Nanci, the ship's AI, says, coming over the internal speakers, "but there is a young man at the airlock door. His wristlet scan indicates his name is Kalvin Vidal."

I gasp, and the blood in my head sinks so fast the world spins for a moment.

Saif raises his eyebrows. "Kalvin is here?"

I enter a zombie-like state, pass the bag of food to Saif, and cross the cargo bay with measured steps. Kalvin, who I haven't seen in several weeks, since we last parted on Sonoma after almost dying in the Novato Desert, is outside?

I round the corner into the airlock, and Kalvin's face is pressed against the tiny airlock window. His lips curl up in a cocky smile.

I take one step back and turn off the lights. His face drops, and his lips form the words, "Oh, come on, Skylar!"

I fold my arms over my chest.

"Pleeeeease!" he begs. He disappears for a moment, and two bottles of expensive whisky appear in the window instead. I break into a laugh and turn the lights on.

Dogging the airlock connection, I swing the door open as the gangway retraction alarms and lights start. The flashing white and yellow lights illuminate Kalvin from behind and remind me of why I always thought he was a pretty boy before he became the handsome rogue who held my hand in the desert.

"Hey, Princess," he says. "Did you miss me?"

7

"No."

I turn and walk away from Kalvin, though I know he's going to follow me.

"No? You didn't miss me at all? Like *at all* at all?"

"Nope. I hope you don't mind sleeping on the floor because I have no room for you here."

There are ten open cabins.

"Well, I mean, I figured you were mad at me when you put my contact on your block list, but..."

I whirl around in time to see Kalvin's eyes change from happy to wary as he spots Saif. "I what?"

"You..." He tears his eyes from Saif. "You blocked me. I had to find out where you were through Marcelo." He strides across the room to Marcelo, his hand outstretched. "It's great to finally meet you in person. Sorry about the short notice."

The two shake hands, and the moment of me blocking Kalvin from my Estrela communications center pops into my head. I did it way back in flight school, before we grew close on our desert adventure. My finger hovered over the block button for a breath before I committed to it. He was so annoying in class and in messages. I just didn't want to see them anymore.

"Oh shit," I say, closing my eyes and shaking my head. "I blocked you."

"You did." His smile pulls up on one side. "But I take that as a challenge." He touches his chest. "I figured you were making it difficult to see if I had mettle, gumption. You know, courage. I've got mettle, baby. Lots of it."

I glance at Saif, and Kalvin stops his prattling.

Kalvin inhales and turns his smile up a few degrees. "This is Saif Bhaat." Again, he strides across the cargo bay with his hand out. "It's good to meet you."

I brace myself for a problem, but Saif's smile is good-natured, if a bit amused, like he's looking at a puppy doing tricks.

"You as well," Saif says, taking Kalvin's hand and shaking it. "I've... uh, I've heard a lot about you."

I cringe, remembering the things I told Saif in the quiet hours of the night about my relationship with Kalvin.

"All good things, I'm sure," Kalvin says, laughing and letting go.

He spreads his arms wide and puts on a dashing smile. "Skylar, don't be mad. I had a lot of shit going on at home. I saw you two on the gossip sites, and I knew you were okay." He gestures to Marcelo. "Plus, I was in contact with him. I figured I would take care of my family and meet you wherever you were."

The clunk of the fuel and air hoses disengaging from the Amagi echo through the cargo bay.

"I didn't think I'd make it by the skin of my teeth, though."

I inhale and lift my shoulders. "Well, as you can see, I need to get ready for departure. Why don't you two get settled in, and I'll get us underway?"

"I'm going to —" Marcelo jerks his thumb at his shuttle.

I nod. "Meet me on the bridge?"

Marcelo considers this for a moment before inclining his head and leaving to return to his shuttle.

I want out of here as quickly as possible.

"Sure. Where can I stay?" Kalvin asks, hoisting his bag on his shoulder.

I point to the rear of the cargo bay. "There with the sheep and the chickens."

He tilts his head and narrows his eyes. "I'm allergic to wool."

"Sucks to be you."

I turn to Saif and smile at him. The difference between these two men could not be more apparent at this moment. Kalvin is brash and ebullient, Saif is quiet and kind. They are complete opposites. But I like them both. They bring out distinct qualities in me, and in our relationships, more than I ever thought anyone could.

But let's not get ahead of ourselves yet.

Kalvin is here, but he's not done any of the hard work that Saif has done. Even so, Saif is a new man in my life. He hasn't plumbed the depths of my insecurities yet. I haven't been introduced to his family, and he has seen mine in all its glory. Ugh. My skin crawls, and I'm embarrassed by how my mom treated him. That would have been enough to send anyone packing.

He's still here.

"Skylar." Kalvin steps in front of me. I feel Saif tense next to me. "Skylar," he repeats, his voice softer. He reaches out and runs his hands down my arms to my hands, taking them in both of his. "I'm sorry. I could have been with you here sooner, and it just didn't work out. My mom is in a bad way. I... I didn't want you involved in that, with everything that happened with your family."

I relax a little.

"I thought the block was funny at first. That you were playing hard to get, or we were joking around. And then things got tense, and I lost sight of my promises to you." He tugs at my hands. "It won't happen again." He looks at Saif. "I want to be here."

"So do I," Saif says.

My face heats, so I clear my throat. "You both are completely insane."

"I'll take that as a compliment," Saif says, chuckling.

"Same," Kalvin replies.

I sigh. "Saif, can you set up for dinner? Is there enough for Kalvin, too?"

"Plenty," he says with a big smile. Being hospitable is one of Saif's favorite things. "I bought extra curry in case we had guests."

I eye Kalvin, and he raises a hand. "I love curry."

"Great. Saif will take care of dinner, and you can drop your bags in cabin eight." I point to the lower level of crew quarters. "The number is on the door."

He steps forward. "I can't join you on the bridge?"

"Not now." I need to get away, not have him hovering over my shoulder asking about every detail of the Amagi.

He pouts but nods his head. "Okay. But I really want to see it soon."

"You'll have to wait."

I turn on my heel and stalk away.

Just like you made me wait. Two can play at that game, Kalvin.

* * *

WHEN I REACH THE BRIDGE, I'M SURPRISED TO SEE MARCELO sitting in the captain's chair.

"What are you doing here?" I ask, laughing. "I thought you were going to your shuttle first."

I slip into my pilot's chair and swipe through the communications screens.

"I made sure my shuttle was fine. I came here to make sure *you* were fine." He glances over his shoulder, so I close the bridge door from my console.

"I'm just great, thanks." I return to the consoles and scan down my launch checklist. "Now, instead of one man I adore, and I'm sure is going to realize I'm a basket case and leave me, I have two."

Marcelo's face falls. "You can't believe that. Not after everything that's happened in the past two weeks."

I stare down at the consoles, noting that we're number eleven in the queue.

"My mom wants the Amagi back," I whisper, not raising my eyes. "And without the Amagi, I'm nothing. I'll fight her in court, but I don't have the money for a sophisticated lawyer."

"Neither does she," Marcelo points out. "Remember that she's in debt up to her eyeballs. You're actually better off than she is."

"Yeah, well, tell that to the lawyer she hired who's already in my inbox telling me not to leave Ossun."

I raise my eyebrows as I remember the contents of the letter. They didn't threaten me with legal action, and they didn't send the local authorities to stop me, which tells me they *can't* stop me. They can only *ask* that I not go anywhere.

And I am just petty enough to ignore all their letters.

"And we're leaving Ossun?" Marcelo asks.

"That we are. We're number six in the queue now."

He nods and sits back in the seat to strap in. "Good. Your mother has lost her marbles, and sticking around here to find them is a waste of time."

I breathe a sigh of relief. Knowing Marcelo believes me is a tremendous weight off my shoulders. I think I would have to give up if he thought I was lying about everything.

Swiping to my internal comms, I call up the engine room.

"Nisrine, we're now number three in the queue," I report, powering up the stabilizers and checking the engine status.

"We're good to go, Captain. I noticed a crack in one of the instrument panels down here. Then I followed it to a backup air exchanger. Now, it's just a backup, *and* it's just a crack," she starts.

"I hear you. When we arrive on Rio, please track down a replacement. I want everything at one-hundred percent."

"Got it."

"Hope the ship isn't too boring for you, what with all the new equipment," I say with a smile.

"This ship is just what I needed. I'm doing yoga with Lia in an hour. Want to join?"

"No, thanks. I have stuff I need to take care of."

"Yes, I'm sure you do," she says with a chuckle. "Engine room out."

I pull my lips in and press on them. "I get the feeling Nisrine finds my romantic situation amusing."

"She's not the only one," Marcelo says. "What are you going to do about Kalvin?"

My screen flashes with a countdown, so I prep for departure.

"Nanci, please tell everyone to buckle in and get ready to leave Sakata City Spaceport," I ask my AI... and I wait for the inevitable.

"Yes, Captain. No one will be injured on my watch."

And there it is.

"I have Ossun Orbital Station One's Emergency Medical Unit on call in case anything happens," she finishes.

That's a new one. I roll my eyes. It's not every day I purchase an AI obsessed with death and mayhem.

"Thank you, Nanci. Everything will be fine," I reassure her.

"But we could explode into a fiery ball upon ascent into orbit, Captain. It's best to be prepared."

"Is Nanci preoccupied with our imminent demise again, sweetheart?" Ai, my other AI, chimes in.

"Oh my God, yes. Can you please talk with her? And don't bring up sex," I warn Ai. As a former sexbot AI, she's the one fixated on dirty talk and the best vibrators.

"I'll do my best."

My screen blinks with an incoming message, and I accept it. I know Marcelo is waiting for an answer, but duty calls.

"Amagi cruiser, this is Sakata City Spaceport Command. You are cleared for departure. Please follow markers to lane 6C. You have four minutes to clear local airspace. Thank you."

"Acknowledged. Thank you!" I chime into the speaker.

My instincts kick in for the flight out and to orbit. I keep my eyes on everything for the ascent because I do not want to die in a giant fireball like Nanci seems to think we might.

Of course, she's wrong, and I sigh back into my seat once we're on route for the Ossun-Rio jump ring. We booked an early slot this time, and we'll be through within an hour.

"So?" Marcelo asks, unlatching his harness. "Kalvin."

"Yeah, Kalvin." I reach forward to power down the stabilizers and close the air intake valves. "I guess he's here, huh?"

Marcelo is a well of restraint. "He's here. And I won't tell you what to do about him. I see all the pros and cons. Pros — he's a fellow pilot and could fly more ships if you acquire them someday, he loves his family, and he's not in any kind of debt that I can tell."

I hold my tongue about his last job.

"Cons — he seems to bounce from job to job, he doesn't have much money, and he has no real ex-girlfriends, which makes me think he's afraid of commitment. Then there's the business with his mother. I thought it was a money debt, but now I'm unsure. He hasn't been forthcoming about the subject."

I inhale and exhale and try to find my calm.

"Okay, then. I'll eat dinner with them both, and send them each to their rooms tonight. I'll deal with the drama of him being here after a good night's sleep."

Yep. I do not want to deal with this right now. I have enough problems as it is, and I need to sleep more than anything.

"Skylar," Marcelo says, his voice low with warning, "you cannot ignore this indefinitely."

"Can I ignore it until after I get a good night's sleep?"

He sighs. "I'll allow it."

"Good." I lock down the bridge, open the door, and gesture to it. "Because that's all I can do right now."

Right now, it's curry, jump ring, and then bedtime.

In that order, and not deviating from the plan.

Stick to the plan, Skylar.

8

I OPEN the airlock and step out onto the covered stairs locked to the side of the Amagi. The sun is shining, and the air is rich with moisture. I inhale deep into my lungs and let it all out with a smile. Back on Rio. Back in Primeiro.

I'm dying to get off this ship, even if it means crawling through the jungle and getting attacked by dragonsnakes.

I have just spent two awkward meals with Saif and Kalvin, who are already not getting along. Last night's dinner was slow and quiet, with neither of them talking to the other. They did breakfast this morning in shifts. First, Saif sat with me and chatted about meeting with his family later in the week. He also kept hounding me about the lawyer who wanted me to stay on Ossun. Kalvin took Saif's place right after, and he did nothing but gush over the Amagi.

At this point, Kalvin should marry the Amagi, not me.

"Ah," I breathe out. "A beautiful day on Rio."

A peal of thunder rips through the air, and I turn to face the opposite direction. Yep. A storm's coming. I should have known better. We're never far from the rain.

Saif arrives through the airlock with our bags. He sets them at my feet.

"Are you sure you want to do this?" he asks, looking at the oncoming storm. "I think that, instead of trekking through the jungle, we should return to Ossun and deal with this lawsuit head-on."

I inhale and hold my breath, annoyance clawing at my chest. Saif is the responsible one around here, and I am not having any of it.

"Fuck the lawsuit. My mom can scream and stomp her feet until she's blue in the face. She's not getting anything out of me. Nothing. Not one thing."

His face falls.

"And I'm not putting my life on hold so that she can drag this nonsense on for months or years. I'm going to get on with my new life, and if they come for me, they'll come for me."

Three steps down the stairs, I realize Saif hasn't moved. I squint up at him. Being on a planet is always challenging for the first few hours. They're so bright.

"Are we good?" I ask him, gentling my voice. I tilt my head to the side.

Saif looks at the ground and rubs his lips together. I don't like his hesitation. "Yeah. Yeah, we're good."

But the tone of his voice tells me he's not sure.

I weigh my options. If I force Saif into the jungle with me, it may not go well because he's having doubts. The jungle is not the place to rid yourself of doubts. If anything, it'll make you run for the nearest spaceship and never come back.

I reach out for my bag.

"Hey, why don't I head out there alone this first time?" I wrap my fingers around the strap. "I'll get the lay of the land, and then you can join me later." I tug on the strap, but he doesn't let go.

"Sky, I said I would go." Annoyance touches his voice.

Ouch. I cringe. I hate this. I hate knowing that I'm the source of his ambivalence. "I just..."

He looks out over the city in the direction of home, I think.

His home. Maybe he's regretting not visiting with his family before doing something dangerous. He's close with his mother, father, her network mates, his sisters and brothers. Just because I'm not close with my family anymore doesn't mean I should run my life like other people are the same.

India Dellis, my new boss, didn't give me a definite start date. I could switch around my schedule.

"Okay," I say gently. "How about we go visit your family now, and we'll take the mining shuttle tomorrow instead?"

"My family? I don't want you to be late," he responds, his knee bouncing.

"I won't be." I shake my head. "India will be happy if I show up anytime soon."

Of course, I want to rush there and get the miserable days of trekking through the jungle over and done with as quickly as possible. But I guess it's not just me anymore, is it? Now I also have to consider Saif's and Kalvin's feelings for the time being. I mean, not permanently or anything. I doubt either of them will be around for long.

"I don't know," Saif says, avoiding my eyes and looking out across the city. "I'm beginning to think this is all not a great idea."

All of what?

Anger rushes up my back. This is such a waste of time. All of it. Everything. This new job. This trip to Rio. This meeting of the family. Everything is a waste when I'm going to end up with nothing anyway. I grew up with nothing. I'll die with nothing.

"Fine," I say, ripping my bag out of his hand. I pivot on my heel and storm down the rest of the stairs. "I'll go find the shuttle and be on my way. I'll call you when I get back." I lower my voice. "If I get back."

"Skylar!" he calls out, running down the stairs behind me. Lightning sparks through the air a few kilometers away, and thunder rumbles after it. "Please, don't misunderstand me."

I come to a halt, remembering Marcelo's advice. He told me that Saif was devoted to me, but he would leave if I continued to push him away.

And you know what? If this relationship ends, it will *not* be my fault.

No.

I will not be the one to end it.

I stop and turn around. The anger in my chest is so hot I could breathe fire. But I draw a cool breath of air and try to calm down.

"What am I misunderstanding?" I set my bag down. "Please explain it to me. Explain to me what's going on, so I can make the right choices here."

He pauses a meter from me, but he says nothing.

I lift my chin. "Because I want to make the right choices."

"Then why did you leave Ossun when you weren't supposed to?"

I pull back. "Who's telling me what I'm *supposed* to do? Huh?"

"You're supposed to be making good decisions that protect you and your crew," he says, anger reaching a new level in his voice. "And running off to Rio when you have a pending legal action on Ossun is *not* a good decision."

I breathe steadily, in and out, in and out. "What, pray tell, was I supposed to do? Sit around on Ossun until someone finally got around to suing me?"

He leans towards me. "You should have left the Amagi there and hired a different ship. Come on, Sky. This is not brain surgery. The Amagi's legal ownership is in question here, and you flying it off to Rio will not look good." He sighs and turns his eyes to the blue sky. "I knew you were hot-headed and compulsive, but I never thought you'd do *this*."

Ouch. That hurts.

Hot-headed and compulsive — I've heard that too many times in my life. Maybe I should have been the model daughter and just handed over the ship. But the Amagi is mine. I have spent the last few years working on every detail of its rehabilitation. My mom didn't come to look at it even once while it was in spacedock. I was ready and willing to take over the business, and then she screwed me.

No, no, no.

"Saif," I say, calming my voice, "there is no money to hire a ship. My balance is rock bottom. I spent my last credits on the docking fees, and I don't get paid unless I show up at the Patras camp." I reach out and lay my hand on his arm. "I know that for you, you have access to funds, and you can solve any problem with money."

He grimaces.

"But my life doesn't work like that. I have nothing. My family has nothing. You've seen Vivian's farm. The fall festival was lovely, and a good sign things are going well. But they are just barely scraping by." I heft my bag. "This bag has all the clothes I own, minus a few fancy dresses and shoes. I told you I'm broke with no inheritance now. I need to get to the jungle and get paid. The Amagi is all I have left to make a living, so that I can..." I lose my breath for a moment. "So I can have a family someday."

My heart hurts, wondering if that's even possible.

"Look at you," I say, gesturing to his new camping wardrobe and impeccable style and poise. "What the hell is someone like you doing with a down-on-her-luck tramp like me? I still have literally no idea what you see in me when I am nothing but trouble."

"Don't talk about yourself that way," Saif says, and I think I've finally gotten through to him.

"Skylar!" Kalvin leaps from the Amagi's airlock and runs down the stairs to meet us. He huffs and puffs for a moment before pushing his hair into place and smiling. "Hey. Didn't want you to leave without me."

I sigh as I glance at Saif. Saif turns so he doesn't have to look at Kalvin. "Why does everyone think they're going to come with me? Huh? Since when is this a group tour?"

Kalvin presses his hand to his chest. "I have survival skills."

He also has a slight heart problem, which I learned about in the desert. But that's a topic for another time.

Saif sighs and turns to Kalvin. My shoulders prickle with goosebumps.

"Come on, man." Weariness has set up camp in Saif's voice. "You weren't even there for her when she needed you. What makes you think you're coming along on a dangerous trek through the jungle? Stick with the ship."

"Uhhh —" I start, but Kalvin laughs.

"Skylar doesn't need help from anyone. She's an independent woman. Isn't that right, Sky?" He turns to face me, and I swallow hard. He jerks his thumb at me. "This here is a woman who can do anything. She's as hard as stone and rules her kingdom with an iron fist." He nods once. "I came when I could because I knew she would be all right."

Despite Saif's cold and unhappy face, I can't help but smile at Kalvin. That's the kind of independence that I like to exude, though not too much. No one will ever want to date me if I don't need them.

I actually *do* need support. I need people in my corner for this fight I have ahead. I need the close times, the heart-stopping looks across the room, the hot sex, and tender moments… I need it all.

"I'm glad you made it," I say to him. "Ruling my kingdom is tiring."

He cocks a sideways grin. "That's why I'm here to help."

Saif looks between Kalvin and me. "So, Skylar's an independent woman who can do anything, huh?"

My skin grows cold, and I open my mouth to deny it, but nothing comes out.

In Saif's brief from Marcelo, he said he wanted an independent woman, but he also said he wanted someone willing to ask for help. Saif loves to help. It's his favorite thing.

Honestly, at this point in my life, enough people have let me down to never want to ask for help ever again.

But I've enjoyed the last week or two with Saif and having him around to guide me. I should have listened to him about the Amagi too. And now this situation is just going to make things worse.

I can see his thoughts swirling. Kalvin is making him think twice about me.

Kalvin's smile is slight. "She doesn't need me to come along with her into the jungles, but I'm going anyway because it sounds dangerous, and I love danger."

"Right," Saif says, taking a half step back. I would laugh, but I'm still stuck wondering what will happen next.

"Don't be scared." Kalvin slaps Saif on the shoulder. He stops, narrows his eyes, and reaches out to lay his hand on Saif's upper arm. "You work out." He nods slowly. "Good. We're going to need that where we're going."

"And just where do you think we're going?" Saif asks him.

"*The... jungles...*" Kalvin says slowly like he's talking to someone who doesn't understand the language.

"No, actually." Saif picks up his bag, his lips in a straight line. "We're going to visit my family first. We'll get on the shuttle to the gemstone mine tomorrow morning."

My stomach bottoms out. Oh no. He's angry again. This is

63

not how I want to meet his family. He's going to cause a scene, isn't he? He's going to punish me, right?

Wait, no. This is Saif. He cares for me. I have to trust that he would never do anything intentionally to hurt me. He may make me feel a little uncomfortable or tease me, but he would never hurt me.

Trust him. Trust him. Trust him. I repeat it in my head.

"Can I at least go inside and change first?" I ask, jerking my thumb at the ship. "I don't want to show up looking like this." I gesture to my ripped and stained jeans, old t-shirt, and boots.

Saif doesn't smile. "You look fine."

I'm about to object and tell him I'd like to make a good first impression when Kalvin steps between us.

"Will we eat Indian food while we're there?" he asks.

"We call it just food," Saif responds.

I huff a short laugh.

"Curries, rice, fried pockets of goodness?" Kalvin asks, his eyebrows climbing as he looks at the darkening sky.

"Yes, all of that," Saif says, smiling.

Well, at least they're getting along.

"Great. Let's go." Kalvin jerks his thumb over his shoulder. "Looks like it's going to rain, and all the autocabs will fill up if we don't get in the queue soon."

He and Saif turn and head off down the walkway, not looking back to see if I agree or if I'm coming or anything. My heart sinks to my stomach as I remember the way Vivian's network dotes on her, supports her, and cares for her, the way they all work together because they love one another.

That's just another thing I can't have, isn't it?

I grab my bag and follow them, picking up my pace as the rain begins to fall.

9

The Bhaat estate takes up half a city block on the outskirts of Primeiro. I can see it from a distance in the autocab as we speed across town. Kalvin and Saif exchange small talk the whole way, and I sit in silence, preparing to meet his family. I wish I had known about this ahead of time. I really wanted to go inside and change since I'm not wearing anything remotely flattering. I thought I was leaving the Amagi for a shuttle and the jungle. I am not dressed up to 'meet the family,' but that's the situation I'm now stuck in.

This is what I get for trying to be softer and easygoing. I look into the middle distance, and all I see is myself in the mirror of my bathroom as an eight-year-old. That promise I made to myself — to be strong with no feelings — is wearing away, centimeter by centimeter. I don't know if that's good or bad.

I try to calm my racing heart as we approach the front gate. When I imagined this meeting taking place, I saw myself in a smart dress, looking radiant and happy on Saif's arm. I would smile and make jokes and charm the pants off his mother, enough for them to excuse my poor family and business prospects and give their permission for Saif to date me.

That moment slips from my grasp as we enter the side garden. Greenery, flowers, ponds, and patios dominate the space. Everything is fresh and sparkling after the brief storm. I stare at the garden, and a pit grows in my stomach. This is a lot of wealth.

Kalvin walks ahead with his mouth open in awe, and Saif closes the gate behind me.

"So, um, your family is home? Do they know we're coming?" I ask, keeping my voice quiet.

"Yep. I messaged them while we were waiting for our autocab."

"Okay," I nod and take a deep breath. "How do I look? I regret not wearing something nicer." My hand shakes as I try to finger-comb my hair.

"Well, if we had done this my way, we would have come for a fancy dinner with all the relatives. We would have made a proper night of it, and you would be dressed up and the center of attention. And we would have gone out for your birthday in a few days, instead of you denying me this opportunity to spoil you. But you're an independent woman, Skylar. You don't need that pomp and circumstance stuff, right? You make the decisions, and I just follow along."

I sigh and deflate as he walks away. "Wait, Saif. That's not how this is at all."

"Oh yeah? Tell me it's not so."

I swallow as I remember how I ordered him not to celebrate my upcoming birthday, and I ignored his advice on leaving Ossun. But those are personal decisions that only affect me. So why am I getting this treatment?

When I don't answer him, he says, "That's what I thought. Good luck with my mother."

He walks off and joins Kalvin on the patio.

You know what? I could walk away right now. I could turn and run out the gate and never come back. And maybe I should.

But I told Marcelo, and Vivian, and Saif, and pretty much everyone that I was going to give relationships a chance. I was going to trust men. I trust Saif, right? He would never do anything to purposely hurt me.

This must be a test. He's testing me to see if I'm going to run.

I draw a deep breath. Yes, this is a test. That's what it is.

And I can pass this test.

I will not run.

I walk forward to join them both on the patio and set my bag down next to theirs. The doors leading out onto the deck open and a young woman a few years older than me comes sweeping out. This must be Sejal because she's with Nadine, dressed again in black. Sejal is more colorful in a bright orange silk beaded top and flowing wide pants. She's covered in gold jewelry, including a nose ring and rings on almost every finger.

"Saif, what are you doing here? I thought you were touring the gemstone mines."

She does a double-take when she sees me standing off to the side. I'm a total schlub next to her. At least I'm wearing the elephant charm Saif gave me.

"I thought I'd go tomorrow. I wanted you all to meet Kalvin and Skylar beforehand. Kalvin, this is my sister Sejal and her friend Nadine. Kalvin is a pilot and a friend of Skylar's."

Sejal's eyes are on me, calculating and assessing every slight twitch of my face. Embarrassment grows in my chest. Saif introduced Kalvin first.

Nadine comes forward and smiles as she shakes hands with Kalvin. "It's a pleasure to meet you," she says gracefully.

"And this is Skylar Kawabata," Saif says, waving to me from

across the patio. Wait, not even a proper introduction? His eyes are hard on me, daring me to rock the boat.

Of course, I'm not going to.

Trust, trust, trust, I repeat in my head.

"Hello." I step forward and try to summon up a smile from fucking nothing. I am fuming inside. I hold out my hand to shake Sejal's. "It's so nice to finally meet you."

Sejal's grip is firm, but her manner is cool as she looks me over from head to toe.

I pull my hand away before things get awkward and run my fingers through my hair.

"So sorry about my appearance," I say with a laugh. "I swear I clean up just fine. I didn't know we were coming here, or I would have dressed nicer."

I would have rented another dress and put on something more than a tinted moisturizer and a swipe of mascara. Sejal and Nadine look like they're ready to head out for a business luncheon.

Sejal tips her head, and her long ponytail shifts over her shoulder. "You didn't know you were coming here?"

"Nope," I say, shaking my head. I smile anyway. "Came as a complete surprise." I glance past her to Nadine. "Hi again, Nadine. It's good to see you."

Nadine leans in and kisses me on the cheek. Oh, we're doing that? Okay, then.

"It's good to see you too, Skylar." She turns to Sejal and lowers her voice. "She does usually look a lot better than this."

My laugh comes out breathy and shaky. I press my lips together and shrug.

Kalvin's smile drops to a frown, and he crosses the garden to me in a few great strides.

"Skylar," he whispers, his smile tight as he angles me away from Sejal, "is this the first time you're meeting Saif's family?" We walk several meters off while she stares us down.

"Uh yeah. I thought that was obvious." I glance over at Sejal and smile at her, hoping I appear confident and sure of myself.

I am not confident nor sure of myself.

Anger grows in Kalvin's eyes. "It was not fucking obvious." He closes his eyes, and his jaw sets. "He let you come here like this to teach you a lesson."

My apprehension about the whole situation cools and becomes as hard as stone.

"Skylar," Saif says, approaching us, "this was your idea."

Now, this is really embarrassing. Sejal narrows her eyes at her brother.

I raise my finger. "I did suggest we visit your family first. But if you had agreed when we first spoke of it, I would have prepared myself. In fact, I suggested I get changed before we left. Instead, you and Kalvin left and expected me to tag along."

Kalvin brings his hands to his chest. "I wasn't aware this was the first meeting. You guys seem so tight. I figured she was already buddy-buddy with your whole family."

He turns his eyes on Saif.

Saif pauses, and my blood boils. "Sorry, Sejal. It appears we've miscommunicated about our plans today."

Sickness claws at my belly. This is how I was treated my whole childhood, and now I'm hearing the same thing from someone I'm falling for. He's insinuating that I lie to get what I want or to make him look bad, and that's not what happened at all.

My knees start to shake, and my vision tunnels. I can't believe this is happening to me. My eyes fill with tears as I stare at Saif, and I watch his haughty demeanor crumble. Kalvin is silent. Too silent.

Sejal turns and grasps my upper arm. "Darling, what's going on here?"

"Nothing." A tear rolls down my cheek. "I, uh... I trusted Saif, and it appears that was a mistake." I take a step back out of her grip. "I'm going to leave now." I grab my bag. "I'm sorry to have interrupted your morning unannounced. This is not... This is not how I wanted to meet you."

"Skylar, wait," Saif says as I turn to go.

My back is to the patio as I hear an older woman's voice lift over everyone else's. "Do we have company? Saif, you're home!"

This must be his mother, but I'm not going to turn around to find out. I hasten my steps and disappear before she can spot me.

"Skylar, wait!" Saif calls out.

I break into a full sprint along the side of the house and push through the gate at lightning speed. Two sets of feet pound on the pavement behind me as I turn and run in the opposite direction of the house.

"Skylar, stop!" Kalvin calls.

I whirl around to face them both.

"How could you do that to me?" I ask Saif as he comes to a halt in front of me. "How could you throw me to the wolves like that and then call me a liar?"

I wipe the tears from my cheek with my whole hand. Thankfully we appear to be alone on this residential street, although Sejal is standing at the gate.

"I trusted you," I say, bringing my fist to my heart. "I thought, this is Saif. He would never do anything to hurt me."

"I wouldn't," he starts, but I cut him off with a flash of my hand.

"You just did. You know, it was just the other day, I was thinking about how I was getting used to having a kind and gentle man in my life, someone I could trust, who was a man of his word. I'm not sure I see that anymore."

He closes his eyes as if I've slapped him.

I lower my voice. "The reason I don't celebrate my birthday has *nothing* to do with you and denying *you* anything. The last time I 'celebrated' my birthday, I was fucking eight. And Dom ruined it by throwing my birthday cake on the floor, blaming me for it, and then convincing my mom I needed discipline. And guess what?" I widen my eyes with pretend shock. "He took away my room, my clothes, my books, my meals, and I haven't celebrated my birthday since. And Dom used to do *that* to me, too." I point back at the garden. "Call me a liar when I never did anything but tell the truth."

His face pales. "I-I didn't know. I was just —"

"Of course, you didn't know." My voice has turned mocking now, and I can't stop it. "Because if I sat down and told you *all* the ways I was screwed over and manipulated as a kid and a teen, it would take years to go over every moment of abuse, and you would run for the hills. But maybe I should have done that, right? Should have scared you away, right from the beginning."

I heft my bag onto my shoulder. Kalvin adjusts his stance from one foot to another. His eyes bounce back and forth between us.

"Listen closely to me because I'm only going to say this once." Saif's eyes widen at my stern tone. "You have no right to question decisions about my business if we're not in a contract. Period. This power trip you tried to pull today will never happen again. I trusted you to be kind to me, to treat me like I've always wanted to be treated, *deserved* to be treated. Not like this. This relationship is on seriously rocky ground right now, but I will not end it because I promised myself I would give relationships a chance. If it ends now, it's because *you* fucked it up, not me. I'm going to work. Don't follow me." I look past his shocked face at Kalvin. "You can come with me."

I turn and stalk off.

And just like I demanded, he doesn't follow me.

10

I ARRIVE at the shuttle to the gemstone mine, and thankfully, my reservation is still valid.

"Is Saif Bhaat joining you?" an attendant asks as we check-in

"No." My curt reply makes the man blink and pull back, but he leaves me be.

"Come on. Let's grab a seat," Kalvin says, gesturing to an empty row in the middle of the ship. I was quiet the whole way back to the spaceport, and he's been watching me warily.

Once the shuttle is in the air and Saif is not aboard, I sink into my seat and close my eyes. Of all the stupid, asinine, mean things to do. I can't believe Saif tried to humiliate me in front of his family. For what? To show me my veneer of independence was fake? That I actually do *need* people, even though I've built up a reputation that states otherwise?

Yeah, well, I did need people. I needed my mother and father. They were supposed to care for me and protect me. And I trusted them too.

Now look where that's gotten me.

I was ready to put my trust in Saif. But maybe it's too soon. He came out of the gate strong, determined to be my knight in shining armor. It looks like he's realized the armor is heavy and chafes and will cost a fortune to fix if it ever gets damaged. It's clear now that I should have urged him to go slower.

Slow, like not at all.

Okay, then. Maybe I don't need Saif. Hell, maybe I don't need Kalvin, either, but at least he's here. Though, probably for not much longer after this little dust-up.

I'm better off being a loner. No one to obstruct me. No one to tell me I'm a horrible human being. Yeah. I mean, I'll miss the sex... and the late-night chats... and the heart-stopping smiles... and the way they make me laugh. Or having someone around to eat with or sit with, share space with.

But that's all fleeting, anyway. My heart aches.

It was never going to last. Just look at today. Those things with Saif didn't last even a few weeks.

Yeah, I don't need them. I'll avoid Saif, and when Kalvin breaks things off with me too, eventually Marcelo will give up. That'll be it.

I just need to make this job work until I can quit and take my credits and buy myself a new ship to add to my fleet.

I sniff up and stare out the window of the shuttle.

Okay, yeah. That's a good plan. I like that plan.

"Do you want to talk?" Kalvin asks, reaching for my hand.

I pull my hand from his, and he frowns. He scoots forward in his chair, so he can turn to look at me.

"Hey Princess, don't turn into an ice queen," he says, his voice kind.

I make eye contact with him and remember everything it took to find the kind side of Kalvin. We were adversaries in flight school, and then we became close in the Sonoman desert. Now, he's finally here, and the first thing he witnesses is a power struggle between Saif and me.

"I'm not," I say softly. "I'm just..." I turn my head to peer out the window. "I'm disappointed."

"That might actually be worse." He tries for my hand again. This time, I let him take it. He laces his fingers with mine, and my heart melts a little. Wasn't I betting on him leaving me?

"Listen to me." He squeezes my hand. "This is one little hiccup. From the look on his face, I'm sure Saif regrets this. Let's continue on, and maybe he'll catch up to us."

"What if I don't want him to catch up to us?" I grumble.

He chuckles. "Then you would have told him it was over. You didn't." He sighs. "Men are assholes. I should know. But the good ones realize when they've fucked up and ask for forgiveness. And they don't try to blame it on you, either. Never let someone do that to you. I bet he turns things around soon enough. So, just chill for now."

He leans back, squeezes my hand again, and closes his eyes. Look at Kalvin giving me advice about men. What strange world is this I'm living in?

I concentrate on the choppy, shining waters of Rio's ocean as we speed over it until I'm no longer devastatingly sad about everything. I'm now just very sad. Hopefully, by the time we land at the gemstone mine, I'll only be somewhat sad. Being somewhat sad won't be hard to hide, and I need to go into this new job in control and ready to rock.

I hold my breath as land approaches. As the water below us gets shallower and shallower, I make out shapes under the surface.

"Oh my... Holy shit," I breathe out as I let go of Kalvin's hand and press my face to the window.

Giant whales swim languidly about, hoisting their fins into the air above the surface. Rio's whales are legendary creatures, and scientists have been studying them for hundreds of years. These whales resemble Old Earth whales so closely that they have been a mystery forever.

"Wow," Kalvin breathes out, pressing his face to the window next to me. "Rio is fucking weird."

Totally weird.

I went through an animal phase in my youth, thinking I might even want to be a veterinarian one day. So I started studying Rio animals, of course. Until they started giving me nightmares. Then I shelved the books and never looked at them again.

The Rio environment is always fascinating for people who love animals. Arriving here in the Brazilianos System, we only had to terraform Ossun. Belem, Rio's moon, came later. But the animal diversity we experienced on Earth is not something we will ever have again. Replicating large animals is extremely hard, and they don't always breed independently. Complex life forms are also a challenge. Vivian explained it to me once, and I still don't understand it despite my attempts. Physics is more my area of expertise than biology.

I sigh as we cross over the beach to the jungle. This lush jungle gives me the chills. There could be a million things in here that could maim or kill me. I close my eyes and tick them off on a list in my head. There are Old Earth animal analogs like monkeys, birds, boars, snakes, spiders, bugs, tigers, and on, and on, and on. They all have odd names and frightening characteristics. The animals are often in pairs, too, so if the green snake doesn't kill you, its hawk pair will finish the job. And if the animals don't kill you, the plants might. I am glad I stopped studying Rio plants and animals when I did, or I might not be here right now.

The shuttle banks out and around a mountain and several buildings come into view. This must be the barracks and offices for the gemstone mine. It doesn't look as scary as I thought it would. They razed the ground around the buildings, flattening them into walkways and safe areas. The trees and jungle growth are cut back far from the buildings, and an electrified fence surrounds everything.

Movement out on the horizon catches my attention.

"Look," I say, pointing into the distance. Kalvin leans over my shoulder.

Smoke rises from a few kilometers away, and birds circle in the air above. I wonder if those are my colleagues or if that's the military. It could be either.

I guess there's really only one way to find out.

I sit back and wait for the shuttle to land.

* * *

"Skylar Kawabata?" A man jogs up to me on the paved landing field. I raise my eyebrows at him, and he laughs. "Hey, I'm Luca Rey," he says, holding out his hand for me to shake. A smile brightens his face, and a dimple appears in his left cheek. "I'm the Patras blockade runner."

Ah, so *this* is the man India Dellis has in charge of keeping people out of the military's hands. He's tall and lanky, and his muscles are taut cords running up his bare arms and legs. It's hotter than hell down here in the jungles, which is an excellent opportunity to wear short pants and shirts. Especially when you have the body to show them off. His dark, thick hair is combed neatly up and over. His russet skin is a good sign he spends more days outside than on a ship, and his upright posture shows a healthy upbringing.

I wish I had worn shorts as well.

I shake his hand. "Nice to meet you."

"How was the flight?"

"Uneventful," I reply. "Just the way I like them. This is my companion, Kalvin Vidal."

"Hey." Kalvin reaches out to shake Luca's hand.

"Nice to meet you." He looks around. "I thought Saif Bhaat was supposed to be with you." He waves at the buildings in the background, all Bhaat Jewelers' property.

"He couldn't make it. It'll just be us."

Luca's lips twist. "Well, I suppose that's fine. But if he arrives at another time, he'll have to wait until I can come get him. Is he delayed? Or not coming?"

"I'm sorry. I don't know. Hopefully, he'll get in touch." I shrug and try to seem nonchalant about the situation.

"I thought he was a member of your network?" When I say nothing, he frowns. "Or maybe I got the intelligence wrong. Sorry."

I notice movement in my peripheral vision and turn in time to catch Kalvin making a slashing motion across his throat. He smiles and turns his hand up to wave at me. Sigh.

"Nope. He's not a member of my network. Sorry for the confusion."

Luca glances around at the buildings, the people coming and going, the guarded landing pad away from the jungle proper, and I can see the calculations in his head. This was an excellent setup I had. I had a safe entrance into the wilderness, away from the military, and finding something this good again will be tough.

"Trust me," I say, butting into his thoughts. "It's not ideal, but this may be the only time I'm ever able to do this. So we should take advantage of it now before someone comes out from those buildings and tells us to get back on the shuttle and return to Primeiro."

He sighs. "Okay. I'll figure it out. Come on."

He's quiet all the way to the fence. The hum of the electrified wires from a dozen meters away pains my ears. The powerful energy raises the hair on my arms and sends tingles down my back. Eek. I don't like the look of it.

"In here." Luca waves to a small one-room building inside the fence's perimeter. He opens the door, and I step in. Inside, four men dressed in camouflage are waiting for us, sitting around and killing time by either fidgeting or reading. They are all dressed for battle with guns slung over their shoulder and knives in their belts.

Luca gestures to me. "We have camouflage for you, too." He opens two lockers on the other side of the room and hands me a shirt and pants. I hold them out and stare at them. He slides a shirt on over his t-shirt and drops his shorts to pull on the pants. All I can do is smile.

"Boss, you're embarrassing the lady," one man says, and the others chuckle.

Luca glances up at me; I keep smiling.

"It's nothing she hasn't seen before." Kalvin laughs.

"I'm not embarrassed in the slightest," I say, rolling out my speech into a drawl. "But you all will be vacating this little hut so I can get dressed."

Luca hops as he pulls up his pants and zips up the fly. "First things first. Let's go over the rules. When we get outside the fence, your whole life becomes being aware of your surroundings. You watch where you step. You watch where we are. You look up at least a meter every so often to make sure nothing is going to come down on top of you."

I shiver, and Luca nods. Kalvin groans.

"If we're attacked, we will handle it." He points to his men. They wave. "You should crouch and stay low unless we tell you to run. Then you run in a straight line in the direction we point."

I can't believe I voluntarily signed up for this.

"Got it," I say, nodding.

"Uh, yeah. Got it." Kalvin leans over to me and whispers, "I said I like danger, right?"

"You did," I whisper back.

"Just checking." He clears his throat.

"How are you in high-stress situations?" Luca asks, his stare drilling down into my brain. I suddenly feel naked. "Do you handle them well, or are you going to faint or breakdown, or..."

He stops at my hardened face. "Please don't think this is sexist. I ask everyone this when they come through here."

I glance at the men behind him. "Truth. He asks everyone."

Okay, well, at least it's not some 'hysterical women' stereotype.

"I'm a pilot, so I handle high stress well. But, I gotta be honest. Rio freaks me out, so I have no idea how I'll be if a snake attacks me or some jungle cat pounces on me."

"Same," Kalvin says, raising his hand. "Also a pilot, and also freaked out by Rio."

He nods. "Fair enough. Okay, we're going to leave you to get dressed. Take your time. I'll call into the camp before we leave. Communications are spotty in the jungle. It's an hour hike, and I don't expect any trouble. Many animals have vacated this area because of the electric fence and the repeated shuttle flyovers. We *should* be okay on this trip, but it's important to stay alert."

I don't like how he stressed 'should' in that last statement.

When the door closes behind them, I sit down on the nearby bench and take a moment to make sure this is what I want to do.

"You okay?" Kalvin asks.

"Ugh. I don't know. This all feels weird without Saif now."

He was so enthusiastic about going, and he secured this location for me to fly in and everything. How do I reconcile that sweet guy with the one who screwed me over this afternoon?

Kalvin sits down next to me.

"How long have you two been dating?" He looks at his hands clasped together.

"Three weeks? Four? You know time…"

"Yeah, it's malleable when you're zooming around in a ship." He sighs. "I apologize. Because I don't think he would have gotten that bright idea to test you if I hadn't said you were an independent woman."

"It's not your fault," I say, standing up.

"Saif had an ax to grind with you, but it's nothing I haven't seen before. You'll just need to be careful."

"Are you… Are you trying to give me relationship advice?" I lean over the back of the bench and look him in the eye. "Because you don't have the best track record there either."

He stands up and faces me, the bench between us.

"Come on, gorgeous. Everything was great until I left. Shall I remind you?"

Before I can respond, his hand reaches for my jaw.

I'm tempted to let him in after the day I've had, but no. Not yet. We connected in the desert, and we were getting somewhere… then he left. He doesn't get to waltz back in and pretend like nothing happened in the meantime.

I lift my chin out of his reach, and his wry smile only grows.

"I see." He chuckles and reaches for the clothes he was given. "You're going to make me work for it."

"Of course I am. Why wouldn't I?"

"Well, I don't know how you'll resist my charm, but everyone needs a hobby."

I shake my head while holding back my laughter. He makes me laugh quite a lot with his roguish humor. Watching him undress now, I remember why I thought he was the handsome flyboy in the first place. He's tall with lean and long muscles he built in the gym. I love when his hair is messy because you can see how the ends curl. We haven't slept together, but I can imagine what it'll be like once I finally let him in. Mmmm, I can't wait for him to wrap his long legs around me.

"Get dressed, sweetheart," he says, interrupting my thoughts of sex. "And stop staring at me like I'm a piece of meat."

He winks, and my face heats. Damned blush response. I hate it.

He mock salutes as he opens the door to step outside. "She

just needs another moment," he says to the guys waiting outside before shutting the door.

Sigh. I need to get dressed and get going. Things can only improve with the men in my life, right? Kalvin is here, and I'm sure Saif will be in my inbox in no time. This is an obvious low point, and assuming the jungle doesn't kill me, everything should work itself out.

Yes. That's what I'm going to choose to believe.

I change and join the men outside.

"Okay. I made this trip only two days ago, and it was an easy trek with no animal attacks. Let's hope for the same today." Luca ushers me forward towards the electric fence's gate. I fall into step next to Kalvin.

"Oh yeah? You had new people in only two days ago?" I ask, trying to calm my nerves by making small talk.

"Yeah, some hot-shot millionaire who's teaming up with Ms. Dellis. Takemo something-or-other."

Fuck.

Did I just say that my life with men can only improve?

I was wrong.

11

Our trek through the jungle is strange and surreal. I keep my eyes peeled for animals along the way, but I'm lucky enough not to spot any. Luca's men lead our party through the brush, careful to clear the plants away, but even that is not a hard job. This is a well-worn path, and this gives me pause. Nothing about Rio is supposed to be this tame. Usually, the jungle reclaims everything humans try to do to it. A well-worn path here means India's teams have been using this route a lot. That's bound to catch the attention of the military, sooner rather than later.

I stick to the path behind the lead men, but I also hold out my hand to the various plants as we walk past. I brush my fingers along trees, ground cover, flowers, bushes — anything I can reach. As we observed on the Amagi, when we carried Vivian's Rio plants and back in her greenhouses on Ossun, Rio plants will move towards their human pairs. If the human has a pair. Ken and Vivian each have Rio plant pairs. Ken's gives him heightened empathy when he consumes it. Vivian's allows her consciousness to jump out of her body and go other places. It's wild. She's only done it a few times, but it's worked every time.

I wonder what my pair is.

"You should keep your hands to yourself," Luca says from behind me. "Some of these plants are poisonous. This type of behavior will get you in the hospital."

He's right, and I should draw back my hand, but I will never find my pair if I'm not always looking for it. Maybe Luca doesn't know this bit of information about the Rio plants. Not many people actually do.

"It's fine. It's what I'm here to do," I reply, stepping over a giant fallen log. I'm careful to look up and around, and I spot nothing but plants.

"What *are* you here to do?" he asks, moving in a little closer. Kalvin turns around in front of me and slows down to listen in. He's only heard the overview of my job.

"I'm... I'm not sure how much I'm allowed to talk about. If I tell you, I may have to kill you."

He jogs up a little closer. "I have full classified clearance."

"And I'm supposed to take your word for it?" I glance behind us, and something about the size of a dog with many, many legs skitters across the path we just traversed. I shiver.

"I suppose you shouldn't." The dimple in Luca's cheek grows.

"Good. Then we're on the same page."

We're quiet for a bit, but Luca slows down next to me, so I slow my steps to match his. He stops, cocks his head, and blinks a few times. "Hear that?" he asks, his hand out.

I can't hear anything over the rush of my breath.

Luca whistles low, and the men around us stop. He gestures to get down, and my stomach drops along with my knees. Oh God, what's going to happen? My back sweats as distant chittering and squeaking grows louder by the second.

"Put your head down and pull your bag over your head. Don't leave your hands or skin exposed." He pulls his arms into his shirt and draws it over his head like he's a turtle in its shell.

"Aw shit," Kalvin says, resigned. "Skylar, over here." He gestures to a fallen log as he does the same thing as Luca.

"What is it?" My voice shakes.

"Starbats. A swarm of them."

The chittering has turned to high-pitched screams now. Starbats? What the hell are starbats?

One flies past me, and I panic and don't dive for Kalvin. I hurriedly tuck in my shirt, pull my bag over my head, and fold my hands underneath me. I get as low as I can, remembering child's pose from my yoga practice, but tighter and more ball-like.

The noise of the starbats crescendos, and one thumps into my back.

I cry out and burst into a sob as it tears my shirt before flying off. *Thunk, thunk, thunk, thunk whap thunk.* Each time another hits me, I flinch and cry some more. My back stings with pain, but I stay down. Whatever's happening, I don't want it happening to my face.

A starbat hits the ground next to me, close enough for me to see from under the cover of my bag, and I immediately wish I had kept my eyes closed. The thing looks like a Franken bird-bat-spider combination. It has a head like a bird with no feathers, but each eye is compounded like a spider. It opens its beak, a screech comes out, and the sound sucks the air from my body. When it spreads its wings to retake flight, I understand where the 'bat' part of the name comes from. The wings are leathery and thin, with several sections. White dots along its torso remind me of the stars in the night sky.

Fuck. Rio is weird as hell.

I concentrate on my breathing, in and out, in and out, until the screeching and chittering grows quiet. Looking at the dirt, I wonder how many times I'm going to end up like this on my trip, cowering in fear and wondering if I'll live through whatever Rio throws at me. It could be a daily occurrence, or this could be the only time it ever happens. I have no clue.

"Ms. Kawabata," Luca says, his hand on my shoulder, "you can get up now."

I drag the bag off my head and hiss at the pain radiating off my back. I lift my head to look at Luca, and he winces.

"You got really scratched up." His eyes scan over my tear-soaked face. "Are you okay?"

I press my lips together. I don't want to cry anymore in front of him, so I pull a breath in through my nose before letting it go. Sitting up, I wipe the tears from my face, and Luca winces again. Ugh. My hands are covered with dirt, so I guess my face is dirty now, too.

Kalvin stands up, unscathed. I should have sought shelter next to him.

"Are they poisonous?" I ask Luca, wondering how much time I have left to live.

He shakes his head, and I sigh in relief. "They just scratch. Sometimes they bite, too, but not if you cover yourself. You're going to need some bandages and antibiotics, otherwise, they'll get infected."

I blow out another long shaky breath and try to pull myself together.

Skylar, it was just starbats. No big deal.

Not that I had any idea starbats existed until five minutes ago.

"Oh no, Sky," Kalvin says, approaching me. He reaches out and wipes the dirt tears from my cheeks. "We'll fix this. It's a simple patch-up job. No worries."

The pilot speak is comforting, more than I ever thought it would be. But I should have left Kalvin with the Amagi where he belongs. He doesn't belong in the jungle.

Neither do I.

"We should go, boss," one of the lead men calls out. "We're almost there, and kites will be incoming."

"Kites?" I ask, picking up my bag.

"The starbats' pair. Snarl-toothed kites. They always follow a flock of starbats within a few minutes. The two are natural predators of each other, and the kites are a lot more vicious. So we should go."

Without a word, I hustle forward with Kalvin and follow the lead men, even though I can feel the blood dripping down my back.

Later.

I'll deal with it later.

* * *

We enter the camp without further incident, thank the heavens. We pass through the gate at an electric fence being run off generators and walk to temporary houses amongst the long grass. I take mental notes of everything as we walk past — the heavy machinery parked outside the fence under the trees, the hum of activity from the furthest buildings, the smell of onions and garlic cooking, a group of five men playing football along the corridor between buildings, another man in full PPE gear leaving a lab.

"Ms. Kawabata, we should go straight to the infirmary." Luca gestures to a temporary building three down the path.

"Yeah. That's a good idea." I'm starting to feel faint from the blood loss and shock of the starbats' attack. I didn't think I'd run into Rio wildlife so soon after landing.

I'm learning hard lessons today, for sure.

Stumbling forward, I blink my eyes to stay conscious. Kalvin trots up next to me and takes my arm.

"How about I escort the princess to her castle?" he asks. I

want to smack him, but I take the proffered arm without saying anything.

Luca pulls open the door to the infirmary, and blood runs down his arm. I touch his torn shirt and pull back the fabric. He's pretty banged up as well.

"It's nothing." He jerks his head at the doorway. "Happens to me all the time." His smile tries to reassure me that this is no big deal, but his face falls as he catches sight of my back. "Shit. We should have dressed those cuts on the go."

I trudge into the room like a zombie on autopilot.

"Doc!" Luca calls to the rear of the infirmary. "We've got someone who needs help!"

Through the clear panel on the door, a woman with her hair in a ponytail is stuffing pasta into her mouth at a hurried pace with one hand while grabbing gloves with her other hand. She tosses her fork on the plate, wipes her mouth quickly, and glides out of the office like she's ready and raring to go.

"Who do we have here?" she says, smiling as she approaches me. "You must be new." She narrows her eyes. "I recognize you, I think." She looks at Kalvin. "You, I don't recognize."

"Fine by me," he says jovially. "I like to be anonymous."

I shuffle and set my hand on the nearest table to stop from falling over. Both Luca and the doctor lunge forward to catch me. Kalvin holds on tighter.

"Oh, wait. Hold on there for a second." She guides me back a step to sit on a stool. She leans to the side, looks at my back, and hisses. "Ouch. You've got yourself quite the bloody back there."

"Skylar," I mumble. "Skylar Kawabata."

She raises her eyebrows as she crosses past the nearest cot to the locker full of medical supplies.

"How did this happen, Luca?" she asks, her face falling into a frown. "I was hoping Ms. Kawabata would arrive in one piece. We need her desperately right now." She waves to the five occupied beds at the rear of the infirmary, partially hidden behind a cloth screen.

Luca shrugs. "I do my best. But starbats can't be controlled. Next time I'm bringing a canvas blanket to throw over people. Ms. Kawabata was right in the center of the swarm."

"Bad timing." She extracts a few bottles, some gauze, sterile bandages, and other instruments from the locker. "Better go get India." She shoos him off with a wave of her hand.

"Those starbats came too fast. I wasn't able to get to Skylar in time to help her." Kalvin pulls up a chair next to me.

She smiles kindly at me, and I can't do anything, or I'm going to pass out or puke.

"I'm Dr. Emily Arzon." She sets everything she needs on the shining steel table. "You can call me whatever — Doc, Dr. Arzon, Dr. Emily — or just drop the 'doctor' altogether." She shrugs. "I don't care. It's the main reason I'm here and not working in some fancy-ass hospital."

I huff a small laugh. "Fucking starbats fucked me up, Doc."

She throws back her head in a laugh. "A woman with the same vocabulary I have. Excellent. We'll make good friends." She holds up a finger as she trots off to another locker and grabs a hospital gown. "We're going to cut that shirt and bra off of you, and you can wear this. I'll tie it in the back."

"Don't cut the bra. It's one of the few good ones I have left."

Her hesitation is less than a second. "Yes, of course. They're so hard to find in the right size, too."

We make the switch, and I'm impressed that Kalvin doesn't ogle or embarrass me when I'm exposed. He has a bedside manner that's kinder than his hot-shot pilot self. An unexpected bonus.

I hold the hospital gown against my chest as the doctor gets to work on my back. Just when I'm finding my calm, the door opens and in sweeps India Dellis with Takemo Diaz right behind her.

"Oh no," she moans, coming straight to me. "Already? You hadn't even made it to camp yet."

She glides to my side. I'm amazed this woman has poise in almost every situation, even when she's wearing the plainest of clothes with no makeup and no jewelry. I touch the elephant charm under the hospital gown, and tears well in my eyes again. I wish Saif was here.

"She'll be okay," Kalvin says, squeezing my hand.

Takemo's eyes zoom straight in to our locked hands, and his jaw tightens. I blink, and he's back to normal. Did I imagine that?

"And who are you?" India asks, pulling away from Kalvin's megawatt grin.

"Kalvin Vidal, pilot and friend of Skylar, at your service." He reaches out to shake her hand.

"India Dellis," she says, shaking his hand and smiling with a knowing glint in her eyes. "You're the one who was stranded in the desert with Skylar."

"That was me, indeed."

"I see." She looks back and forth between us. I play comatose. "Is it painful?" she asks me, looking at Dr. Emily doing her work. "Give her more meds, Doc."

"Sure thing." Emily sets down her instruments and returns to the lockers and the fridge for painkillers and juice. I drink down what she gives me and turn my mind away from Kalvin, Saif, and this whole mess.

"So, starbats, huh? Luca filled me in." India takes my free hand in hers.

"Yeah. I'll be fine." I sniff up and glance at Takemo. His expression is stern. "It was just bad timing, that's all." I sigh and then wince as Emily disinfects another cut. "What sucks is that I sleep on my back."

Takemo huffs a brief laugh. "That *does* suck. You have the worst luck, Skylar. I came in two days ago with no problems."

"Aren't you a lucky bastard, then."

"Always." He grins and briefly looks at Kalvin.

"Takemo Diaz, this is Kalvin. Kalvin, Takemo," I say, waving between them.

Kalvin reaches over to shake, and it takes Takemo a beat to match his hand. I don't know what's going on here. I don't really care.

"I'd give you a few days to rest, but we need to get started. Sorry. We're on a schedule," India says, keeping her smile light. "But I'm sure we can make anything work. Whatever you need, just let me know."

"How about a giant glass of gin, a sleeping pill, and a comfortable place to sleep?" My words are already slurring, so maybe I don't need any of that.

"You've got it." India turns to Luca and squeezes his arm. "Thanks for getting her here in one piece. She's important to the mission."

Luca frowns. "Well, now I feel bad that she arrived in this condition." He sighs as he stuffs his hands in his pockets. "If it makes this any better, that was one of the largest flocks of starbats I've ever seen." He shrugs.

"Oh yeah, that totally makes me feel better," I say, my voice flat and lifeless. I sigh. "It's not your fault. It's Rio." I try to shrug and regret it.

India tips over her wristlet and rolls her eyes after a moment. "It seems I'm needed in the lab. Are you okay? Do you need me to stay?" She squeezes my hand.

"No. Go ahead. I'm in good hands." I wince from the deep cut in my lower back that's being cleaned. "Ow, fuck," I growl.

"Sorry!" Emily sing-songs as she moves onto something else that I'm sure will hurt just as bad.

"Takemo will show you to your cabin after this. Yours is next to his. Will Kalvin be staying with you?"

"Sure," I say, feeling lightheaded.

She leans in close to whisper in my ear. "Should I ask why Saif Bhaat didn't join you? His mother is not a fan of mine, so if this is my fault, I'm sorry."

I shake my head and pull away from her so she can see my face. "It's not. It's my own fault."

"Okay. Call me if you need anything," she says before she leaves.

I grip the table and try to hold still, but it's hard to be so complacent in the face of such a strange turn of events in my life. I'm supposed to be out flying the stars with the Amagi, meeting men, and starting my own relationship network, not trudging through the jungles. I'm losing the men I care about and most of my family. And I'm about to lose my ship, the one thing that was going to be my savior.

I sniff up and look away from Takemo.

He sighs and picks up the position India just left by my side.

"You were right," I tell him. "Saif was too good for me. It only took him a few days to want to embarrass me, the unworthy and undesirable mate, in front of his family." I swipe my hand up and under my nose, and then laugh at the state of my dirty hands... and now my face. I glance at him sideways, and he's staring at the floor at our feet. "I bet you're pretty proud of yourself, huh? You called that one weeks ago."

Before Takemo can say anything, Kalvin squeezes my hand. "Shhh, Skylar. You're too tired to talk."

I feel a hand on my shoulder. "Ms. Kawabata, I'm done. Get some rest, and try not to touch your back for a few days. Sorry to say that a shower is out of the question for a day while the bandages cure. You can wash from the waist down and use a washcloth on the rest. Come see me in two days, and I'll check on everything." She slides something across the steel table.

"Here's that sleeping pill. Don't mix it with alcohol, or you'll regret it."

No gin for me.

"Thanks, Doc," I say, taking the little cup. "And it's Skylar. Ms. Kawabata is what my matchmaker calls me."

"You got it." She leaves to go tend to the men at the rear of the infirmary.

I throw down the pill and swallow it with the rest of the juice. I should be settling into my room by now, unpacking my bag, laughing with Saif and Kalvin, getting ready to eat whatever smells so good out there. Instead, I'm this wrecked piece of trash.

I suppose I deserve it.

Sliding from the stool, I waver on my feet, and Takemo's hand whips out to steady me. I grab his arm and pull him close to me.

"You've been an asshole to me, Takemo, even after I won the tournament for you."

He raises his eyebrows at me.

"The least you can do is walk Kalvin and me to my room."

"I took your mom off trash hauling duties," he reminds me.

I look up and remember how my first impression of him was of how handsome he was, and he's still pretty stunning, with his perfect hair, glowing skin, and clean clothes. I've obviously set the bar sky-high, haven't I? It's too bad that I remember all the nasty things he's said about me. How I'm worthless. How I'm a conniving bitch. How I'm lazy, hotheaded, and undesirable.

"Yeah, I got your message. Thanks for that. But don't go easy on her again. Okay? If she's busy, maybe she won't try to take away my ship."

His eyebrows pull together, but I wave away his questions.

"Ask tomorrow." I nudge him forward.

"Sure. Whatever you say, Skylar."

He sighs as I jerk his arm towards the door.

12

I SLEEP on the edge of the bed all night, and Kalvin sleeps on the sofa in my suite. When I get up in the wee morning hours to dress for the lab, I pull him from the couch and stick him in the bed. Before I leave, I stand at the door and watch him, his thin face, long nose, and lips I'm dying to kiss, if it doesn't backfire on me.

What am I thinking? Of course, it'll backfire on me.

I leave the suite quietly, making sure everything is buttoned up tight before heading out.

"You said to ask tomorrow, so here I am, asking. What's going on with your mom and your ship?"

Takemo hovers over me as I sit in the lab and await my first meeting with the lead xeno-plant biologist. On this side of the divider, I don't have to wear PPE. I stare into the lab window and watch all the scientists bustle about, cutting plants, mixing plants with solution, putting solutions in lab equipment. I don't know what they're doing, but it all looks impressive.

Instead of ignoring him, which won't get me anywhere, I turn to face him. "Why do you care?"

His jaw hardens. "I probably shouldn't, but I promised you I would do better." He sweeps out his hands. "So, here I am, doing better by giving a fuck."

I almost laugh because it *is* laughable. Takemo should be long gone from my life, but he's stuck here with me, whether or not he likes it.

"I see." I pause to gauge him for a moment. I suppose I could confide in him because it's not likely he'll even admit to anyone that he knows me. "My mom is disinheriting me and has retained a lawyer to get the Amagi back."

"What?" he pulls away, shocked. "She can't do that."

I laugh. "She's gonna try, and knowing my luck lately, she'll probably succeed." I point at him. "Though not without a big, ugly, public fight, I can tell you that much."

Rage burns in my stomach, and the need for revenge swells in my heart. If my mother thinks she's going to get away with this robbery, then she is sorely mistaken.

"No," Takemo insists. "I mean, she really can't. I know because I tried to get the Amagi." He shrugs at my death glare. "What? It's a great ship. I saw it was being overhauled and thought I could take it instead of the Mikasa."

He raises his hands as I get to my feet. This little shit. He could have totally screwed me over if he had taken the Amagi.

"Skylar," he says, warning me, "that was Past-Takemo, okay? Current-Takemo wouldn't dream of taking your ship from you. I already regret most everything that's happened between us. Don't get even angrier with me." He inhales a deep breath. "Please," he stresses.

Hmmm, there's a Past- and Current-Takemo? What does that even mean? He seems unhappy with his previous asshole behavior. Maybe he'll be nicer now? But maybe there'll be a Future-Takemo, a time in which he will dig deep and find his dickhole behavior, long lost and forgotten about but ripe for reanimation.

I still don't trust him, but he's growing on me.

"Okay. I'm not angry," I say, calming my breathing. "What do you mean, she can't take my ship? I thought it was a done deal. She gave it to me, but I saw no legal documents. Ken Mata was going to look into it for me, but, well, he's busy."

Takemo nods. "He's a busy man, but I can tell you, one-hundred percent, that ship is yours. Your mother transferred the title to your name four years ago. It was a good move on her part because she didn't have to pay taxes and fees on it anymore. I'm sure you know how expensive those are."

I nod and stare off into the lab. I try to keep the fees down by accessing the jump rings at off-peak times, and I always choose the slips at spaceports that are farthest from the terminal. Still, I'm scraping by week to week until I get my first payment from Patras. Fees and taxes could bankrupt me before lawyers do.

"If she's trying to get back the Amagi now, she'll need to prove she handed over the title to you under duress or something else." He shrugs. "This is a pure power play on her part. She's doing it to teach you a lesson."

"No shit, Sherlock." Why is everyone trying to teach me a lesson nowadays? Haven't I learned enough?

He sighs. "Sorry. That sucks. But the good news is they can't send the local police after you or detain your ship. They have no legal right to do that."

I sink in relief, and the background anxiety I've felt since Mom showed up at Vivian's dissipates a fraction. She's still going to come after me for the Amagi, but at least she can't just take it. I was worried she could.

"Good to know. They tried to keep me on Ossun, and Saif wanted me to stay and deal with it." I should feel elated that I was right and Saif was wrong, but instead, I'm just sad. I wish he was here. "He's angry with me for not being more careful and methodical about my choices."

Takemo laughs. "You so are not either of those things."

"Hey now," I say gently. "I could use that in my life. I'm willing to listen to other people's opinions about my business. I may not always take their advice, but I listen."

He steps away as someone finally enters the room. "Listening is a good start. Hey, does the pilot know all this?" He jerks his chin at the door. I turn and look, though I know no one's there.

"That I'm losing my family and business? Yeah, some of it." Not enough, though, when I really think about it.

"He's the one who was marooned with you, right? You saved each other's lives?"

"Yeah, that's him." I step to the side as the lab tech puts stuff on the table. "Why?"

"Just checking," he says, waving my question away. He scans my back. "How's your back? Did you sleep okay?"

"Not really." It was hard to stay off my back all night. I was restless sleeping on my side, and sleeping on my stomach is never a good idea. "And my back itches and it's painful." I shrug.

"You should get it looked at then," Takemo insists.

"Do you want to start this experiment later, Ms. Kawabata?" the lab tech asks as he sets a tray on the table in front of me.

"No. I'm fine." I wave off her concern. "I want to get to work as quickly as possible. Have the doctor stop by later when she can."

"Good." He pulls a thermometer gun from his pocket. "Because we're breaking camp tomorrow and waiting any longer means we need to wait several days."

"We're breaking camp?"

"India moves us about every six to seven days," Takemo fills in. "It's not good to put down roots. We have to keep moving, or the military will find us."

My skin cools. "What happens if they find us?"

"I don't want to know. But it's a real pain in the butt to move. We have to shut everything down, including the duonet data points, which means we lose communications for about twelve hours. Then it takes longer for supplies to reach us because we work farther into the jungle each time."

"So I should check my messages before the blackout. Got it."

I wonder if Saif has messaged me yet. I quickly tip over my wristlet to check my inbox. And yes, there's a message from him, almost a day old now. I'm tempted to watch it, but Takemo is hovering next to me. There's a transcript attached to the message, so I download both to the local storage on my wristlet and swipe away.

Then I remember my brief plan to just let him go, ignore him, and hope he would forget about me. Listening to his message, though, is fine, Skylar. I'll listen and not respond. That's avoidance right there.

"Skylar," Takemo says, knocking me out of my daze. "You ready?"

When I nod, he asks the lab tech, "So, what's first?"

"I should take your wristlet now," the lab tech says, holding out his hand. "It might cause problems with today's plant."

I turn it over to the tech and jerk my head at Takemo. "You don't have to stick around. I know you have your own work to do here."

"Nah. It's fine. I have employees out there doing the work. You shouldn't have to do this alone." His tone is damning, and he's wondering why Kalvin isn't here.

"I made Kalvin sleep on the couch last night, so he's in bed now. I'm sure he'll be here later."

"Sure, Skylar." The 'whatever you say' is left off. He already doubts Kalvin's sincerity, even though we survived the desert together.

I wonder if Kalvin understands how his personality comes off to other people. I don't think he does.

I open my mouth to protest, but the lab tech butts in, not seeing my hesitation.

"Okay. Up first, we have a specimen of lily. We've found an array of interesting plants around a freshwater pond about a ten-minute walk from here. All the plants seem to have the same properties as the fish and other creatures in the same water. This particular one is pretty neat. It changes a person's skin at a cellular level to become electrocytes."

I gasp and bring my fingers to my lips.

"You mean I'll produce electricity?"

"Yep," he says with a wide smile. "We suspect it'll be anywhere up to four hundred volts. The effects seem to last a few hours, so you'll be here all day."

Looking around at the room I'm in, I realize they furnished it especially for me. I can relax on the oversized, plush couch, watch something on the wallscreens, and grab food from the stocked fridge. I'm not supposed to go anywhere because someone will observe me to ensure I don't get sick.

Well, all of my worries about this job were for nothing. Looks like I'll be sitting around bored, going from one guarded building to another, over and over. I thought this entire trip would be a lot more adventurous.

Not that I'm complaining. My trek to the camp from the gemstone mine was enough adventure for a lifetime.

"Did you witness this electric effect in other human test subjects?" I ask, excitement brewing in my chest.

"Yes, we did." His mood sobers. "Unfortunately, he fried his scalp and ended up with second-degree burns."

Yikes. Okay. Maybe I spoke too soon about this being boring.

More like possibly dangerous.

"We've analyzed your DNA, though, Ms. Kawabata, and we don't expect any issues. You have a gene mutation that makes this all possible. If we have good luck here, and the luck continues, we may be able to make this work for the masses. We'll see."

"Okay." I nod and shake out my arms. "Okay. I can do this."

I hold out my hand for the crushed leaf encased in a gel pill, throw it into my mouth, and swallow it with a glass of water.

"I'll call the doctor now," the lab tech says, heading back inside.

"I think I'll stick around," Takemo says, ambling over to the couch and testing the cushions with his hand. "This looks comfortable."

Suppressing my desire to be snarky with him, I cross to the fridge once the lab tech heads back inside. "Water?" I ask, leaning in to see what's on offer. "Uh, black or green tea? Iced coffee?" I grab one of each and turn to see him, his head cocked to the side, staring at my ass.

I clear my throat and point. "My face is up here, asshole."

His smile is self-satisfied. "I'm familiar with the anatomy of a human being, Skylar."

"Could have fooled me. What do you want?" I ask, holding out the various cans.

"Coffee, thanks."

I hand him his can, and I open a bottle of sweetened black tea.

"Didn't really peg you for a tea drinker," Takemo says as I sit down on the opposite end of the couch.

"I prefer coffee, but I like it hot, not cold. I only drink it hot, ever. Even if it's blazing like the face of the sun outside." I sip my tea. I hope the conversation dies soon and he leaves.

"How much time do you even spend outside? You're a spaceship captain." He tucks a leg up underneath him, turning to me.

I suppress a sigh.

I want to tell him to go, to find something else to do. Because I know this game. We'll talk for a bit, and then he'll say some-

99

thing insulting, and we'll end up fighting with each other. But I can't just order him to leave because that will also result in a fight.

"I like both ships and planets, but ships are more comfortable for me." I drink more tea and set the bottle aside. "I didn't spend much time on planets as a kid, so I'm trying to make up for it now."

Takemo is quiet for a moment. "So, you really grew up on that ship?"

I close my eyes for a minute and rewind my memory to when we played cards on the Amagi. He had asked me why I hadn't gone to boarding school on Ossun or Rio, and I had ignored his question.

"Right," I say out loud, opening my eyes. "Yes, I grew up on the ship, and no, I did not go to boarding schools. Dominic insisted we stay aboard and be tutored instead."

Takemo's jaw flexes. "I don't like that guy. He gives me a bad vibe."

"Because he's a bad person." I sip my tea again and grimace at the pain in my back. Where is the doctor? "I got to go to far-school a few times. That's how I met Saif."

"Then how…?" He stops in mid-sentence, opens his mouth, grunts, and hesitates.

"Cat got your tongue?" I ask, trying not to laugh.

"I'm afraid if I ask this question, you'll hate me."

Ah. Shit. What's it going to be? I inhale, lift my chin, and smile.

"Go ahead. I promise not to be angry or hate you."

He seems to assess me for a moment before he nods.

"Okay. Then how did you cultivate this personality on the duonet of being a high-society princess? The fuck-em-and-leave-em type?"

My lips twist as I remember how it all started. I actually laugh, and this relaxes him a little.

"I went to far-school pretty regularly from six years old onward. The dads hated it, but my mom insisted I get to know other kids. Well, she did, at first." I sip my tea again to cover my awkwardness. "Anyway, there was this girl at a camp on Rio when I was nine who just *instantly* hated me." I roll my eyes. "She was so petty and insecure. She had some kind of dictatorship running with the other kids, and she saw me as a threat. When she heard my family had a small fleet of ships, she started the rumor that I was some high-and-mighty kid of a wealthy spacefaring family. That turned into 'princess,' and then all the kids were calling me that."

I stop for a second, remembering the tears I shed in the bathrooms when no one could see me. That was the hardest few years of far-school before I met Saif.

"So, yeah. I didn't know what to do. I spent little time with kids my own age. I didn't have the playground to try out my strategies on or anything. So, I went with it. I couldn't get her to stop, so I just let it happen. I played it up. If they thought I was snobby, I was even snobbier."

"Ugh. I hate childhood bullies," he mumbles.

"Yeah? How do you feel about adult bullies?" My face heats with anger for a moment. "Because I distinctly recall you saying awful things about me and calling me a bitch."

He pales and raises his hand. "I know. I'm sorry. I became the thing I hate, and I'm still trying to get past it."

I sigh, pushing the air out of my nose. "The rumor grew and grew. They passed it through every social circle, every primary school. The kids had mouths, and it just could not be stopped. When I got older, men wanted to sleep with me *because* they thought I was some princess with money, and instead of telling them no and freezing them out like I should have, I let it happen. I was just happy for the attention. Nothing good ever happened at home, and this way, I had control over what I wanted. I never dreamed it would backfire on me so completely."

"Your mom," he says, nodding.

"Yeah, my mom." I sigh as I lay my head back on the couch and rub my arms.

"I'm sorry. I feel like I was a party to all those rumors by believing them," he says, looking away from me.

Ugh. I have permanent goosebumps, and my scalp is prickling.

I glance at the clock, and it's been about thirty minutes since I took the pill. My whole body tingles, and I smell ozone. It's so weird. And forgetting the body sensations for a moment, I feel like a new relationship has opened up between Takemo and me. Maybe he's willing to listen to me now. Maybe he's even ready to be friends.

What if...?

I slip from the couch and approach Takemo. I peer down into his eyes as he lifts his chin to look at me. Softening my smile, I step right up to him.

"I know how you can make it up to me."

His lips part slightly, but he doesn't move. If he tells me to stop right now, I will. But I can see it in his eyes. He's grown to like me, trust me.

Let's see if he really trusts me.

"Hold out your hand, palm up," I say, and he hesitates only a moment before complying.

I reach out to hover my fingers over his.

Closer, closer...

An electric current jumps from my finger, an arc so bright I gasp in surprise.

"Shit!" he cries, pulling his hand back and shaking it out. "Oh my God. That fucking hurt."

I pull my hand up and cover my mouth, so I don't start hysterically laughing. My fingers are numb, and they smart with pain. Stepping back from Takemo, I hold my fingers out to look at them. They're singed.

"Oh shit."

I whirl around at Kalvin's voice. He's standing in the doorway with two takeout cups of coffee and a paper bag.

"Sky, your fingers. They're..." His voice drifts away on memories of our time in the desert. Quicksand had sucked him into the sandy abyss, and I shoved my hands into the sand to save him. Something shocked me and downloaded my memories, like flashes in my brain. I thought maybe the thing holding Kalvin was intelligent, so I asked for him back. I don't know why I thought this. It was instinct.

And my fingers ended up the same. Singed. Red hot and almost black.

I laugh, holding up my hands to him. Kalvin pales.

Takemo blinks a few times, his breathing deepening.

"I saw something when you did that." His voice is dreamy and light. "You were a kid, crying in a dark room... asking for food because you were hungry?"

My laughter dies quickly. "What? What did you say?"

"It was Dominic," he says, smacking his lips and closing his eyes. "He used to lock you in the closet and not feed you." He stands up, his face livid with anger. I'm stunned into silence. "What the fuck, Skylar?"

"I..." I reach out, hoping to calm him down, and another bolt lances off my hand and hits him in the upper arm.

"Ow!"

Takemo flies back on the couch, and my vision turns white for a second, like a giant flash from a camera has gone off. A wave of dizziness rolls over me as my head spins, and I collapse to my knees.

A flash of insight hits me — Takemo, in his early twenties, drowning his sorrows at a bar. He had just been dumped by someone he loved, I'm sure of it.

"Whoa!" Kalvin's arms are around my chest and hauling me up. "Oh my... Shit. Help!"

I blink a few times as the world comes back to me. But I see Kalvin this time, sitting at his mother's bedside? Yes, she could be his mother. She's wasting away, barely breathing. Oh no.

"Get her on the couch!"

It takes a moment to realize the doctor has finally shown up, and she's just in time to witness my first attempt at metabolizing the Rio plants.

I smell smoke, and Kalvin curses again. "Jesus, stop electrocuting me!"

"Back up," I whisper. "Let go."

He drops me to the floor, and I curl up and shout, "Stay away!"

Between Takemo and my past and now this, nothing about this day has gone well.

Nothing.

13

"Hey, Skylar! I saved you a spot!"

Is that Kalvin? I haven't seen him since I passed him sleeping on the couch again this morning. It wasn't safe for him to be anywhere near me, and even though another room opened up for him to take, he refused to go. He insisted on sleeping in the same room as me, 'just in case.'

The entire camp is in upheaval. Workers are disassembling all the buildings into flatpacks, and staff members are running every which way. A huge flatbed truck backs up to a crane that lifts flatpacks and stacks them on the back. I step out of the way of a bulldozer that trundles by and duck under the branches of a tree to get into the open field.

"Skylar!"

I turn around and around until I find the source of the voice calling for me.

Kalvin is waving from the front seat of a giant all-terrain vehicle about ten meters away. Takemo is sitting next to him, of course. Because I'm sure these two bonded over me repeatedly electrocuting them. I sigh and try not to show my hesitation. I think Kalvin and I are fine, but I figured I was on the outs with

Takemo. This is not out of the question since sometimes my very presence seems to annoy him, but he's waving to me as well.

Is it a trap?

I dodge puddles of rainwater and hoist my bag farther onto my back as I approach the vehicle.

Looking up at Kalvin makes my neck ache.

"It's like you're on a throne or something," I say, squinting into the sunlight.

"Well, I am a king, baby," he says with a wink.

I groan. "I walked straight into that one."

"Come up here and be my queen. No more princess for you."

I huff a laugh as he leans out to grab the ladder and offer me a hand.

Fine.

I climb up the three ladder rungs, and instead of putting my hand in his, I give him my bag. I'm wary of touching anyone right now.

Yesterday, it took four hours for the effects of the plant to wear off. I'm finally no longer electrocuting everyone and everything I touch. Emily bandaged my fingers up, and they're still sore. I hate that plant. Hate it. There was nothing even remotely great about what it did for me. When I took the plant that allowed me to use telekinesis, I could control the effects. But this electro-plant? I couldn't control it at all. Maybe with time I could learn, but the side effects were too much for me.

Takemo backs into the truck and leaves room for Kalvin and me to sit next to him, but it's not enough.

"Can you move over just a little more?" I wave at him to indicate Takemo should push back.

"Did I suddenly develop cooties overnight?" he asks, scooting over a few more centimeters.

"You've always had cooties. But after yesterday, I need some distance from everyone."

I settle my bag between Kalvin and me so we can't accidentally bump into each other. Two men climb into the front seat, start the vehicle, and drive us off into the jungle. I cringe as we trundle through and make a path, mowing down trees left and right. Birds scatter and take flight. Monkeys flee from the area. We're causing quite the ruckus.

"Hey, do you think this is a good idea?" I ask Takemo. "Not only are we doing damage to the forest, but this could be a signal to the military that we're on the move."

"They're on the move too," Takemo responds, lifting his voice over the roar of the engines. "India flew drones over their camp early this morning. Now is the perfect time to move out."

I sigh and stare out the window. Takemo leans forward to talk to the driver, and Kalvin joins him, so I have a chance to finally watch Saif's vidmessage from yesterday. I wanted to watch it last night, but the lab tech cautioned me not to put on my wristlet for a few hours after the plant wore off.

When Saif's face appears before me, my heart aches. Damn it. I was just getting used to having him around, and then here I was becoming accustomed to not seeing him. And now? Now I want him more than ever.

"Skylar, I'm so, so sorry. What can I say except that I'm an asshole, and I made a foolish decision the other day out of spite and jealousy. I even dragged Kalvin into this mess, and he hadn't seen you in weeks. I'm sure he hates me now too, and that's not what I wanted at all."

Shit. This is such a mess. I rest my head back in my seat.

"I won't go into this in a message because that's not how I want to apologize to you. I'm going to figure out where you are, and I'll be there with you because I promised to be from the beginning. I'm angry at myself for breaking that promise. I swear it'll be the last time. I hope to see you soon."

The message ends, and I sigh. I don't know how he'll find

me now that we're on the move, and though I saw his face and heard his tone of voice, I'm not sure how genuine he's being. I've been played before, too many times to count, and each time, it was because I gave someone the benefit of the doubt, and then I let them walk all over me. I'm tired of being a doormat. But I'm also tired of being so hardcore that no one will touch me. Why can't there be a middle ground somewhere?

"Feeling okay?" Kalvin asks, sitting back in his seat.

"No." I close my eyes and lean my head against the window, but the vehicle rocks, and I'm thrown to the side against him.

"Hey now." He holds my shoulder and steadies me. "No need to throw yourself at me. I'm right here." He chuckles when I sneer at him. "Sorry, sweetheart." He pushes me back upright to my seat. "At least you're not electrocuting me anymore. That sucked."

"Yeah, sorry about that."

He waves off my apology. "It's not your fault."

"It was really wild, though," Takemo says, getting into the discussion. "It was a flash of pain and then the scene from your childhood."

"I saw you in the flight school simulator," Kalvin says like the information is no big deal. "I had no idea you were so nervous. It never shows."

"That's the way I like it." I turn my face to the outside.

Unwillingly sharing my memories with these two is so embarrassing. I wish I could rewind time and erase the entire experience.

We're quiet for a few minutes as the vehicle stops, and someone runs out in front of us with a rifle. The man shoots the rifle into a copse of bushes, and a pair of giant squids slink out from underneath and slither away to a creek to our right.

"Holy shit," Takemo breathes out. "I didn't know they came on land."

The man in front turns around. "Yeah, mating season is a

little weird around here. We need to scare them out of the underbrush, or we'll squish them."

Good. I do not want to think about how many times they made a trip like this before they figured that out.

The man with the rifle outside pops a thumbs up and runs back to the vehicle in front of us.

Once we're moving forward again, I clear my throat. Might as well deal with this embarrassment once and for all.

"So, Takemo, you saw bits of my childhood when I shocked you the first time?"

"I did." His jaw works back and forth. "Did that bastard really deny you food and a bed?"

I shrug like it's no big deal. I have to hide the trauma somehow. "Yep. I slept on the floor of a closet for several months."

"What?" Kalvin's eyes are wide. "What are you talking about?"

I pluck at my pants and don't meet Kalvin's eyes. "There's a lot you don't know about me yet."

"And he wants to take the Amagi away from you now?" Takemo asks.

"Yeah." I sigh and turn to face him. "My mom is the face of this operation, but I know it's him. He's been jealous of me since I was a baby."

"I know men like him," Takemo says, nodding. "They can't make a life for themselves, so they take from other people instead. They justify it with things like 'she doesn't deserve her success' or 'she wronged me' or whatever. And even if they get everything, they're never satisfied. That's why I've always concentrated on my own businesses."

"You got pretty mad at me when you assumed I cheated the auction. And you were happy to take my mom's business because you thought I didn't deserve it," I remind him.

"Yeah, but —"

"Don't 'but' me." I tap my temple. "Do I need to repeat back everything you said to me?"

Kalvin points to me. "She has a mind like a steel trap."

He scowls. "Fine. You're right. Unfortunately, I lost sight of what was important because your mom and Dominic were such horrible borrowers."

"I can imagine," I grumble.

"The absolute worst." He runs his hands through his hair. "Most people borrow money and then just pay it back with some interest. Or I invest in their business. But your mom? She kept coming back and coming back and asking for new terms and more time and on and on. And that Dominic? He was manipulative at best, threatening at worst. I had to ban them both from my office."

Ugh. I can only imagine the rumors out there about my family now because of the way they handled things. I wouldn't blame Takemo's staff for talking, especially if Mom and Dom were rude to them.

We could have solved this all had Mom believed in me and not kept the dads on a tight budget and made them crazy for any credits they could get. One thing's for sure, when I finally have my own network, I'm doing things differently. I won't ever leave them without suitable compensation. Ever.

"They made me so angry. I saw red every time I saw your name anywhere."

Kalvin leans over and drops his voice. "What's going on with your mom and the family business?" he whispers.

"I'm sure you're catching on, but Mom sold the business out from under me. To him." I jerk my chin at Takemo. His face is a blank slate. "And now she's taking me to court for the Amagi, too."

"What?" Kalvin's voice climbs. "You can't be serious."

I press my lips together to halt a sarcastic remark. "We, uh, should sit down and talk when we get to the next place."

"Skylar," he warns, but I shake my head to stop him.

He sighs. "Fine."

Time to change the subject. Takemo's figured out the error of his ways, hopefully, and Kalvin is brimming with questions.

"Who did you date about, oh..." I glance over at Takemo. "About five or six years ago? I know you haven't dated anyone in a while."

His eyebrows draw together. "What are you talking about?"

"You were younger, maybe early twenties, and she dumped you. Then you went to a bar to drown your sorrows." I smile politely at him as the vehicle rocks side to side. "The electric shocks went both ways."

He draws back. "You saw my memories?" He glances at Kalvin. Kalvin grimaces.

"Only the one. So, who was she?"

I'm not giving him any room to wiggle out of this. If he's going to have insight into my life and my past, then I get to peek into his.

He pauses, and I wonder what he's considering before telling me anything. I could jump on the duonet next time I have access and search for his past lovers, but I'm going to do this the old-fashioned way — pump him for information.

"Elizabeth Brooks. We went to school together."

He turns away from me and stares out the window. I give it three breaths before I reach over Kalvin and whack Takemo on the arm.

"Come on. Spill it," I demand. "I'm sure we're going to be in this car for another twenty minutes, at least."

He sighs. "Fine. Liza and I dated for most of secondary school and into university. We just had that spark, you know? And I was prepared to spend the rest of my life with her, and anyone else she wanted to add to her network. She had everything I wanted in a woman — a good family, excellent taste, the right social connections, and a kind heart. My friends gave me such shit about her because she..."

"What? Go on? Nothing you can say will shock me now."

Kalvin is sitting, facing forward, not participating in the conversation.

"Well, she wasn't very pretty," Takemo says, cringing. He puts his hand to his chest. "I never said that, not once, to her, to anybody. But, for fuck's sake, everyone said it to me all the fucking time."

Takemo dated someone who wasn't the standard of beauty he seems to love now? Say it isn't so.

"What happened? It sounds like you loved her."

"I did," he insists. "But she fell into the vanity trap. New nose, new lips, new body, new attitude. She got the whole Adonis makeover, and suddenly, everyone wanted her. Liza was wined and dined by most of the elite Rio social set. She dumped me not long after, and now she has a huge network. I haven't dated anyone else since."

I nod slowly. "Huh. Your girl got a glow-up, a new sense of pride, and decided she wanted more than you."

He stays silent.

"And you've not dated anyone since?" I ask, thinking back on everything I know about him.

"Nope. I've had dates, like for dinners or parties or events, but that's all they were. One event and a thank you. Occasionally, we'd sleep together, but I kept it business."

And he owns sexbot love hotels, so there's that.

"I see." I nod slowly and consider the situation. "I think it's interesting the memories that were chosen for exchange between us, don't you?"

"What did you see from me?" Kalvin blurts out. He was holding it back, but he couldn't wait a moment longer.

"Your mother," I say simply.

"Oh." His face falls. "I didn't want to tell you about that. At least, not yet."

"Sorry," I whisper.

Takemo looks at us both and narrows his eyes. "Are you suggesting there was a rhyme and reason to what we each saw?"

I peer down at my hands, singed and bandaged up, and I remember the entity in the Sonoma desert, the one Kalvin and I ran into when we were marooned. It shocked me too and flew through the memories in my head.

Huh. I wonder...

"We're approaching the new campsite," the man in front says, turning around to face us. "I need you to stay here in the vehicle until we reestablish the fence." He reaches for his rifle. "Three people were attacked and wounded on the way here. I don't want any more casualties."

Yikes. Takemo, Kalvin, and I glance at each other.

The vehicle trundles to a stop, and both men upfront open the doors and drop to the outside.

Takemo grabs his coat and bunches it up into a ball. "Now seems like a good time for a nap." He sandwiches the coat between his head and the door, slouches down, crosses his arms, and closes his eyes.

Okay, then. I'd love to nap, but I don't do that in public.

Vulnerability is not the kind of emotion I'm used to. And now both of these men know things about me I would never tell them. Kalvin is warm next to me, and I want some of his warmth to stop the coolness creeping into my heart. It may be hot and sticky in the jungle, but I am slowly becoming the Ice Queen.

I reach over to take his hand in mine, and he pulls away from me. Disappointment covers me from head to toe. I glance at him out of the corner of my eye, and he's looking out the window on Takemo's side.

Sigh. Fine. I get it. I wouldn't want to be with me either.

The disappointment doesn't fade. Instead, it seeps into my pores and decides to stay for a while. Nothing has been going right lately. I'm wary of my own memories, and none of my relationships are flourishing like they should be. I wish I could get a do-over.

I prop my elbow on the door, stare out the window at the jungles of Rio, and try to forget the two frustrating men in the car with me.

Rio, Rio. Something about this place just does not sit right with me.

Scientists have been trying to figure this planet out for a few hundred years now, why Rio has so many analogous flora and fauna to Old Earth. And besides a theory about aliens seeding a bunch of similar worlds, no one has ever figured it out.

But I have different pieces of the puzzle than those scientists do, and a picture of Rio's history is forming in my head. It's hazy and unfocused, though, and I'm unsure what I'm looking at.

But I need to figure out what it is.

Fast. Before anyone else gets hurt out here.

14

ONCE THE FENCE is up and running, we're allowed out of the vehicle to stretch our legs and help with the setup. I need a break from the men in my life, so I walk around and look for people who need help, but everyone here knows what they're doing because they've all done this before. India Dellis hired enough qualified people to keep everything operational. I hope to see her and talk to her soon. I have questions. Lots of questions.

A group of men across the flattened jungle grass are erecting the individual dormitory buildings, much like the one I slept in for the nights before this trip. I approach them with a wave.

"Hey there. Can I help?"

One turns with his hands out at arm's length. "Ah, no, miz. You should stand back."

"I can help. I promise I'm not a complete weakling," I say with a bright smile.

"Oh, it's not that. It's —"

"Coming through!" Another man yells as he strides past us, holding a cloth sack out away from his body. A high-pitched shriek comes from the bag, and I jump away.

"It's that we still need to remove some native animals before we can get started," the man resumes. "But honestly, I would feel so much better about things if you went over there to the buildings that are already up. At least over there, we've already cleared the grass."

I raise my hands. "Got it. I will definitely back the fuck up and go over there."

His returning smile is wry. "Thanks, miz."

Oh well, so much for helping.

I walk over to the buildings and pace instead of forcing myself on other workers. I'm so unsettled and out of place. I should be on my ship, flying the stars, having dinner and drinks with Saif and Kalvin, sleeping with each of them, making a name for myself with a new business and a new life. Talking with Takemo only makes me want this more. He's reminding me that there are a lot of misconceptions out there about me, and the only way for me to fight them is with the truth. The whole truth.

I begin to sweat as I consider what outing my family will be like, telling everyone that my mom's network abused me as a kid. I imagine the concerned faces, the misunderstandings, the shock or the disbelief, and I want to curl up in a ball and not do anything. I wish I could call Marcelo or Vivian and talk to them about this, and I will once the data points have been restored. But my guess is they'll tell me to listen to my gut and do what's right for me. It's what I would say in their shoes. And with no one in my network, I'm not sure who to go to for advice anymore.

Kalvin appears around the corner of the building I've been pacing.

"Hey," he says, stepping into my path. "You all right?"

I stop and narrow my eyes at him. "No. Do I look all right?"

"No. Sorry. It was a dumb question." He jams his hands in

his pockets. "At flight school, I saw nothing but confidence from you. This is a little odd."

"Yeah, I'm sure it makes you happy to see the princess cracking at the seams."

"No. It doesn't." He huffs a short breath. "What's with you, Skylar? I thought we put that rivalry behind us."

Shit. I see what I'm trying to do, annoy him enough to make him go. It's time for honesty.

"I have nothing left, Kalvin. My mom sold the business out from under me to Takemo. And now she's coming after the Amagi. My family repeatedly ignored and abused me for years. If you thought I was a good pilot, well then, soon I'll be a good pilot without a ship and no family either."

Kalvin is silent for a few moments, his face screwed up in concentration. "Sorry. None of what you just said made any sense." He rubs his face with one hand. "You know, I heard what you said to Saif, back at his parents' house, and what Takemo said today in the vehicle. This is the second time you've told me, and I still am not understanding the situation. Dominic is one of your mother's consorts, right?" I nod. "And he abused you, the first daughter, because he's a selfish asshole?"

"Basically."

"Then you can't let him win," he says, matter-of-factly.

"Win what?"

"Life, Skylar. Hell, I was an asshole to you, and you did not let me win at flight school. You just kept on flying perfectly, waiting for me to screw up." He laughs. "Brilliant plan, honestly."

Takemo was an asshole to me, too, but I won that Bridge tournament. And things may have changed with him as well.

"Soooooo, the answer to my problems is to win?"

He nods, his eyebrows lifted. "One hundred percent. And don't forget Saif. You have to win that, too." He shrugs. "Winner takes all."

I laugh at the simplicity of his reasoning. Usually, I'm not interested in winning. I'm interested in being the most competent and intelligent person for my job. I'm not out to win awards; I want to master things. Becoming a master pilot, someone like my friend Asteria, is a dream of mine. But if I had wanted to be a doctor, I would have wanted to make breakthroughs, save lives, or conquer risky surgeries. If I had been an author, my stories would have charmed millions.

But I have never thought of life as a competition. I'm sure that's not healthy, but maybe it's what I need to get through things. I need to be the master, and I need to win.

This is like playing cards, Skylar. Take all the tricks. Leave nothing on the table.

"Winner takes all," I repeat.

"I've played enough craps to know when someone is going to win it all, and I'm just feeding their bank account," he says, slowly approaching me. "I will gladly keep paying to watch you win. It's thrilling as hell." He rests his hands on my upper arms. It's been days since I've felt any clarity in my life, and his closeness right now puts it all into perspective.

"It's not emasculating for you?" I ask, rolling my eyes.

He throws his head back with a laugh. "Please. Men who say that shit have small dicks." He raises his eyebrows at me twice.

Hmmm, I still haven't slept with him yet. I let my eyes travel down his front. Sigh. He's one fine-looking man.

He brings his hands to my face. "Hey princess, my gorgeous eyes are up here."

"Queen," I remind him. "Are you going to kiss me?"

Our connection is so intense the ground rumbles beneath my feet. Kalvin smiles as he leans in, his lips close to mine for a moment before they make contact. I draw in a long breath through my nose and press close to him. We shared moments like this after we returned from the desert, but being with him here makes this all seem real, natural.

Kalvin wraps his arms around me and pulls me close as his lips expertly move over mine. He nips at my lower lip and drags his kisses down my neck. I hum and melt into his embrace. Saif taught me to let men hold me, something I never allowed before. And though this feels right, anxiety buzzes in my chest. The evil doubt in my head says things like, "He'll never last. You'll just push him away like the rest."

And then my back smarts with pain as his hands hit a healing cut from the starbats.

"Ow." I hiss and pull away from him. "Sorry." I clutch his arms and rest my forehead on his chest. "It's my back."

He brings his face down close to my ear. "It's not my horrible kissing?"

I inhale. "Oh hell no. That was not horrible kissing, though I don't kiss much."

He smiles, and it lights up my insides. "Good. Because I thought I lost you there for a moment."

I shake my head and place my hand on my chest. "My gut wants this. My heart is willing but tired. And my brain? It doesn't trust anyone or anything anymore."

"Then we'll have to teach it differently."

"Hey, you two," Takemo says from behind me. I close my eyes and blow out a long breath. "Didn't want to interrupt or anything."

Without seeing his face, I can tell he's annoyed.

"It's fine," Kalvin says, cupping the back of my neck and pulling me to him for a kiss on the forehead. I never thought this man could be sweet. He's always just been a rogue pilot, untouchable.

My face heats.

"But I thought you might want to come around and have a beer? We've got chairs set up in the shade."

I'm about to say yes when I realize the rumble under my feet wasn't imagined. It's grown in intensity, from a slight vibration to a knee-knocking tremor. When Takemo looks to the jungle and Kalvin looks over his shoulder, I look at the sky. I can't see anything in the trees, but birds take flight, squawking and fleeing. Monkeys squeal and swing away through the canopy.

"Shit," I say, glancing around.

What is it? And where is it coming from? And whatever it is, how do I hide from it?

"Stampede!" someone calls out, running past our building at full sprint. "Run!"

Kalvin and I run for each other and knock heads.

"Ow!" One hand flies to my head, and the other grabs his hand. "Come on!"

We take off, Takemo falling into step next to us, our legs pumping and following other people as they flee for their lives.

"What is it?" I shout over the roaring coming from the jungle.

Takemo points to the right.

"I don't know!" he yells back.

"Where are... we going?" I am not a runner, and I'm huffing and puffing while my legs scream in protest.

"The vehicles!"

A massive trumpeting sound comes from our rear, and I almost pee my pants with terror. It's so loud, it pushes us forward. Kalvin stumbles but catches himself before he falls.

I cast a glance over my shoulder as we angle around one of the already erected buildings. What the...

They're large, twice as big as the vehicles were running to. Mottled gray skin, six or eight legs, a long nose, a mouth full of fangs, and eyes that are the stuff of nightmares. Are they elephants? Are they spiders? I have no fucking clue, and I don't want to stick around to find out.

One beast tramples a building to our left as we run. People scream, and building materials scatter everywhere. Something hits me in the back. I stumble into Takemo and almost knock him down.

"Skylar!" he shouts, grabbing me and yanking me up to run again.

Kalvin lets go and taps into a burst of speed to get ahead of us. He'll reach the vehicles before we do and hopefully before these beasts.

The trumpeting and shouting crescendo as more beasts pile into the compound at a run. Dear God, I never expected this. Snakes in my bed, yes. Spider-Elephant-Beasts in a raging stampede, no.

Up ahead, the vehicles are parked along the edge of the forest behind the electric fence, which is now offline and half collapsed across the wild grass. The door to the nearest vehicle opens, and a man leans out.

"Come on!" He's waving us to him, so I call up my last reserve of strength and speed and pull Takemo along. My lungs burn, and my face is on fire from exertion. But we have to get there quickly, or we're dead. Kalvin reaches the vehicle first, swinging his legs in, grabbing on, and holding a hand out.

My skin prickles as my brain focuses on the heavy breathing coming from behind us. The ground shakes, and I'm so close to giving up and crying that I can already feel the tears burning in my eyes. Terror and I do not get along. When I'm in space dealing with a stressful situation, I follow procedures. I assess risk and make decisions. This run for your life shit? It's so not me.

The beast is getting closer, and my steps are wobbling because the ground is shaking with each of its strides. How does a spider and what looks to be an elephant become this? What the hell happened on Rio to make it this way?

"Go," Takemo yells, throwing my hand off and urging me forward towards the vehicle.

Five meters. My legs pump. Three, two, one.

I leap to the first rung of the ladder, throw my fingers into the awaiting hand of Kalvin leaning out, and he pulls me up and in quickly. I scoot back in the seat, and Takemo is right behind me.

"Close the door!"

Takemo pulls the door closed as Kalvin leaps into the front seat and crouches down in the front footwell.

"Holy fucking shit," Takemo breathes out as the beast continues to approach us. "Is it going to stop?"

Takemo backs up, putting his body between the beast outside and me. I lean back against the far door and wince in pain. Whatever hit my back is still there. I try to reach up over my shoulder to see what it is, but I stop when I realize the beast is not slowing down. It's not diverting. It's heading straight for us.

Takemo lunges for me as the beast reaches us. He throws his arms over my head and sandwiches me to the floor, covering me with his body. I scream as the building shrapnel bites into my back, and the beast hits the vehicle. The vehicle rocks and creaks as it climbs over the top and falls to the ground on the other side.

Takemo and I freeze in the silence, with only our labored breaths filling the vehicle's cabin. He squeezes me and rests his cheek on mine for a moment. I hold still, not wanting to injure myself further nor break the spell. No doubt about it. He just saved my ass. I guess he doesn't hate me as much anymore.

Skylar, people can *change, huh?*

I burst into tears now that the adrenaline has worn off and I'm safe.

"Shhh," Takemo says, holding me tighter. "It's over. It's okay."

"Skylar? Is she okay?" Kalvin asks.

Gunfire pops in the distance, and the acrid stench of smoke wafts over the vehicle.

Takemo slowly lets me go. I open my eyes and watch him pull away from me. His hands are covered in blood.

"Skylar, you're hurt."

I press my lips together and nod through my tears.

"Something hit me in the back," I mumble, my lips tripping over the words.

"Sorry." He grabs my shirt with his bloodied hands and pulls me up to a sitting position. Leaning over my shoulder, he looks at my back. "Shit. Something is lodged just below your shoulder blade. We need to get you to a medic."

I nod, my gaze focusing on the world outside the vehicle.

"Oh shit." Kalvin's eyes are wide. "Let me go make sure the coast is clear. You help her get out." He points, and Takemo nods.

My heart rate spikes as Kalvin opens the door. Everything in camp is in chaos. Many of the buildings survived, but the trampled ones are nothing but rubble. A fire burns close to the electrified fence, and people are limping across the grass to the infirmary at the far end of camp.

"Come on. I think we're safe now," Takemo says, watching Kalvin out the window.

I huff out a short laugh. "Rio is never safe. Hey," I say, grabbing his shirt. He stops, and I pull him close. "Thank you."

I lean forward and plant a kiss on his lips. It's short and not at all romantic, but it feels like the right thing to do. He's been kinder the last few days, and he saved me from rampaging beasts. I think a kiss is an acceptable payment, especially since I don't kiss just anybody.

He pulls away, and his smile is sweet, an expression I haven't seen on his face before.

"You're welcome." He sighs as he pulls me forward, inching me out of the vehicle. "Let's go before you bleed to death."

15

"Are you... glowing?" India Dellis leans away to scan me from top to toe.

"That I am," I say with a wide smile. "You should see me in black light. I am a sight to behold."

"Well, shit." She fills my glass up with ice and gin. "That's a new one. The last plant we tested before you showed up made the man grow hair all over his body. All over, Skylar. He was almost blinded."

I hiss as I try to imagine my eyelashes growing at an exponential rate. That sounds incredibly uncomfortable.

"Yeah, well, so far, it's the Rio animals that have been a problem for me, not the plants."

India nods. "Those spiderphants are really unpredictable. We think a jungle cat spooked them." She sips from her glass. "We lost two people and four buildings to the stampede. How's your back?"

I shift and feel the second skin beneath my shoulder blade. "It's been better. But since Emily has use of all the Athens Industries medical technology, I'll be healed in no time." I hold out my hands and gaze at the pretty blue hue of my skin. "I don't know how long I'll be glowing, though."

"I'm glad you're here and that you're okay," she says, lifting her glass to toast mine. I touch my glass to hers. She throws back a mouthful before she circles her index finger at me. "Though I'm not sure what we'll do with a plant that makes us bioluminescent."

I shrug. "I'm not here to expound on what you should do with the plants. I'm only here to test them."

When she raises her eyebrows, though, I laugh.

"But bioluminescence has a lot of advantages in the animal kingdom. Animals use it to lure prey. They use it to attract mates. They also use it to disappear in brighter situations."

India draws a deep breath. "Really? That's fascinating."

"Imagine using it to colonize new worlds. If the world has a long, dark cycle, people can glow and provide their own illumination." I drink my gin and then stare down into the glass.

"I love this idea. I'm going to send it along to Vivian tomorrow." India makes a note of it on her datapad. When she's done, she props her chin on her hand and stares at me. "You have hidden depths."

"There's an abyss in me, didn't you know?" I smirk at her and turn the glass on the table.

The cafeteria is subdued at this time of day, turning the usually bustling space into a low-light bar and lounge area. I look around at the other dozen tables while I gather up some confidence to ask India a serious question. Four men play cards (pinochle from the looks of it) at the farthest table, and two other men sit on the sofas, drinking beers and working on their datapads.

"India," I start, but I lose my voice.

Her smile widens. "Yes, Skylar."

I take a deep breath. "Whatever happened to the work your company did on the jump rings?"

Her smile fades as she pulls back a few centimeters. "I thought you were going to ask me about the Bhaats, considering Saif is not here with you. What happened?"

I laugh lightly. "I suppose I should ask, but let's come back to that." My chest heaves with measured breaths. "Please. I have a vested interest in this, and I'm hoping we're on the same page."

"Huh. I admit I've thought little about the jump rings in my lifetime." She sips her drink. "Hmmm, from what I know, this is how my company was started, by my great-great-however-many-times grandparents. Patras Technologies, as they called it at the time, pioneered the jump rings and the focusing technology. It was one of my ancestors that figured it out." She sits up, pride lifting her chin. "But you know how it is," she says, waving her hand. "A technology like that can't be kept under lock and key. They sold it to the military, and the military spun off the STRA to run everything."

Shipping and Trade Regulation Authority runs and maintains the jump rings as an offshoot of the military. It's really the only military establishment that stretches between each system. The Brazilianos military is a power-hungry and out-of-control nightmare. The Californikos military is more of a humanitarian organization that's around for disaster relief, medical research, and search and rescue. They have agreements to move between systems, but otherwise, they're separate entities. They both let the STRA keep the jump rings running smoothly. Even though the STRA are independent now, they weren't always.

"So the military had the technology in its hands for a while then." I hum as I stare out into space.

A few years ago, Vivian and I, with a team of people, broke into a military base on Neve. Yes, yes. It was dangerous and reckless. We got what we needed for Athens Industries, and we blew the place up on our way out. But I saw one thing that has stuck with me since, and I can't stop thinking about it now.

"What's going on?" India asks, sitting forward.

"There's something that Vivian and I never told you or Renata about our mission to the Neve military base."

Renata sent us there to find out what they were doing with the Rio seeds. She didn't bargain for everything else.

Her face hardens along with her voice. "Go on."

"Sorry. It all seemed so fantastical at the time. I'm sure Gloria told you about the jump ring in the basement of the military facility."

Gloria was a soldier who came with us on the mission but reported directly to Renata and Athens Industries. She saw what we saw, but she didn't hear what Vivian heard from Nina Correa, a colonel in the military at the time and Vivian's consort Gus's mother.

India nods, but her eyes are wary. "Gloria told us that there was a jump ring that bore through space and needed the nuclear power plant for power."

I reach forward and squeeze her forearm. "Can you imagine how this could help with terraforming other worlds?"

"Well, yes. Gloria saw a bunch of artifacts that the military teams brought back from other worlds, so Renata and I thought maybe this was something we could do, too. But..." She shakes her head.

"Yes, we both saw them," I say, sipping my drink. "So, we were out of the room when Nina Correa told Vivian that the jump ring did not *just* tunnel through space, but it could also tunnel through time."

"What?" Her mouth drops open, and her face pales.

I lick my lips as my heart pounds in my chest. "India, the military has figured out how to send people through time."

She sits up. "Which direction?"

This is her first question? I file this away in my head.

"I'm not sure. We didn't get many details before we left."

She stares out into space, and I take a few breaths to calm

my racing heart. Seeing the jump ring in the basement of that military base has haunted me for years. The possibilities for its use are endless, and the sheer power of it tugs at my soul. I'm not sure how Vivian feels about telling India Dellis everything, but I *have* to. Because we need this technology more than the military.

"India," I say, breaking into her thoughts, "we need this. We can't let the military have this technology."

"I... I hear you." Her voice is light and breathy. "Damn, Skylar. Why didn't you or Vivian tell us this ages ago?"

I shrug. "Sorry. We had a lot of shit going on. Better late than never?"

"I need to go speak with Renata," she says, standing up. "You'll be around? I'm sure she'll want to talk to you."

I lift my glass. "If I'm not passed out, I'm happy to speak to her."

A peal of thunder rips through the sky, and several people lift their heads to peer at the ceiling. One man sitting on the couch jumps up, grabs his stuff, and charges for the door. He probably wants to get to his bunk before it starts pouring. The early evening light filters in, turning everything into a wash of pink before the door closes.

"Seems like now is a good time to head to bed." India looks me up and down. "Though if you get caught outside, you'll be able to find your way in the dark. Come on."

I stand up and bus our glasses to the kitchen counter. I guess I'll have a quiet night in bed and sleep in tomorrow. I'm not expected at the infirmary until ten for a checkup before moving onto another plant.

As I'm on my way back to meet India, the door snaps open with a rush of wind.

I catch my breath.

"Look who I brought in from the gemstone mine," Luca says, stepping to the side.

Looking tired and chastened but uninjured, Saif waves from under a rain poncho, trying not to be too overbearing.

"Hey," he says. He narrows his eyes at me. "Are you... glowing?" he asks.

I sigh. So much for that quiet night in bed I was going to have.

16

WE RUN BACK to my suite as the sky opens with a thundering downpour. I take the lead, and Saif is right behind me all the way into the double-door entryway. The two barriers to my living space help keep out any Rio wildlife, but they're a pain in the ass when two people are trying to get out of the rain. I lightly leap over the second door's threshold while Saif drops his stuff inside the first door. I frown at the water I've tracked in before I shuck off my boots and throw them into the vestibule.

"What's going on here?" Kalvin asks, standing up from the couch. He's been reading and hanging out all evening while I was drinking with India Dellis.

"Sorry to just show up like this," Saif says, running his fingers through his wet hair and stepping over the threshold behind me. "It took forever to signal to Luca since you were on the move. I've been at the gemstone mine for three days."

I glance at Kalvin, and I remember his words.

I have to win this.

But how do I do that?

"What are you even doing here?" I ask, throwing my hand

out to the side. "I didn't think you were going to come after what happened at your parents' place."

The shame of his humiliating treatment burns my cheeks again. Sejal's pitying eyes will be stuck with me forever. I force the images away. No.

"You got my message, right?" He nods at Kalvin. "Hey, Kalvin."

"Saif," Kalvin says. "Glad you made it in okay."

Shit. I never responded to him. "Yes. Sorry. I got your message. We left before I could reply, and then it took a while for the data access point to get up and running. I'm not allowed to wear my wristlet while I'm testing the plants either, so that's eight hours a day when I'm unavailable."

I sit down on the edge of the bed and wait for his explanation.

Saif grabs a chair and sits across from me. "I understand. I was a complete asshole. I don't know why I did it. It was like this deep, primal stirring of jealousy in my chest, and I... I lost sight of what was important. I think I wanted to punish you for making decisions without me. For, uh," he glances at Kalvin, "moving forward so quickly with your network. I was wrong."

"*We* were wrong," Kalvin stresses. "I stepped in without giving a thought to what was going on in your life. I made things worse."

Kalvin already apologized to me, but hearing him admit it to Saif warms my cold, dead heart.

"Kalvin is not to blame." Saif's expression is serious, something I rarely see. "I... There were a lot of things going on at once, our relationship, the Amagi. But after giving it some thought and talking it over with Sejal, I realized my insecurities need to be set aside. I need to learn to be a better partner in a network."

In my head, I can hear Sejal telling him this. Did he really listen?

"Hell, with everything going on, you're just trying to get by." He shrugs. "Your ship is your livelihood, and taking that away would be devastating. You're just doing the best you can. The universe has given you a pretty serious handicap, Skylar. I don't want to add to it."

He puts the chair aside, crosses the suite to the table with chairs, and sets a bag down on top of it. "Come sit, both of you," he says, gesturing to the table. "We need to work some things out."

Kalvin smiles sadly, approaches me, and puts out his hand. "I remember what we talked about in the desert, about the expectations of your family, the stress you've always been under." I slip my fingers into his and let him pull me to my feet. "You saved my life out there. We can work this out."

I sit down at the table as Saif empties his bag of goodies — orange fizzy soda, butter biscuits, a box of chocolates, and an assortment of nuts. "Sorry about the random food. I grabbed what I could before I left." He falls into his chair with a sigh.

When I stretch out my hand to grab the biscuits, I notice I'm not glowing as much anymore. It seems to be wearing off. I turn my hand over and look at it on both sides, wondering how long I can stall and delay the inevitable.

Saif opens the package of butter biscuits. "Here." He pushes it across the table to me. I ignore it as I pull my hands to my lap.

Silence blankets the table for long enough that I sigh.

I don't know how to win people over. I haven't had enough practice in this area of my life. With my cloistered youth and brash early adulthood, I never learned how to make people adore me. That's a skill that's honed over time and many thousands of little interactions. That's not me.

I can only be me.

I pick up my chin. Be brave, Skylar.

"Let's be honest here, okay? We don't have to do this. We

will all be totally fine on our own. Saif, you're wealthy and sought after. You'd find someone better in a heartbeat. Kalvin, you're an ace pilot, and any ship would be grateful to have you. Me? No one who cares ever sticks around, so it's not like I expect you to, either. I'm good for nothing but a quick fuck and a see-you-later, and that's about it. You are not getting anything special by coming after me. Just a whole lot of trouble, okay? So tomorrow, you can both turn around and go back to the safety of the city and leave me to figure out this mess alone."

There, I said it. I put the truth on the table. All of it is true. Every word.

"Skylar, I'm not leaving," Kalvin says.

I make eye contact with Saif and say, "I'm sorry. Really sorry. I tried. I told you I wasn't going to run from you, and I held on as long as I could. But I never expected to be treated that way by you." I deflate. "And I just won't stand for that anymore."

His face is grim, so I turn to Kalvin. "You *should* go. We'll all be much better off without each other. And bonus, you won't have to deal with my crappy family coming after you too for everything you have. If you hitch your ride to my star, you'll only be pulled into their lawsuit, eventually."

"I've got nothing." Kalvin shrugs and drinks from the soda bottle.

I press my lips together.

"You're right," Saif says, breaking into the conversation. "I treated you poorly. You didn't deserve that. I hate myself for it because you put your trust in me, and I fucked it up. You saw I was struggling and thought a trip to see my family would help me. Instead, I turned it into a humiliating experience for both of us."

Usually, Saif is the picture of health with bright eyes and glowing, rich sandy brown skin. But he's subdued sitting here, his eyes dull and his skin a pale gray.

"Oh yeah?" I ask, crossing my arms over my chest. "How was it humiliating for you?"

He rolls his neck side to side, stretching it out, weary after days on the move. "Sejal and my mother yelled at me for *hours* after you left... in several languages. And I am not welcome at home until I get my shit together."

Saif is super close to his family, so this is shocking news. I can understand my own family forgetting about me, though not Vivian, obviously. But a family as tight as the Bhaats? That's unthinkable.

"So I'm here, and I'm hoping we can start over. Because despite my behavior the other day, everything I've ever said to you holds true. I want to be here with you."

"Me too." Kalvin pushes the butter biscuits at me again. "I did nothing but think of you for all those weeks we were apart, and it's been quite the adventure being here with you. I don't want it to end."

His wry smile does nothing to defrost my chilly attitude.

"Really? Looking to run for your life every day?" I say with a huff of a laugh. I shift my shoulders, aware of my injuries. They itch, so I hope they heal soon. "I don't know. I'm sick of being manipulated by men, and I'm tired of being hurt over and over by the people I love and trust." I press my hand to my lips, unable to believe I've said that out loud. Usually, I pretend I don't care and tell everyone to fuck off. My little eight-year-old self would be disappointed in me right now.

"How can I even trust you again?" I ask Saif. I close my eyes and remember us in bed together. He held me, even though I never let men do that. He treated me like I was deserving of love. Then the scene in his parents' garden plays out in my memories again, and I gasp.

I jolt out of my head as I feel his fingers on mine. "I'm going to show you that you can trust me again. What I did was a horrible mistake. If you really don't want me in your life, I'll leave, but if there's even a glimmer of a chance we can repair this, then I'm staying."

I look at Kalvin, and he nods.

I guess this is a win.

"Fine. But I have to warn you that I've heard all of this before. Lots of promises that never come true. You'll only get this one chance, and that's it. I will not be a doormat."

Saif winces. "You should never, ever feel that way. I promise things will be different."

"I've heard that before, too," I grumble, getting to my feet.

When I glance over at them, they're both frowning. "Sorry. It's been a long day, and I'm still healing from being attacked by starbats and almost trampled by a family of spiderphants."

"Starbats, and what now? What happened?" Saif asks, alarm growing in his eyes. "Are you okay?"

"I'm fine. I'm just a little scratched up."

Kalvin stands up and comes to me. "Her back took a heavy hitting yesterday, but she'll be okay." He runs his hand down my arm. I shiver from the contact, and if Saif notices, he doesn't mention it.

I close my eyes. I should tell them to leave and never come back. That would be the sensible thing to do. I could really give Mom the shove off by denying her heirs from her first daughter. I could swear off relationships and tell the universe I'm going celibate because of childhood trauma. That would be a great way to end my life and career.

Or I could let them stay and open myself back up to love and acceptance. My belly churns with anxiety about this, but it's probably my best bet for a long and happy life.

No relationship is perfect, right? We're bound to hit some snags along the way, make some wrong decisions, say the wrong things. That's how it's supposed to work, I think. At least, I've seen this in fiction, certainly not from my family. I should give

Saif and Kalvin this chance. I developed a shaky truce with Takemo. Why not them?

"We'll start over again tomorrow, then," I say, and Saif melts with relief. "Kalvin, will you make sure Saif has a place to stay?" I lift my chin, daring Saif to challenge me for a spot in my bed and intrude on my space this early in our makeup process.

"Uh, sure." Kalvin nods to Saif. "We'll go speak to someone about getting him a bunk."

I say nothing as they suit back up to return to the rain outside.

But Saif turns around at the double door and nods to me. "I'll see you in the morning. Sleep well, Sky."

Kalvin salutes. "I'll be back, gorgeous."

The door closes on them, and I stand in my room, not sure what just happened.

Saif is back, and I kissed Takemo today. Kalvin will be here at any moment. I went from not trusting men to having three of them in my close circle instantly.

What the heck is going on with my love life?

Hell if I know.

But I can't just let it happen to me. If I want the same kind of life Vivian has, then I have to do something about it.

Starting with the sleeping arrangements.

17

Rain pummels the roof of my suite, and the door opens as a peal of thunder cracks the sky.

"Woo. It's really coming down out there." Kalvin shucks off his wet coat in the vestibule. "I got Saif a room two buildings down from here. He should be fine."

Rummaging through my bag, my hand grazes the box of cards before I grab them and hold them up triumphantly.

"Gin? Let's enjoy the evening before I make you find your own place, too."

He raises his eyebrows. "You mean I get to sleep on an actual bed instead of the couch? How novel."

I move some of the snacks Saif left and place the deck of cards on the table. "If you can beat me at Gin, then you can sleep with me tonight." I raise my finger to his wide eyes. "Be warned now. I am very good at cards."

"Sleep with you. You mean, close my eyes and lose consciousness in the same bed with you? Or tear your clothes off and make sweet love to you all night long?"

I cringe. "Never use the phrase 'make sweet love' ever again. And yes, both."

Who the hell is this guy, anyway? Who says 'make sweet love' sincerely and still manages to capture my attention? He must be possessed by a god or something.

He nods slowly. "I'll accept your challenge despite you disliking my choice of words." He cracks his knuckles and sits down opposite me. "Soda?"

"Yes, please. I'm sure it'll go great in my stomach with all the gin I put there an hour ago."

He hands over an orange soda, and we lean across the table and knock the glass bottles.

"Cheers," he says, making eye contact with me while sipping.

I can't help but smile. I remember when this man made me so furious that I would avoid him between classes and sit far away from him at the flight school cafeteria. Now I'm considering sleeping with him and adding him to my network.

I shuffle the cards as I consider this turn of events. I've never discussed this with Kalvin. He may not want to be a part of a network, come to think of it. He may just want to sleep with whomever he wants and keep on flying.

There's no time like the present to find out.

I deal the cards, ten to each of us, and then create the discard pile.

"Best two of three because I'd like to go to sleep eventually." I arrange my cards into like suits and then from highest to lowest value. Committing the cards to memory, I set my hand down and watch Kalvin.

"So..." I drum my fingers on the table. "What do you have planned next?"

"Next? Like tomorrow? Next week?" He finishes rearranging his cards, looks at the top card, picks it up, and discards it from his hand.

"Like, after this little Rio adventure." I flip over the top card, and it's one I don't need. I add it to the discard pile.

"You're not even going to look at your hand?" he asks, peeved.

"Nope. I don't need to."

He sighs. "You're too smart for your own good." He chooses a new card and lays it in the discard pile.

"I've heard that a lot in my life." My turn. This is a card I need to round out a three-of-a-kind. I discard.

"Uh, I don't know what I'm doing after this Rio adventure. I need to check on my mom, but..." He shrugs while looking at his cards again. "I suppose it all depends on where you're going." He draws and sets the card down.

I lean back in the chair and watch him sip his soda.

"Where I'm going?"

"Yeah, Ms. Obvious. I said I wasn't leaving. I am a man of my word. Are you going to draw a card, or what?"

I sigh as I draw a card. Oh good, another one I need. I discard.

"How do you feel about relationship networks?" I ask, and he tries to stop a smile. "You didn't come to me via Marcelo, so I have no idea. Maybe you hate them."

"Maybe I love them." He draws another card and discards from his hand. I suspect he's close to Gin. So am I.

"Maybe you do. What's wrong with your mother?" I ask, my tone of voice soft.

He sighs, sets his cards down for a moment, and rubs his face.

"She has a wasting disease. Seen a million doctors." He waves his hand and sighs again. "There's nothing that can be done. I've rushed home several times in the last few years to be with her, thinking that was it, the end, you know? She just keeps holding on."

I pull a card, and it's not one I need. Damn.

"Marcelo thought you or your mom had money problems, and that's why you left."

"I kept it vague on purpose. My mom is a private woman." He draws another card, smiles, and lays his cards down. "Gin. Must be my lucky day."

I flip my cards over. "Must be. I was one card away." I gather up all the cards and pass them to him to shuffle.

"So, you have a birthday coming up?" he asks, shuffling the cards.

I tip my wristlet over and check the date. "Yep. It's in a few days." I keep it vague on purpose.

"How old?" He cuts the cards and stops to take a sip of soda. He shuffles the deck like someone who plays frequently, so sometime soon, we'll have to discuss cards.

I laugh. "Usually, that's a loaded question, but I'll allow it. I'll be twenty-nine. You?"

"Thirty-one in four months. We can always celebrate my birthday. I love a good party." He lifts his eyebrows and begins to deal.

Looking at Kalvin's face as it falls back to neutral, I can read the deep concern for his mother and the family stress he's been under. We're both facing family stress of different varieties. But he's here with me, instead of at home.

I decide to lose the next hand.

I want him. I want him for good. Does he want that too? When I think of how my mother built her network, it makes me want to do things differently. I want to be sure my mates are happy, not like Mom's men. How can I make that happen?

Once the cards are on the table, I rearrange my hand like I'm playing to win.

"Does your mother have a network?" I ask, picking up the first card and replacing it with something in my hand. I'm not paying attention.

"She has two husbands." He moves the card he picked up to the discard pile. "One of them is estranged. The other is a constant worrier. He's there with her, but he's terrible at this sickness stuff."

We continue playing.

"It's not easy to watch someone you love get sick and waste away." I observe him over the top of my cards.

"That's very true. It's tough on my brothers too. My mom never had a girl." He laughs as he rearranges his cards. "She absolutely doted on my older brother's wife. Not a mean bone in that woman's body."

I stop and stare out the small horizontal window near the ceiling. The rain is really coming down now.

I wonder what it's like to have kind and loving parents. It must be... fulfilling. Yeah, that's the right word. I've always felt like there was a part of my life that was missing, empty. I tried to fill it with booze, and flying, and sex, but that never worked.

"Sorry," Kalvin says, exchanging cards. "You know I talk too much."

"Oh," I say, pulling myself back to the game. I flip over the next card and discard it. "No, it's fine. I asked. I'm just sitting here wondering what that must be like, having a loving family."

"And then to lose it," Kalvin says.

"Yes, well, I lost my family ages ago. I just have my cousin now. Even my siblings are lost to me." I look up at him. "You have Gin. You had it two cards ago."

He lays his cards down, and I was right. Gin. Best two out of three.

"I want my own family, Kalvin. I want to break the cycle. I want men I love, children to dote on and laugh and cry with. I want to give my children all the stuff that was denied to me as a kid. I want to fly the Duo Systems and learn everything. Absolutely everything. What about you?"

His smile is slight, warm, kind. "I want those same things."

"And you can share?" My stomach is tied in knots. If he's

going to cause problems with his pilot ego, then I should cut him loose now. I don't want to.

"My mama taught me to share my toys," he says. His eyes crinkle with humor.

I sigh with relief. Kalvin is game, and he's here with me. Saif has come around, and he's not far. Hell, even Takemo has mellowed out some, though he is far from being in my network or a desirable mate.

I stand up and round the table. Kalvin angles his chair away from the table, and I straddle him to sit in his lap. He smiles as his hands slide up my thighs to my hips. Taking his face in my hands, I look him in the eyes.

"Don't play me," I say, my voice gentle. I stroke my thumb over his cheek, and the sandpaper stubble soothes an anxious part of me. "I won't be manipulated."

"Not me," he whispers. "I know I play the high-flying pilot, but with you, you get just Kalvin." He squeezes my hips. "I don't want to play games anymore. You're the only one for me. I knew it right away, as soon as I opened my eyes and stopped listening to rumors. I won't fuck it up. I've learned my lesson the hard way." His eyes are dead serious. Ah, there was a woman he tried to charm, and it didn't work out. I wonder what happened there.

I lean in and kiss him, inhaling through my nose and wrapping my arms around his neck. His hands clutch my hips, pulling me towards him. His pants bulge between my legs, and my head swims with lust. Yes. This is what I've been waiting for. A meaningful connection with Kalvin. We had a spark in the desert, and now that spark has grown to a roaring flame. If I can trust him to be gentle with me and my heart, I can trust him with other things as well — the Amagi, my eventual other network consorts, my business, my life choices.

His hands travel up my back, and I draw a sharp breath and

pull away. "Ow. Oh no." I rest my forehead against his. "My back is still messed up."

He raises his eyebrows. "Then you'll have to be on top." His fingers pull at the hem of my shirt and lift it up over my head. I lift my arms and let the shirt go.

With a slow, gentle pressure, he drags his hands up my sides and pulls my chest to his lips. I let my head drop back as he kisses along the top of my bra, and his fingers skirt my bra straps to release the hooks in the back. He sighs as he drops my bra to the floor.

"I've dreamt of this for weeks," he says, cupping one of my breasts and teasing the nipple. I inhale as all the blood in my body pools low in my abdomen. He leans forward and draws my other breast into his mouth. I groan as his tongue swirls around my nipple. Grinding my hips against his groin, I'm desperate to relieve the pressure growing between my legs.

"We need to move," I say, my voice light and breathy. I can't take this anymore. I have had the most stressful few weeks, and with this lawsuit hanging over my head, my brief fallout with Saif, and everything that's happened in the jungle, I just need a release. I won't treat Kalvin like a sexbot, but for fuck's sake, if we do not do the deed right now, I will explode.

He pushes my hips off his lap. "To the bed, gorgeous."

I back up, but he's right on top of me. He takes my face in his hands and pulls me to him. Our lips crash into each other, and I open up to let him in. His tongue slides over mine as I pull his shirt from his pants and struggle with his belt. Why have we invented nothing better to keep our pants from falling down?

I pull my lips from his. "Gah, your pants are trying to kill me. Take them off right now," I demand.

"Yes, Captain," he says, humor touching his voice. He unbuckles and pulls his pants and underwear off. My knees shake. His dick is full and long, and... I can't see straight. I rush to him and take his shirt off. There. He's naked, and I'm so aroused. I'm going to burst.

"Come here." He unclasps my pants and slips his hands in the back, cupping my ass. "I remember that bruise you got right here from falling off the life pod. I saw you in your underwear that day, and I knew I wanted you." He dips down and pulls everything off.

Oh yes. Yes, yes. I inhale, close my eyes, and reach out for his dick. He groans as I wrap my fingers around it. "I wanted you too. I just didn't know it yet."

We stand there for a long time, our lips moving together, my hand stroking him, his hand migrating to between my legs. I don't think I can orgasm and stay on my feet, though. I'm sure I'll collapse. So I push him to the bed and let go so I can press on his shoulder and get him to sit. Wasting no time, I straddle him again and guide him into me. I gasp as he rocks and hits me right at the most tender spot.

That's it. I won't last long. I drop my head down to his.

"I'm going to come quickly. I can't hold back. Keep going to the end."

He leans forward and nips at my collarbone. Our hips find a rhythm, and I let go. I just let it all happen. I let him hold me. I let him guide me. He finds the spot swiftly, and with a few thrusts, I'm tipped over to the other side.

"Keep going," he growls, holding the rhythm strong.

I orgasm again, twice more in succession before he comes too. I'm panting heavy breaths, in and out, in and out.

"Sky." Kalvin pushes back my hair, so I look down at him. "I don't know what you see in me." His eyes are scared, worried, vulnerable. My heart aches. "But I will never leave your side again. If this is our life together, then I want it."

With a deep kiss, he lifts me off of him, holds my hand, and guides me into the bed. I lay down on my side with my back to him, and he snuggles up, close enough to feel his heat. He kisses my neck as his hand comes around to cup my breast and then head to between my legs again.

Yes, yes. Again.

I will not sleep tonight, and that's fine with me.

18

THANKS TO INDIA, I'm given a day off between plants to rest and let my system reset. At some point, Kalvin rolls over, kisses my bare shoulder, and leaves before the sun is up. I roll over and go back to sleep. I'm tired after a night of sex, and talking, and after days of being on the go. I dream of the desert, long stretches of sand as far as I can see. Kalvin is with me, and my heart hurts to see him so unwell. I wake up mumbling something and stare at the ceiling. I think I care more for him than I initially thought.

Once I'm up, I use the tiny shower, clean up, and take my sore and broken ass to the cafeteria for carbs and caffeine. Everything a growing girl needs.

But I open the door, and I'm met with all of my romantic decisions from the last week.

Saif, Kalvin, and Takemo are all having breakfast together at a table littered with plates, half-eaten food, and generous cups of coffee. They're talking and laughing, getting along. What the hell alternate universe did I just walk into?

I almost turn around and leave. Carbs and coffee? Those are for the weak.

But no.

Don't run, Skylar. Stop. Running.

I listen, but my feet itch with the desire to leave and avoid the awkwardness in front of me.

"Hey, look who it is," Kalvin calls out. He jumps up from the table and approaches me. "Did you go back to sleep?" He swiftly leans in and kisses my forehead before I can stop him.

"Yeah. Yeah, I think I got another two hours. Thanks. Where did you disappear to?"

"The gym," he says with a smile. Yeah, his hair is wet. He must have showered there.

"Smart. Though I'm not sure where you found the energy for it," I whisper. "I came for breakfast and coffee."

"I can grab that for you." He jerks his thumb over his shoulder. "Me and the chef are already tight. He's going to make hash browns tomorrow."

I blink a few times. "You've been here a few days, and you're already ordering around the staff?"

"Pshaw, Skylar. It was not an order. It was a mutual love of fried potatoes."

In the background, Takemo and Saif rearrange the plates at the table and make room for me. I guess I can't just leave.

"Well, who doesn't love fried potatoes?" I say, trying to chase away my impending sense of doom. "Fine. Get me whatever looks good and a giant cup of coffee, okay?"

"We already have a carafe at the table." He gently nudges me forward.

Saif stands up as I approach, and Takemo leans over to fill an empty coffee cup.

"Morning, Sky," Saif says, pulling out a chair for me. "Sleep okay?"

"Yeah, fine, thanks." I sit down and pull the coffee cup to me. I look around for the cream and sugar. Takemo finds both without me saying anything and puts them next to the cup. "Thanks," I mutter, doctoring up my drink.

"It seems both of your men made it here," Takemo says with a chuckle. "I was surprised to see Saif here this morning."

"You weren't around last night when he came in." I take a sip of coffee. Oh, blessed coffee.

"Yeah, someone told me to bugger off so she could drink with India in peace." He chuckles again. "I spent my evening, cold and alone, in bed with my quarterly reports."

"I hate to tell you this, but there's nothing even remotely cold about Rio." I look up, and Kalvin is approaching with two plates. "I have not stopped sweating since we got here."

"Correct. This place is the second circle of hell."

"Isn't that lust?" I ask, knowing full well the answer.

"Well, there's plenty of stuff here to lust after," Takemo replies, his eyes on me.

Saif nods as Kalvin sets the plates on the table. "Eggs, protein printed bacon, some kind of citrus fruit, and waffles. I got you a little of everything." He sits down across from me.

I rearrange the plates so the waffles are front and center.

"So, I see you two made up," Saif says with his eyes on Takemo.

"Yeah, I..." I'm not sure what to say about Takemo and me.

"I think we did." Takemo sits back in his chair with his coffee. "I apologized for my asshole behavior, Skylar probably forgave me, and then we all ran for our lives from a stampeding pack of spiderphants. It was quite the illuminating day."

I douse my waffles with melted butter and sugar syrup, say a quick thanks for the meal, and dig in with both fork and knife. Mmmm, the carbs hit my mouth, and my body melts with happiness.

"It was quite the terrifying day." I hold my hand in front of my mouth while I chew. "I hope that never happens again."

"I don't know," Takemo says. "It wasn't too bad. I got a kiss out of the whole ordeal."

I stop chewing for a moment and then resume. "I did kiss you. I must have been high."

Kalvin chuckles and shakes his head. Saif looks away for a moment, but then his eyes meet mine.

"So, this is what it's like," he says, his tone matter-of-fact.

"What?" I fill my mouth with waffles again.

"Sharing someone you care about with someone else." He nods at both Kalvin and Takemo. "It's not as bad as I thought it would be."

My heart hurts for Saif. He only had me to himself for a few weeks, if that. And then we ended those weeks on a negative note. Now, he is a part of an unofficial network, not a couple. Networks are always more complicated, especially in the beginning.

Takemo raises a hand. "You don't need to worry about me. I'm not a part of this network. I only got a kiss because she was in shock. She still hates me."

I open my mouth to deny this when Takemo leans forward and grabs the citrus fruit off my plate.

"Speaking of hateful things, I have more quarterly reports I need to look at. Later."

He saunters off, tossing the fruit in the air and catching it over and over.

"Do you want another one of those?" Saif asks, pushing back his chair.

"No. Don't worry about it."

But Takemo's statement sits in my gut like one-hundred-year-old cheese. He thinks I hate him. I mean, I don't really like him all that much because of everything he said about me. But I've forgiven people for worse over the years. It makes me a bit of a doormat, but I'm guilty of my own terrible temper, and I've said things in the heat of the moment that I have regretted. I try to give other people that grace too.

I went to war with Takemo, though. He thinks I hate him because I made his life miserable for a while. But we've been on good terms since we won the Bridge tournament. Still, that doesn't erase everything that came before.

I thought he hated me, not the other way around.

Now I'm more confused than ever. I don't know whether I'm coming or going with him. I should hate him for the part he had in my family's demise, or the way he's treated me, or his arrogant attitude, but I can clearly see why he made each decision he did.

Ugh. Takemo. He's so frustrating.

Forget it. This is something I'm going to worry about later. I have enough on my plate right now.

Speaking of which, I need to get back to eating. I look at both Kalvin and Saif, sitting quietly and drinking coffee.

"So, um, I'd like to have dinner with you both tonight. I've got stuff I have to do this afternoon. My inbox is a mess, and I have to fill out my reports for the plants we've already tested. Why don't you grab us food and meet me back at my place this evening?"

"Sure," Saif says.

"Sounds great." Kalvin's smile is sweet and satisfied. He's still flying high on last night.

"Perfect. Now, why don't you two go find something to do?" I shoo them away from the table. These two men need to figure out how they'll be friends. I can't have them at odds if they're going to be in my network together.

"Sure," Kalvin says, jerking his head at the door. "Come on, Saif. Let's go hang out with Luca and his men. They play cards all day and swap jungle stories. I've been eavesdropping, and it sounds fascinating."

Saif stands to join him, but I reach out and grab his hand. Smiling up at him, I squeeze his hand and let go.

The healing begins now.

19

Filling out forms is annoying and tiresome work. There's nothing I want to do more than crawl into bed and sleep, but I have calls to make.

The connection to the data access point is up and running at one-hundred percent, so I sign into my Estrela view and move access to the tablet to give my ocular implant a break. If I use it too much, I often get a headache, and I don't have time for that today.

I want to call Amira. It's been a long time since I talked to her, and I miss her. But she's running shipments for her family in the Californikos System, and universal time puts her in the dead of night. I shoot off a quick text to her, telling her we'll meet up soon. Maybe I can convince her to join me for a vacation on Laguna? I could really use a break.

When Marcelo's face appears before me, everything relaxes. I sink down into my chair and smile. It's nice to smile because I'm happy to see him.

"Oh, good," he says with a deep sigh. "You're alive."

I throw my head back with a laugh. "That is so not the

greeting I was expecting. Did you think I had perished in the jungle?"

"Yes. Yes, I had." His face is serious, with a deep frown. "You would not believe what's been happening here."

My stomach jumps up into my throat. "What? What's been happening?" My face cools as all the blood leaves my head. Whatever it is, it's serious. "You got my update reports, right? I had to send plain text because our data access point was getting shitty reception to the satellites in our last camp."

"We did get them, and that's how I knew you were alive. But Dominic has been here three times, the last time with the local Rio police, saying they had found you dead in the jungle, and he owns the Amagi now."

"What?" My voice cracks on the word.

Marcelo shrugs. "You were unreachable, and he had some kind of certificate? I'm not sure what he hoped to prove, but Lia and Carlos refused to open the ship for him each time. We all had your updates, but Dominic kept saying they were faked."

I close my eyes and push out a long breath. "For fuck's sake, that man is willing to kill me, both metaphorically and physically, in order to get his way. It's insane."

"You have to be careful, Skylar. If he doesn't get the ship, he'll come after you." Marcelo rubs his chin. "You should have more security wherever you are."

I shake my head. "I'm unreachable. We move every few days because the military catches up to us, but I don't think he'd sneak through the jungles to find me."

That would be suicide.

But didn't I just say that he's insane?

"Don't put it past him." Marcelo sighs. "It's a good thing you got the AI upgraded on the ship. Nanci is watching the ship's security night and day. And Ai, well, she's trying to keep everyone entertained as we sit here under siege."

"Are you not leaving at all?" Oh, now I feel bad. I'm out and about, and everyone back on the ship is stuck there when we're sitting on a planet.

"Lia goes out to get groceries. You know she has no fear. I have powered up my shuttle and flown to Segundo a few times. We're getting out. Carlos is the only one holed up with his work."

I frown at this. Carlos is always in a better mood when he can get fresh air frequently. He goes stir crazy if he works too much. I will need to call him next.

"What did you go to Segundo for?"

His frown lightens, and he relaxes a little. "To see some family. One of my network brothers was in town. I also needed to meet up with someone I'm considering for your network. Then I went back to Segundo to pick up Yan Martinez."

Yan Martinez is one of Carlos's old friends. His hobby is reviving ancient Earth tech, but his main job is doing database work for security companies.

"Yan's there? What's Carlos got him doing?"

"Uh, looking at the videos he's been mining from your family's security network, I think."

It's telling that Marcelo doesn't want to make eye contact with me through the call.

"You think? Did you see them?"

He sighs. "I'll let Carlos fill you in."

I run my fingers through my hair and consider his reply. Either he saw the videos where I'm abused, and it made him mad or uncomfortable or whatever. Or he saw doctored videos, and now he thinks I'm a big fat lying liar. I twist my hair up off my neck and tie it in a messy bun. My suite is air-conditioned, but it's still too hot and humid in here at all times.

"Okay," I say, drawing out the word into many syllables. "And what's this about someone you're considering for my network?"

This loosens him up a bit, and he produces a smile. "Believe it or not, this one stood out as a suitable candidate because you want to start your own shipping company. But I'm not going to tell you about him yet because he's considering what he wants to do in the long run. Be patient. How are things going with you and Saif and Kalvin?"

"Well…" I grimace.

"Spill it, Skylar. Tell me everything."

I roll my eyes, but I start with the disastrous trip to see Saif's family, the ensuing fight, Kalvin's time with me in the jungle, his family troubles, the starbats, the spiderphants, the kiss I shared with Takemo…

"And then I slept with Kalvin last night," I say with a shrug and a smile.

"I can tell from your smile that went well." He chuckles and shakes his head.

"We have good chemistry. He's still the pretty boy high-flyer, but now he's *my* pretty boy high-flyer." I point to my palm. "I have him right here." I close my hand into a fist. "That is until he flies off to somewhere else."

"Do you really think he'd do that?" Marcelo asks, tipping his head to the side.

"Look at what Saif pulled. Most men leave me eventually. I become boring and annoying, and they salute, grab their bags, and head off into the sunset."

"Skylar, the whole point of this exercise is to find men who are going to stick around for a place in your network. I know you haven't had the best of luck in the past, but it's different this time."

I shake my head again. "I still have nothing valuable to offer them."

"Let me remind you once again, it's not just a business transaction. Even Vivian, who desperately needed the money, found men who fell in love with her and wanted to stay if she got the farm or not."

I want to say, "But who is going to fall in love with me?" Because I still don't see why anyone would. I've been told my whole life that I'm useless. That I'm a terrible person. That I don't deserve what little I have. Maybe Dominic and my mother and the rest of my family are right. Maybe this is all a useless endeavor, and if I just let them have the Amagi, they'll tell me I'm worthy again. My heart aches as I remember the times, long ago, when my mother and father would dote on me, hug me, tell me they loved me, no matter what. They had made me feel valued for a short time.

I turn my face from the vidcall and stare out the window. I'm only here because of some stupid gene that allows me to metabolize the plants. If that didn't exist, I'd be living in the closet on Vivian's farm, the Amagi would be in Dominic's hands, and Saif and Kalvin? They'd be gone. I'm not here with India because I'm a great pilot, because my skills are second to none. I'm here because I'm abnormal. It's completely pointless.

"You will find men who love you. I'm sure of it," Marcelo says, his voice quiet.

I inhale and let the shaky breath out before I turn back to Marcelo. "Yeah, well, I guess we'll see about that."

I sniff up, angry that my emotions have gotten the better of me.

"Keep an eye on Dominic for me, okay? Oh! I forgot. I had Ai keep tabs on him before I left. I'm sure she's got reports saved up in her queue. Why don't you go to her and see what she's been tracking on him?"

"Sure. I can do that. So, do you need anything?" he asks, raising his eyebrows. "Supplies? Chocolate? A trip to Laguna?"

I laugh. "All of that. I need it all."

"I'll see what I can do." His eyes crinkle with humor. Good. I like to end calls on high notes.

"I need to call Carlos now, so I'm going to let you go. Stay safe, okay?"

"You too," he says.

We wave to each other as the call ends.

I sigh and sit back in my chair, drumming my fingers on the desk. Calling Carlos will open a bucket of worms, and they'll all come slithering out. But there's nothing I can do about it. I set these events in motion. Now I have to deal with them.

Carlos answers right away.

"Hey, Skylar," he says, melting into his chair. "You're alive."

My grin is too big to contain. "I didn't realize everyone was going to be so worried about me. Sorry I didn't check in sooner."

He rubs his face with an open palm. "You didn't think we'd be worried about our friend who also gives us a paycheck?"

"Consider me corrected." I press my hand over my heart. "But in my defense, it's been wild here."

Yan Martinez slides into view next to Carlos. "Hey, Skylar," he says with a wave. "Sorry to butt in, but I'm dying to hear about Rio, too."

"Well, I'm happy to oblige. Regarding me being out of touch, we've had stampedes, and we've already moved once. And I'm not allowed to wear my wristlet when I'm testing the plants. The first plant I tried when I got here caused me to shock everyone and everything."

Carlos's eyes widen. "Whoa. Really? Tell me everything."

I repeat the same story to Carlos and Yan that I told Marcelo, and it gets better and more lavish this time. Maybe I missed my calling as a storyteller because it's a lot more fun to tell this story after the fact than it was to live it, that's for sure. And I bet this is not the last time I tell it, so I should memorize it and store the tale away for later.

"That's amazing," Carlos says, his voice filled with awe. "I never want to spend time in Rio's jungles. I barely want to leave the ship while I'm here. Ossun is more my speed."

"I'm partial to space myself," Yan says, and I nod my agreement.

"I definitely prefer space to this bullshit." I blow out a deep breath. "But I'm getting used to it, and we're making substantial progress here, so I'm not going to complain. I don't know how long this job will even last, so I'm taking it day by day."

We're all silent and staring at each other for a moment when I decide to take the plunge.

"So, tell me, what have you found with the video?"

Carlos's face loses its cheer, and Yan glances sideways at him.

"Uh oh. I guess it's bad news?" I ask, trying to keep a smile on my face.

Inside, though, bitterness grows at an exponential rate. If I lose this path to the truth, then what's next? What else will be taken away from me? What more will Dominic do to keep everything hidden and drive me mad with doubts? I drop my eyes and stare at the table for a moment. I already question my sanity every day about what I remember from my childhood and whether or not I imagined it.

"Well, it's both good news and bad news, unfortunately."

Yan clears his throat. "Skylar, the video surveillance from your mother's ship is there in the family's archives on Laguna. It's decades' worth of data, and we've combed through a lot of it already. But..." His voice trails off for a moment. "But there are no videos of the abuse you encountered."

"Fucking hell," I whisper. I turn my eyes from them both. Then I imagined it all? I'm going insane and remembering a life I never had?

"Here's another 'but.' But it's obvious to me, and to the two colleagues I've shown the videos to, that what's in the family database has been tampered with."

I turn back to them with raised eyebrows.

Yan continues, "There's two decades' worth of data that's

been fucked with. Some timestamps and logs show Dominic has been in the system almost every day for twenty years, making small edits." He shakes his head. "The man was incredibly thorough. He never missed a day when you were on board the ship. I thought maybe he was just doing routine maintenance, but then Carlos had a good idea."

Carlos raises his finger into the air. "I know you didn't get off the ship much as a kid." I nod in response. "But I knew that you went to far-school a few times and then to visit Vivian on occasion. So sometimes you were away, right? I found the receipts for one of your far-school visits, and then I cross-referenced that time with the logs."

Yan butts in. "It will not surprise you to find out Dominic logged out for the time you were away. He went years making daily changes to the video surveillance, and then boom. Suddenly, he does nothing but only because you were off the ship. That's pretty damning." He pokes himself in the chest. "In my opinion, that means he was erasing the evidence every day, evidence of your abuse."

A little of the tension I've been holding onto eases away.

Just a little.

"Does this mean the evidence is gone, though? What do the videos show now?"

"The videos are confusing," Carlos says, swiping at something on his screen. "Many of them just cut away from conversations you had with Dominic. Others show you yelling at him or defying him somehow, but it's apparent part of the conversation is missing." He shrugs. "Nothing in there damns you, nor does any of it exonerate Dominic either. It's obvious to me that Dominic worked hard to delete the evidence of his abusive behavior, but he didn't build up a case to make him look like a saint, either. He just wanted it gone."

He knew what he was doing was wrong, and if anyone saw the video, he would be out of my mom's network.

"Hey, did you see if he had sent my mother video clips? Were those in the archive?"

Yan nods. "We found many of the doctored videos in archives of your mother's inbox. Several of them are just like what we describe. Mostly you, young, less than ten? Angry and yelling with no context. There was a video of you smearing cake on Dominic?" A smile tips the corners of his lips. "That one was pretty epic, though it looks like it was bad for you." He cringes. "The view count on it is over twenty. Your mother watched it several times. Her reply to Dominic was that he was in charge, and he could do whatever needed to be done to keep you behaving 'in a proper manner.'"

"Uh," Carlos interrupts, "the term she actually used was 'keep you in line,' as if you were some military soldier that just needed boot camp to fall into ranks."

Yan nods. "Yeah, that was some bullshit."

I have no words. Mom just handed me over to him. She thought I was some spoiled brat, and Dominic would cure me. I sigh, hang my head, and rub at my face with both hands.

Come on, Universe. Something needs to go right sometime soon.

"I need good news, guys, or I'm going to walk into the jungle and never come back out." I'm not suicidal, but I'm not feeling very upbeat about my chances here.

"Okay, a little possible good news. Your family's data archive is sitting on Laguna, and no one has ever come and dealt with the solid-state backups." Carlos sits up and starts typing. "This means there may be archives of material that were sent to the backups before Dominic could alter them. They remove backups at this facility from the main network every five years and store them on solid-state drives. The company puts them in storage until someone comes and gets them. I've heard they have data drives from over three hundred years ago stored there."

Laguna. Wasn't Marcelo just saying I could have a trip to Laguna? Hmmm, maybe I can make that happen.

"So, there's a chance we may obtain some original videos that weren't tampered with before they were backed up," Yan says, sliding back into view. "But it's only a possibility. Dominic was pretty thorough, and he's well aware of the backups, even if he's never accessed them."

"It's worth a shot to go after them." I feel deep down in my gut that this is my only option. It's my word against Dominic's and Mom's, and with my reputation around the Duo Systems not being so stellar, no one would believe me. "In the meantime, you should follow any other clues you can find."

Carlos smiles and salutes. "You've got it. I'm following other leads too. We'll crack this case. I promise."

"Thank you, Carlos. Make sure you go outside and get some fresh air, okay?"

He rolls his eyes. "Yes, Mom."

Even though his smile sticks with me after I sign off, I can't help but feel the doubt pull me down.

I need something to go right.

Soon.

20

My door chimes, and I run to open it. It's still raining. But that's Rio for you.

"We come bearing gifts," Kalvin says, lifting two canvas bags. Saif is holding an umbrella over both of their heads.

"Come in quick." I wave them into the entryway. Saif sets the umbrella right next to the outer door and closes the inner door behind him on the way in. They take off their shoes before tracking water into the living area.

Kalvin opens the canvas bag and empties covered bowls onto the main table. He uncovers each, and steam curls in the light spilling from the overhead lamp.

"It's fried noodles night. I had them load yours up with lots of vegetables."

He remembered. I asked for extra vegetables in my pasta when I was recuperating at Vivian's consort's vineyard on Sonoma. Kalvin and I only had one meal there, but it must have been memorable enough for him.

Saif approaches me, squeezes my upper arm, and leans in to kiss me on the cheek. "I got dessert. Peanut butter pie." He lifts the bag he's carrying and raises his eyebrows.

I press my hand to my chest. "Sugar will always be the way to my heart."

"I figured." He smiles.

Kalvin's smile is slight as he sets the chopsticks next to each bowl. I cross the room to him and kiss him on the cheek.

"Thanks for grabbing dinner, guys. I appreciate the help."

I need to be open about how their help is needed and appreciated. They want to help, but I am terrible about asking. Despite wanting to spare them the inconvenience of my crazy life, they signed up for this.

My chest aches as I imagine them leaving, grabbing their bags and high-tailing it out of here, and how much that will hurt when it happens. I take a deep breath through my nose and push the thought away. It's okay. Whenever they want, I will let them go. I promise myself, right here and now, never to be selfish and try to keep them if they want to leave me. I will accept it.

But I hope they're here to stay.

"Of course," Kalvin says, gesturing to my spot at the table. "It's just dinner, Skylar. No big deal."

I sit down in my seat, say a quiet, brief thanks, and pick up my chopsticks. Both Kalvin and Saif wait for me to start before they pick up their chopsticks, too. I capture a mouthful of noodles and pull them up.

"You may think it's no big deal to pick me up dinner, but it is. Really. It's a sweet gesture. It's the kind of pampering I've rarely had from loved ones." I push the noodles into my mouth and sigh at their perfection. Chewy with just the right amount of saltiness, they are bliss. India must have hired one of the best chefs she could find. "Mmmm, delicious."

Saif picks at his noodles, and Kalvin's face is twisted in thought.

"Are you telling me that just giving you food is pampering?"

The table jumps, and Kalvin hops with it. I glance under the table, and Saif is pulling his foot back to his side. Classic.

"Ow. Jesus." He sits up taller, bringing his feet under his chair.

I mix around the noodles in my bowl. "It's okay, Saif. No need for violence."

"I just thought you'd like a break," he replies.

"From what?" Kalvin asks. He shoves noodles into his mouth.

Even though I'm hungry after working all afternoon, I set my chopsticks down.

Here we go. Kalvin knows so little about my past, and I'm sure Saif is sick of hearing about it.

"Besides going to a restaurant or eating at Vivian's house, I have always fed my family first and then myself. Since I was six. And even then, there were many times I fed everyone else, and I was denied food of my own." I stare out the window at the rain. "I have a complicated relationship with food. I always eat now whenever I can." I touch my chest. "There's a buzz in here, when I see food, that I have to push away and ignore every time. I see a meal, a snack, whatever, and I want it, but I fear it'll be snatched away from me at any second. So I always eat, and I never wait for people to bring it to me. It's…" I stop and close my eyes with a smile. "It's a treat for others to feed me and not take it away."

I face Kalvin. "So, thank you. I appreciate it more than you know."

Being gracious does not come naturally to me, so this is a feat. Every time I was appreciative and gracious in the past, my family used those moments to destroy me.

I pause and wait for someone to say I don't deserve this meal, or to steal the food from my bowl, or make a snide comment about how I never reciprocate.

Nothing comes.

163

Silence has fallen over the table, but I won't let it stop me from moving forward with this evening. I pick up my chopsticks and keep eating.

"Maybe you should stop calling them 'family.'" Kalvin's voice is low with anger.

I pause for a moment and find my zen in detachment. "Yes, I probably should. Anyway, we're going to hammer out some things here tonight, between the three of us, so we can either move on together or part ways."

Kalvin and Saif resume eating along with me. Saif grabs a beer from the bag, opens it, and hands it to me. Beer and noodles, what could be finer?

"Thanks." I take a sip. "Okay. I've been going over my financial records, and things will be tight for a bit, but I think I can make this work for the next few months." I chew on the noodles and decide to be open about the financial arrangements. "India Dellis paid me two million credits for being here."

Kalvin's eyes widen, and he and Saif glance at each other. "That's a lot of money. You could buy a decent ship."

"I could," I stress, "but I won't. I will use the money to give you both a stipend and pay for a lawyer to defend the Amagi. I will still make money as I work here month-to-month, assuming I survive the plants and the animals of Rio."

"Skylar, that's unnecessary," Saif says, pausing his chopsticks above his bowl. "I don't need a stipend. I have money I planned to bring to my network."

He looks at Kalvin, hoping Kalvin will back him up. Kalvin quickly chews his mouth full of food.

"Skylar knows the predicament I'm in." He clears his throat. "My previous job stole my wages, and every credit I've saved has gone towards my mother. I have a small amount of savings, but it's not much."

Saif's eyebrows furrow. "Why does your mother need money?"

Before me, I have two men I care for, and they both come from opposite sides of society. Saif's family is wealthy. They are the elite. His mother would never dream of taking money from her children. Kalvin has never been that lucky.

Kalvin clears his throat. "She's been sick for over a decade. She would be homeless without my support."

Saif's cheeks fall, and he stares into his bowl.

I hold up my hand. "We'll get to more of that later. I really feel it's important you're both paid for the work you'll do in the network."

Saif pulls his attention back to me and folds his arms over his chest.

"I don't ever want you to think I'm being selfish or holding back from you," I explain. Anger rises in my belly at his stony face, and it's difficult keeping my voice even and calm. "You will get the stipend because that's what's fair."

"No, no, no," Saif says, pushing his bowl to the side. "You have slaved and suffered your whole life just to get to this point. I should be allowed to contribute funds and spoil you in the way you deserve. And I will settle for nothing less."

I open my mouth to argue with him, but nothing comes out. For once, there are no comebacks to a statement like that.

Because deep down in my gut, that's what I want. I want to be spoiled, and cared for, and watched over. I want someone to smother me with love so I can barely breathe, so I can barely move. Not that I would know what to do with that kind of attention or anything. Just the very thought of it makes me want to hide.

"I will settle for nothing less," Saif repeats, stressing every word. "And you will let me because that's what I was meant to do."

Kalvin is quiet, poking at the noodles in his bowl. I watch him from the corner of my eye.

He thinks for a moment before lifting a helping of noodles. "Let him," he says, stuffing his mouth full of food.

Saif gestures to Kalvin, his palm out and his eyebrows raised.

I actually laugh. "What?"

"Let him spoil you. Let *us* spoil you. I can't spoil you with money and jewels, but I can spoil you with attention, food… I'm a great cook, by the way. My siblings made me cook because my food was the best. I can take care of ships and make sure your business is always running on the up and up. There's no reason we have to keep doing things the way the old guard did."

"He's right." Saif sits up straighter. "Newer networks now are more evenly balanced. They don't rely on just the woman to do everything, and the men become leeches. My mother raised me to be independent and want the same thing in a network."

Kalvin looks me dead in the eyes. "Some of us were lucky to have good role models for mothers. You don't have to be like yours."

His statement knocks the air out of me. I press my hand to my chest as I try to catch my breath.

"Have I…?" I start, but I can't finish the sentence.

Have I been trying to be like my mother, but better? Thinking that if I just paid my men enough, they would be more responsible, more loving, more reliable than Mom's network? When I remember my childhood, a lot of the grief amongst the dads was because of money. They never had enough, hence the gambling and the side hustles. They put me in charge of the kids to pursue their own desires because they didn't get anything from Mom. All she ever did was fly and pop out babies. She was never really a part of the family, and her network didn't make it a family because she wasn't around.

"Oh my God," I whisper, pressing my fingers to my lips.

Kalvin nods. "You don't just make the mold better or stronger or bigger. You break it. That's how the cycle ends."

When did Kalvin become such a wise man?

Maybe he always was. I still have a lot to learn about these two.

"You're right. You're so right." I sigh as I stare down into my bowl of noodles. "I thought that if I just paid you more or gave you less responsibility or asked less of you, everything would be better. Dom, Miguel, my own father..." I press my hand to my lips. "They were never happy, and I figured it was because they never had enough."

Saif's eyes are wide. "Did you think you would just do everything, and we would — I don't know — hang out?"

My neck begins to sweat, and I swallow hard because I think I know the correct answer to this, but I'm still unsure.

I slam the chopsticks down on the table, cover my face with my hands, and groan.

"I don't know!" I yell, throwing my hands into the air. "I don't know." I stress every syllable. "I don't know how to do this. I feel like a complete and absolute moron. I am smart," I say, poking myself in the chest with every word. "I gather data, and I make decisions based on previous experiences. All my life, I watched the dads be restless and angry. They took advantage of me as free labor so they could do their own things. All because Mom was tight with the money. What do *you* think I learned from that, huh?"

Kalvin holds up his hands and nods slowly. "It's okay. We're not here to demonize you for being the way you are."

"No," Saif says, shaking his head. "I'm sorry if my tone was sharp." He closes his eyes and sighs. "I grew up believing everyone was cherished as part of a network. Men and women. Everyone in my mother's network had an equal say, with my mom being the final decision maker. Still, I don't think they ever fought over it because they always came to compromises.

My mother has five men in her network, and they have always all been considered. It's a team effort."

I never saw a team effort growing up. I saw one man dominate the psyches of everyone else and impose his rule. Unfortunately, I was the one who endured his wrath.

Kalvin glances between Saif and me. All I can do is stare into space. I have been lied to for most of my life, lied to and used. How do I even have healthy relationships after all the shit I've been through?

"That sounds pretty great, Saif. Doesn't it, Skylar?"

I swallow and turn to him. I must look like a dying baby bird because his face falls.

"It is pretty great." Saif's lips turn up in a warm smile. "And I think Skylar is going to make a wonderful partner."

"Partner..." The word feels foreign in my mouth. I sit with it a moment until it warms to my soul. "Partner." I nod as the word becomes a friend, not an enemy.

"Yeah." Saif's mood brightens along with his smile. "Let's do things differently. I think it would be great for us to have a partnership. All of us." He gestures to Kalvin. "He's growing on me."

"Same, buddy," Kalvin says, sarcasm dripping off his words.

I burst out an abrupt laugh. Saif's smile grows.

"And I'm sure there'll be others," he continues, nodding. "We can make this a tight family where we all have a say in how it works. My mother came from a family similar to yours, Sky, though she didn't suffer the kind of abuse you did."

I lower my eyes to the table.

"But her mother's network was always so bitter. They lived hand-to-mouth for so long because they invested in the business instead of themselves and their own happiness. When my grandmother died, none of my mother's siblings were surprised. She had worked herself to the bone for years and did nothing but complain for the last ten of them. My mother decided she would never do what her mother did. You can do the same."

I take a deep breath and let it all out. Vivian's network is more like a partnership than anything else. I grew up believing the woman had to be the center, had to pull all the weight, had to provide all the income, had to birth all the babies. But as I've grown older, I've seen other network configurations. I've seen ones as small as single pairings. I've seen larger ones with multiple women. I've seen unhealthy networks and happy networks. The happiest ones were always a mystery to me.

But they don't have to be.

"Do you think we can make that work?" I ask, sitting back in my chair.

They both nod. "I don't see why not," Kalvin says. "It is a partnership by law, anyway. It's obviously not always done this way. Some networks prefer a more traditional style with the woman at the front and center always. But I've seen others where it works out better the way Saif is suggesting."

"Okay." My shoulders start to feel lighter.

Saif raises a finger. "I'd also like to propose that you don't appoint a number-one like some networks do. It seems to work for Vivian because of her farm situation. Still, I think things would be better divided evenly between us all, with you as the ultimate decision maker, especially when it comes to your business and your ship."

"Okay." A smile returns to my face. "I'd like that, I think."

Saif nods once.

My noodle bowl is almost empty, so I pick up my chopsticks again.

"I'm going to make my first decision as part of this network, then." I scoop up a mouthful of noodles. "I'd like for you both to work out a sleeping arrangement schedule. I will not be sleeping with you both every night. In fact, I will only ever sleep with one of you at a time."

"Good," Saif mumbles.

"Thank fucking God," Kalvin says.

"Glad to see we're on the same page. And some nights I would like to sleep alone. Can you take care of that?" Vivian has a similar arrangement, and I think it would be good for us.

"Sure." Saif nods to Kalvin. "He was here last night, and you've done enough emotional labor today. So take the night off. I'll take the next. Fair?"

We all agree.

Kalvin lifts his hands. "Look at that. We made it work." His smile is sweet, and Saif's returning smile is gracious and kind.

How the hell did I find two men like this? Now, if only we can fix the disastrous trip to see Saif's family.

"Finish up because I'm dying for dessert," Saif says, reaching behind him to grab the food bag. He pulls out three helpings of peanut butter pie with chocolate ganache on top. I finish up my noodles in a flash.

Hey now. You can't go wrong with dessert.

My night is looking up.

21

I'M LESS than three episodes from the season finale of *Next Up* when the door to the lab opens and out comes a frazzled lab tech. I don't get up. Most of the time, they're checking to make sure I'm alive. When the door shuts, it falls into place with a loud clunk.

"Anything yet, Skylar?" he asks, glancing at the wallscreen. "Oooh, you're getting closer to the juicy episodes."

I wave at the wallscreen, pausing the show. "It is taking *fucking forever* for these two to sleep with each other. This is the most angsty show in the universe."

"Yeah, but it's so good."

I sigh. "It is. I wish I could stop watching, but it's an addiction at this point." I sit up and roll out my neck. "Nothing yet. I haven't noticed any changes." I shrug. "I feel like I'm wasting your time just sitting around watching dramas, though the pay is fantastic for sitting around doing nothing." I stand up and cross the room to grab another bottle of water from the fridge. Gotta stay hydrated on this hot world.

"Hmmm, I bet." He looks at his datapad again. "We've noticed no changes in your health data either. Everything looks fine." He sighs and drops his datapad to his side. "I think this one is a dud. Nothing happened to our previous test subjects except for a few headaches, so we thought maybe it would elicit a proper response from you. But I guess not. If you get a headache anytime in the next day or two, you can take painkillers for it. Just ask the doc."

"So, I'm done for the day?" This is a first. I'm usually in the lab from late morning until dinner. It's a sunny day outside. Maybe I can get some daylight on my skin and go for a walk. It's been ages since I last walked anywhere for fun. Running for my life doesn't count.

The tech glances over his shoulder at the lab window. Everyone inside is moving around, and storage bins are being brought in from the rear room.

"Yeah, might as well. We have to pack up here, anyway."

"We're moving again?" This is news to me. I thought we had another three days here.

"It looks like it. Sorry. Gotta go." He hastens to the door, and when it opens, the conversations inside come spilling out for a second. I catch someone saying, "Fucking military," before the door closes for good.

Outside, the camp is in chaos. I'm assaulted on all sides by the noise of people moving and shouting, buildings being broken down, and vehicles lumbering through the camp. I step out of the way as a man runs past me with a writhing bag in his hand. When the animals invade the camp, you know things are about to get rough and ready.

"Skylar!"

I whirl around at Kalvin's voice. He's holding up my bag and heading in my direction with Saif on his heels. My heart rate soars at the cacophony, the assault of sound. I squint my eyes and flex my jaw, hoping it'll dissipate quickly.

"We packed everything of yours up and got out before they collapsed your suite." He drops the bag at my feet. Leaning down, he looks me in the eyes before reaching out for my cheek. A moment of panic causes me to pull away. "Whoa, easy," he says, lifting his hand. "Are you all right?"

"No." I clamp my hands over my ears. "I can't... My ears."

I struggle to make sense of the auditory input. It's like the entire world has its volume turned up, and I'm hearing everything at once. I shake my head and try to bring the volume down, but I can't. A whimper lodges in my throat. The lab was so quiet compared to this.

Kalvin looks at all the people milling around us — the vehicles, the power tools, the generators — and turns to Saif.

"Do you have earplugs?"

Saif blinks. "Yeah. I never travel without them." He sets his bag down and unzips it, rummaging around inside until he stands up with a tiny box in his hand. "Here," he says, handing them to me.

I take a few calming breaths before letting go of my ears to accept the earplugs. The sound is deafening. The booming, shrieking, and grinding noises are so pervasive that I feel nauseated and fall to one knee. Kalvin lunges for me.

I squeeze each earplug and jam them into my ears. As they expand to fill out the voids, my heart rate decreases, and the sounds become manageable again. I close my eyes and slowly breathe in and out a few times.

"Oh, thank God. I thought I was going insane." I slip the box into my pants pocket and stand back up.

Saif touches my face and tips it up to get a good look. He smooths out the stress lines on either side of my eyes with his thumbs. "It's not that loud out here. What happened with today's plant?"

I shrug and shake my head. "Nothing."

"Hmmm."

I can hear him perfectly, even through the earplugs. Maybe 'nothing' is the wrong qualifier for today's plant. I should go find the doctor. Except there's no infirmary anymore. It is just a space with collapsed building walls and a crane lifting them onto the back of a truck.

Another vehicle rumbles past us, so I step out of the way. Once it's passed us, it reveals India and Takemo having a conversation on the other side of the expanse of grass. Just the people I need to see. It's time to find out what's going on.

"Come on," I say to the guys, waving them forward.

I jog across the grass and raise my hand to catch their attention. "India! Takemo!" Takemo turns and smiles, and India hands off a datapad to someone else before turning to me. "Hey, so what's happening? I just got kicked out of the lab."

"Sorry." India glances at my earplugs. "It was a split-second decision. The military did a flyover about an hour ago, and I expect them to be here in no time. We need to move."

"Not just move," Takemo insists, turning to India. "We need to consider a different part of the continent. This is way too stressful *and* dangerous."

"No," India says, swiping down with her hand. "We've been over this. I've had expeditions to every corner of the continent and several outlying islands. This area has the most diverse plant and animal life. Whatever happened to Rio to make it this way happened *here* at some point. We have to stay."

"But we're constantly moving, and Skylar is not getting to test as many plants because of this." He glances at me. "I would feel much better about this situation if we stashed her in a nearby city and brought the plants to her."

"Wait, wait, wait," I say, throwing my hands up. "What the hell are you doing? You're not my mother. I'm fine with being here."

His jaw tightens. "You don't *need* to be here. You can do what you do from a place of safety. It was one thing when we were moving every two weeks, and it's another when we're moving every third day. Not only would you be safer in a city, but you'd be able to test more plants." He turns his stern eyes on India. "Which is the whole point of this affair, is it not?"

India rolls her eyes. "He's not wrong, but he's also not right." She takes a datapad from someone who approaches her. "Look, we have nothing set up like that now. And that would require us to have another separate operation and have teams bring the plants to a Rio city, which would further erode our security."

Takemo opens his mouth to object, but India raises her hand.

"I hear your concerns, and maybe we can make it work, but for now, I need to continue doing what we're doing and hope the next location lasts longer." She hands the datapad back and inhales sharply, turning to me. "I have an idea. Why don't you and your network mates take a break? Take three days off and meet us at our new location. Luca is leaving soon to take a crew to a shuttle not far from here. Hopefully, when you return, we can stay in one place for two weeks or more."

As much as I hate the jungle, the heat, the inconvenience of limited communications, and many, many other things about this job, I don't want to leave. I'm in a groove now, and stopping to go back to the city will just make returning here more difficult.

"I'd rather stay and not lose momentum," I tell her, but she shakes her head.

"Nothing lost." India sees my hesitation and smiles. "Skylar, can I speak to you privately?"

"Sure."

I follow her off to the side, away from everyone's prying eyes and ears. I can still hear Saif, though, even from ten meters away and with earplugs in.

"Do you want to go back to Primeiro? To the Amagi or to my parents?" he asks Kalvin.

"I'll go wherever Skylar wants me."

"Good answer."

"You guys are going back to Primeiro? Can I come along?" Takemo asks.

"To my parents?" Saif asks.

"Uh... Am I invited?"

I try not to laugh.

"Skylar," India starts, so I turn my eyes to her, "you're doing a great job. I'm thrilled you're here. But I don't want you to burn out on this. The constant moving is stressful, especially with the bad animal luck we've had lately. You could use a real bed and some downtime. Tell me, you haven't met Ketal yet, have you?"

She folds her arms over her chest.

"Saif's mom? No. I haven't." Do I tell her about my disastrous first attempt to meet his family? No. I don't think so.

"Well, then, you should go do that on your time off. But be sure not to mention me, okay? It's in your best interest."

The mystery is too much. "Why? What happened between you two?"

Her smile is wry. "We were university rivals. It's silly now to think back on it, but we both got inducted into the same 'secret' society, and then we fought our way to the top of it."

"Oh yeah? Who won?" I rub my hands together, ready for the gossip.

She throws her head back. "Neither of us. We both got pregnant our last year, and then Sidney Rodriguez stole the president position from us both. It was quite the coup. But we're not friends, and it would be a good idea to leave me out of it. Just say you're working for Athens Industries. It's accurate enough." She squeezes my upper arm and pulls me a little closer. "I spoke with Renata about the jump ring. We *must* have the technology the military has, or we'll be doomed to failure. Any idea of how we can get it?"

I shrug. "I don't know. That base we were in on Neve

burned to the ground. There was talk about them having more than one gate, I think." I close my eyes and recall the trip. But, details are missing from my memories because of the stress of the low oxygen environment. Most of my memories from late in that day are soupy. "I honestly can't remember, but I'll ask Vivian."

"Well, if you think of anything, please let me know. So, what's with the earplugs?"

"Skylar, we should go!" Saif calls out. "Luca is here, and he's ready to leave."

I back up from India and smile. "Tell your lab techs this plant wasn't a dud at all. Enhanced hearing, but I didn't notice until I was out in the open. I'll give them a report when I return."

"Well, at least we got something out of this trip." She waves before turning away to head back to work.

I wave goodbye and jog up to meet Saif, Kalvin, Takemo, and Luca.

It's time to get out of the jungle and back to civilization.

22

My heels click on the pavement as we approach Saif's family home. I remember my last time on this street, and for once, I'd love to just be able to erase memories instead of having to keep them forever. I can only hope better memories tonight replace it.

"You look perfect," Marcelo says, stepping back and scanning me from top to toe.

"I should hope so. This took three hours to complete."

I skate my hands down my sides, adjusting the black dress until it sits on my hips smoothly. I'm sure I could have gone with many of the colorful dresses that Marcelo would have picked out for me, but nothing is better than a little black dress. This one has cap sleeves, a plunging V-neck line, and the length swishes around my knees.

I lift my arms and twirl in a circle for Marcelo, and he chuckles.

He holds out his arm for me. "Are you nervous?"

We fall into step side-by-side.

"A little," I admit. "I don't always fare well around parents. I just need to be gracious and keep the swearing to a minimum. I think I met Saif's dad once when he came to pick Saif up from far-school camp. But we didn't speak to each other, and I was like twelve."

"That was a long time ago."

"More than half a lifetime ago." I smile at him. "I'm glad you're here. Thanks for meeting me at the hotel. I plan on coming to the Amagi tomorrow, but I've heard Dominic has been there almost every day, and I didn't want to run into him."

"You can't avoid him forever."

"I need to if I wish to keep on breathing. He's going to find some way to kill me. I know it."

Marcelo squeezes my arm in his and looks around. "I'll keep my eyes open. I'm always happy to escort you anywhere. And this was a good idea. The Bhaats will love the fact that you came with a chaperone." He chuckles. "They're a tight-knit family and network, but they love the traditional ways."

I take a deep breath and hold it as we approach the front door. The sun is starting to dip in the sky, and twilight will be here before long. Warm, yellow light bathes the front porch in a golden hue as Marcelo and I wave our wristlets at the door to announce our presence. Saif's elephant charm gift hangs around my neck, so I touch it briefly, hoping its power brings me some much-needed good luck tonight.

The door opens, and a servant smiles at us. "Please come in. Ms. Bhaat is on her way down right now."

Butterflies erupt in my stomach as I brace myself to face Saif's mom.

But his sister comes floating down the staircase instead. Her smile is friendly, and she practically skips off the bottom stair before coming straight to me.

"Skylar, dear. It's so good to see you in person." Her hand is in mine before I'm even aware of it, and she leans in to kiss me on the cheek. "You look ravishing."

"Thank you. I love your purple sari. It's beautiful. Especially the beading." Still holding her hand, I step back to admire her. She's a picture of classic beauty. With her long hair curling around her shoulders and her hands and neck glittering with tasteful jewels, it's no wonder she's a sought-after member of the family. Saif has two younger brothers and a younger sister, but they all do their own thing. Sejal is the only one who still lives here with her network, and she helps take care of her parents. I appreciate their nuclear family situation. It's something I always wanted.

I work hard to keep my smile in place as I think about how I was ready to sacrifice everything for my mother and family when they turned on me.

"Thank you. It's one of my favorites too. Marcelo, it's good to see you again," she holds out her hand, and Marcelo takes it and lifts it as he bows.

"Thank you for inviting us both," he replies.

From down the hall, I hear raised voices speaking in a foreign language. They sound stressed. Maybe angry? I'm not sure since I don't understand the language. Both Marcelo and Sejal smile at each other without a flinch so I ignore it. My hearing is still sensitive anyway, despite having left the jungle over a day ago.

"Please leave your shoes here. Take slippers if you'd like."

I slip my shoes off and spy Sejal walking barefoot, so I do the same. Marcelo stays in socks.

"Come," Sejal says, waving towards the hall. "Saif and his guests are in the sitting room just off the garden. If you want to go outside later, we have slippers at every door." She weaves her arm through mine and leans in. "Saif and I had a little chat last week about you and your business. Let's talk after dinner, okay?" She lowers her voice. "I'm glad you came back. My brother is an idiot sometimes."

"Thanks," I whisper. I glance back at Marcelo, but as always, he's minding his own business and admiring every painting we pass.

The sounds of boisterous talking become more raucous the closer we get to the room at the end of the hall. My ears start ringing before we even open the door. I brace myself for the noise so I don't flinch when the door opens.

The sitting room is a massive expanse of hardwood floors and plush rugs. A piano and sitar have pride of place near the center wall between cases of real books. Three yellow Labrador dogs lie like logs in front of the French doors that lead out onto the back garden. They don't even lift their heads when we walk in. I smile at their laziness. I love lazy dogs. They're the best.

"Skylar's here," Saif shouts over three older people talking at the highest volume ever at the end of the room. He rushes forward and slides to a stop in front of me, his socks allowing him to coast over the slick floors. "Hello, gorgeous." He leans in to kiss me on the cheek, and I let him. The cheek is fine. I want to make a good impression here. "Did you rest at all at the hotel?"

We had parted ways at the shuttle, and I booked myself into a nearby hotel to avoid Dominic for one more day. Neither of the men bunked in with me.

"I got a little rest. I passed out for the night and spent all day getting ready."

On the other side of the room, Kalvin and Takemo are drinking beers with an older man who looks like Saif. That must be his father. And two other men are past them in the kitchen talking at the top of their lungs while people chop and cook.

Kalvin and Takemo both turn to smile at me, and it sends a shiver down my spine. I pull in a quick breath and have this moment where I'm trapped. I should be out flying around the stars — no commitments, no obligations. Just me and my ship and the open sky. What the hell am I doing here?

But Saif lays his hand on my bare arm, and the anxiety in my stomach calms down. This is part of my life, too — meeting people, developing my network, having a family.

You can do both, Skylar. Both of these things can exist in the same universe.

"Come on in. I want you to meet my dad and my mom's other network mates."

I glance between Saif and Sejal. "Sejal, are any of your men here tonight?"

"Yes, Arjun is here. My other two are off-planet right now."

Sejal's smile is gracious, and I could cry from the relief of it. Before meeting her, I remembered Saif's comments about her exacting nature, her Type A personality. He always worried he would never measure up to her standards. It seems his fears were unwarranted.

"Marcelo, join me at the bar, and I'll pour you a drink," she says, leading Marcelo away.

I cross the room on Saif's arm and meet up with Kalvin, Takemo, and the older man.

"Fancy seeing you here," I say to Takemo. "I don't remember you being invited." I narrow my eyes at him, and he laughs. The older man raises his eyebrows.

"I am adept at inviting myself to interesting places. I hope you don't object." He covers his heart with his free hand.

I soften my tone. "Of course not. It seems you are now a part of my life, whether I like it or not."

"That's the spirit, Skylar." He chuckles.

"Kalvin," I say in greeting. I lean into him, and he kisses me on the cheek. If he feels threatened about being the non-dominant man in this situation, he doesn't show it. He looks good in a button-down shirt, sharp black pants, and... socks. I kind of miss seeing those fancy shoes on everyone.

"Sky, it's nice to see you not sweating buckets in the jungle."

"Same."

"I sense a rivalry here I wasn't aware of," the older man says, holding out his hand. "Hello, I'm Saif's dad, Yohan. It's nice to see you again."

"Oh, yes. I met you once, a long time ago. Sorry I didn't recognize you." I shake his hand and let go.

"That's all right. I've gotten a lot more gray in the last few years." He turns his head side to side, and I see more of the resemblance to the fuzzy memory of my twelve-year-old self.

"It's a handsome look. You should keep it." I nod my head and smile.

His returning smile is warm. "Thank you. You can stay." He chuckles. "Let me go break up this discussion in the kitchen and get you a drink too while I'm at it. Is wine fine?"

"Always," I reply.

When he opens the door to the kitchen and the voices spill out, I wince and turn away.

Saif pulls back. "Sorry. I know you're still sensitive to sound, and my family is extremely loud. We speak all Hindi in this house at the top of our lungs."

"It's true," Takemo says, taking a sip of his beer. "They have done nothing but yell since we arrived."

Saif holds out his hand. "Yes, but it's not aggressive. Like now..." He stops and tips his head to listen to the conversation, which sounds like a fight to me. "Arjun is saying that his shuttle to Decimo for tomorrow was canceled, and Ravi is complaining about the usual schedules."

He listens for a moment more.

"Yep. It's a regular discussion." He shrugs. "It's best to just pretend they are speaking at a normal volume."

"Okay then." I smile as Saif's dad delivers a glass of wine into my hand.

We sit on the plush chairs and have a light conversation for a little while. Saif's dad asks me about all the places on Rio I've been to, which restaurants I've liked, which museums I've visited. He spends several minutes telling me about the works of art he's enjoyed the most and what he would love to see in the coming months. I smile, remembering Saif's more creative side. I didn't realize he got it from his father. But listening to this talk of museums and art saddens me. As a kid, I never got to do those things.

"I haven't been to many museums, unfortunately." I panic as his face falls. The man is obviously into the arts and was hoping to find a kindred spirit with me. "Not because I don't like museums," I hastily add. "It's just that I grew up on a space ship and I spent little time on planets like you all."

"Remember, Dad?" Saif asks, leaning forward to touch his father on the shoulder. "Skylar had private tutors on her ship. She didn't attend boarding school."

"Right! Sorry. I forget details sometimes."

Be gracious, Skylar.

"It seems you love museums and art." I touch my chest. "I do as well. Maybe we could go to a museum together sometime soon." His eyes brighten. "You could pick your favorite, and I could meet you there."

"I love this idea," Yohan says, standing up. "Ah, my beautiful wife has joined us."

As Saif's mom enters the room in a red sari, I hasten to my feet. She doesn't wear half as many jewels as Sejal does, but she still sparkles and shines like an early morning sunrise over the ocean. She's diminutive, just a little shorter than me, with her hair pulled back in a bun and her smile turned up to full.

"Welcome, welcome, everyone. Sorry I'm late." She glides across the room, heading straight for us. I suck in a breath and hold it. I'm not sure what to expect or even hope for here. I have never done the whole 'meet the parents' song and dance. Hell, I've never been with one man more than two nights in a row, so already, I am in unknown territory.

"This *must* be Skylar." She approaches me with her hands out. Her fingers go straight to my face, cradling my cheeks between her two worn palms. Saif tenses behind her. I blink away my surprise. "What a beautiful woman you are," she says, tilting my head side to side and peering down into my eyes. "I think maybe you don't eat enough." She pats my face and then drops her hands.

"Come." She adjusts her sari at her shoulder. "I will make sure you don't leave here hungry."

She whirls around and marches to the kitchen, speaking in Hindi at full volume. People in the kitchen scramble to get out of her way and whisk platters into the adjoining dining room. I glance at Saif. He's smiling and brandishing a thumbs up.

Takemo leans in and whispers, "Breathe, Skylar. You're turning white."

I let all the air in my lungs out in a giant exhale and suck in a new breath before I blackout. Kalvin chuckles, and Yohan's smile is sweet.

I glance behind us at Marcelo and Sejal. Sejal is smiling too, and Marcelo seems pleased.

I didn't even say one word to the woman, and she's ready to feed me like some distant family member.

I think that went okay.

23

"I don't think I've ever eaten that much in one sitting in my life."

I groan as I lower myself to a sofa in Sejal's room on the third floor of this massive house. My sensitive hearing from the plants is still hanging on. I winced through most of dinner and had to stop myself from raising my voice just because it felt like everyone else was shouting. It's been a weird reaction. The plant made everything from the quietest whisper to the loudest yell the same volume. I hope it's out of my system soon.

Saif sits next to me and takes my hand in his.

"Mom was so pleased. If you had eaten little bites all night, she would have cast you out. And asking for more chilis was a bold move. Your stomach must be on fire." He squeezes my hand, his eyes gleaming with happiness.

I sigh. "I may regret that decision later, but you know I like it hot." I wink at him.

"Now, now. It's getting too spicy in here for my tastes." Sejal shoos her brother away. "Go now. Skylar and I have business to discuss."

"Okay." He stands up. "Kalvin, Takemo, and I are going to

light up the bonfire on the deck. Meet us out there when you're done."

When the door clicks behind him, I lean back on the sofa and place my hand over my expanding belly.

"You look positively pregnant," Sejal says with a laugh.

"I hope it's just a food baby. I haven't signed any contracts yet." I sit up a little. "Thank you," I say, pressing a serious nature into my voice.

"For what?" She sits up too.

"For the first time I was here. The whole day was really embarrassing for me, and knowing you cared made me feel a lot better. So, thank you."

She smacks her leg. "My brother can be such an idiot sometimes." She blows out an exasperated breath and lifts her eyes to the ceiling. "Watch out for his petty and jealous side. It comes out when you least expect it."

"I'll keep that in mind," I grumble. "Anyway, I don't want to keep you from your family. Arjun is lovely, by the way."

"Thank you," she says, pride lifting her chin. "He is pretty great. You'll meet more of my network in the future. And yes, I asked you up here for business reasons. So, I know about your ship and your... dispute with your mother."

I glance away, shame coloring my cheeks.

"I am incensed with rage about the way you've been treated. I do not take these kinds of transgressions lightly, especially when they are perpetrated against people I hope to call family."

This catches my attention.

"Saif cares for you deeply, and dare I say it, he has for many, many years. He used to come home from far-school and chat about you endlessly. Even when he dated others in the interim years, I knew that he was a goner for you. He would talk about your strength and the things you learned and your humor." She shakes her head. "He has never spoken about anyone else in the same way."

I press my lips together. My belly is so full that crying will only make me sick, so I stay quiet.

"So, I would like to talk business. I am taking over Bhaat Jewelers in two years. My mother is retiring, and this business is mine. Well, it has been for some time, but it'll be official then. I have made a name for this business in the last five to seven years by being in the gossip sites, getting influencers to wear our jewelry, and doing everything I can and could do to elevate Bhaat Jewelry to be the most sought-after business in the Duo Systems."

"You've done an amazing job," I say, reaching out to touch her leg briefly. Her shoulders relax a little.

"But with that notoriety has come unwanted attention, for both my family and my employees. One of my top jewelers was on his way home to Palo Alto last week when he was approached by our competitors and harassed into fearing for his life."

"Really? That's horrible." Who thought jewelers would be so popular?

She sighs. "He was so shaken, and it spurred me into an idea. I hope you will listen with an open mind."

This is intriguing.

"Go on."

"I would like to fund your business in the hopes that you can also buy a second ship and work exclusively for Bhaat Jewelers for a time. Sure, we could hire Flyght ships, but even then, I am dubious about the privacy they afford. Instead, we would use your ships for business and pleasure trips, like getting my staff off public transport and to their homes safely. Or flying the family to vacation spots. That sort of thing." She waves her hand in the air. "Of course, you would not be a family servant. You would be family." She raises her chin. "A trusted individual. You and your whole network, not just Saif."

I think for a moment, drumming my fingers on my knee.

She wanted to eat. They forced her to cook for them and then locked her in the utility closet. She never told me this back then. Only just two weeks ago."

"Fuck me," Takemo whispers.

"She was always eating at far-school. Maybe she hoped to put on some weight so she'd feel less starved back home. I'm not sure. All I know is that whatever she wants from here on out, she gets."

I open my eyes and nod to Sejal. Her face has fallen into a frown. She caught as much of that as I did.

"I'll get the drinks," she says, pulling away from me.

I try to make as much noise as possible approaching the back deck so they can stop talking about me and not feel as if they've been caught. But seeing the far-off haunted look in Marcelo's eyes slows me down.

I was going to ignore it, but I've changed my mind.

"Hey," I say, and they all stand up. "Oh, don't get up."

Kalvin and Saif make room for me between them, so I sit.

"And you can stop guessing. Yes, I ate more away from home, so I had more fat to burn for the long periods of starvation. But they stopped denying me food when I turned fourteen. Mom was catching on and wondering why I was so skinny, and I wasn't developing." I gesture to my body. "Dominic was almost caught then. He hated that I had to eat because he used to devour my servings. The gluttonous fucking pig he is. But the layers of his lies weren't fully built yet." I shrug. "Mom wasn't with him one-hundred percent. She is now."

Sejal arrives with my drink, whisky on the rocks. She taps her glass against mine and sits next to Marcelo. Takemo stares into the fire.

"So, let's enjoy the fire for a bit, and then I'd like to *back to the hotel to sleep."

"Sure, Skylar," Kalvin says, glancing at Saif. "Wh* want."

24

At the spaceport, Takemo pops out of an autocab and trots up to meet Saif, Kalvin, Marcelo, and me on the sidewalk.

"Thanks for letting me tag along to get back to the shuttle," he says, shouldering his bag. "We're just going to drop by your ship first?"

"Yeah, I need to speak with my employees there and swap out a few things from my bag." I lead them all away and into the winding passages of the spaceport.

Takemo pulls up next to me. I set a brisk pace through the spaceport, eager to get moving again.

"Hey, so I've been thinking a lot about... stuff. And I'm wondering what to do with your mom's ship."

"Uh-huh."

"What do you think I should do with it?" he asks, keeping up at my side.

I glance over at him. "I don't know, and I don't care."

His lips twist. "Well, see, I don't feel right owning it anymore. And I don't feel right giving it back to her either."

I stop and face him, anger boiling up in my stomach.

Takemo has been ever present as of late. Why does this man keep hanging around when he doesn't even like me?

"What do you want from me? Permission to do something?" I ask, my voice grating.

He narrows his eyes. "Yes?"

"Is that a question?"

"Yes?" He repeats.

I sigh, and some of the heat in my belly melts away. I'm too tired to deal with this.

"Cut my mom loose with a severance package and sell the ship."

"But it's where you grew up. You don't want it back?"

I slow my steps for a moment. There was a time when I wanted the ship. It was going to be my future.

But now? It only represents my awful past. It's the prison that held me as a kid. It's a sign of my failures.

"I never want to see it again."

"Are you sure?" he asks, and this time I narrow my eyes at him. "You're sure. Okay."

"Besides, it's yours to do with as you please. It's none of my business. I don't even know why you're asking."

"Skylar..." Takemo starts, but Saif directs him ahead of us, and Kalvin falls in next to me.

"Be nice," Kalvin whispers. "Takemo's only trying to be helpful."

I huff. "Why does he care? He doesn't even like me, and he thinks I hate him."

"That's not true," Kalvin insists.

"Forget about what happened in the jungle. He called me a 'lazy, hotheaded, and undesirable offspring' like two weeks ago. He doesn't like me. I have no idea why he's sticking around." I drop my voice. "Probably looking for the right opportunity to piss me off again."

Kalvin's brow furrows. "I can't imagine him saying that."

"Believe it. Saif witnessed most of it."

"But he's been helpful and kind lately. Maybe you should give him another chance."

I sigh. "Maybe. Until he decides I'm hateful again?" My wristlet buzzes, and it's Ai. "Hold on. Ai is pinging me."

"Hello, Skylar. I see you are approaching our terminal in the spaceport. I must inform you that Dominic is here, and he's stationed himself in the bay across from the Amagi."

"Fuck," I breathe out and come to a stop. "Is he there all the time?"

"Pretty much. He seems to be in stakeout mode. There's a log of his movements in your account. But since he hasn't been near you physically, I haven't alerted you before now."

I pick up my pace. "Call the spaceport police, Ai. Send them over to Dominic's location. I'll be right there."

I push past Saif and Takemo. "That's it. I've had it."

My legs move at double speed as I stalk through the hallways of the spaceport and head to the outside gangways. Fury burns inside of me so hot I'm on fire by the time I reach the bay across from the Amagi. I round the corner, and Dominic jumps up from his seat on a construction crate.

"Get the fuck away from my ship, Dominic."

"Skylar," he says, his smile growing. It falters a moment when the guys join me. "I see you're finally back."

"Your petty stalking behavior is the height of desperation. You're not getting my ship, no matter how much you harass my crew."

"It's not your ship." Dom shakes his head. "It belongs to your mother, and you're going to give it back." His jaw tightens, and he takes a confident step towards me. "You are going to end this war of lies and confess to everyone that your mother was a good woman who never hurt you, never laid a hand on you."

I'm so hot with anger my face is ready to melt off.

"So many lies," he says, jabbing his finger at me. "We took

care of you. Clothed you. Fed you. You did nothing but spit in our faces." He laughs at the guys behind me. "And now you've conned these men into believing you're some kind of saint. You should be grateful for everything we gave you."

I'm immobilized by my memories of my childhood, how brutal they were, how my clothes were hand-me-downs from my brothers, and how I went hungry so many days and nights while my family feasted like nobility. Dominic's version of my life is so much kinder and nicer than what I lived.

Am I wrong? Did I exaggerate the things that happened to me?

Doubt tiptoes into the back of my head and plants a tiny seed, one I can't ignore. I've asked myself these questions a lot lately. I had almost shrugged this off just a few days ago, but now, they are more prominent than ever.

"The Amagi was a short-term loan," Dominic insists. "You will give it back. We have the lawyers drawing up the papers right now."

"Fuck you and your lawyers," Takemo says, stepping in front of me.

Whoa. I wasn't expecting that. His hand reaches back to move me closer to Saif and Kalvin.

"If anyone could repossess the Amagi, it was *me* for *your* debts. But guess what? I couldn't touch it because it belongs to Skylar one-hundred percent."

This shuts Dominic up. He opens his mouth to speak again, but Takemo steps into his space.

"Your continued harassment of her is pissing me off enough for me to sue *you*." He throws back his head with an evil laugh. "Oh, I would just love to have you raked over the coals for this bullshit." He points at Dominic. "Your lawsuit threat is nothing but bluster. And if you think you're going to get this ship when I couldn't, then you are sorely mistaken."

Dominic leans to the side so he can see me. "If you think

this is a cut and dry case, then *you* are sorely mistaken. I don't actually have to win back the Amagi. Instead, I can bury you in court cases and drain all of your money until there's nothing left for you but to sell your ship and your body to the highest bidder." He spits on the ground in front of me. "Fucking whore."

Takemo's arm cranks back, his hand curled into a fist. I inhale a sharp breath and leap just in time to catch his arm before he slams his fist into Dominic's face. Dominic scrambles, his eyes wide with fear. He knocks over the construction crate and falls to his ass briefly before jumping to his feet.

Kalvin grabs me and pulls me to the side, and I drag Takemo with me. Saif stands between Dominic and us.

"Everything's going to come out eventually," he warns Dominic. "The starvation, the slavery, the abuse — you will pay for it all."

Dominic laughs, and my blood cools. "See? You *have* conned them with your lies," he shouts at me. "Lying bitch. You didn't get what you wanted, so now you've concocted this story, huh?" He raises his eyebrows. "Good luck proving it."

I hate him, but he's right. The gleam in his eyes tells me he knows he's done a thorough job of scrubbing the video, the only evidence I have against him. I trust Carlos, and I pray that he'll find something, but my stomach is hollow looking at the triumph in Dominic's eyes. Maybe I'll never be able to win this. Maybe I'll never have enough to prove my childhood trauma to others. And over time, more people will become skeptical of me and my stories because, let's face it, they're almost unbelievable. That whole 'believe the victim' thing only goes so far without proof.

The doubt blooms from a small seedling to a budding flower.

Has it all been lies? I thought I trusted my memories. Could Dominic actually be right?

Footsteps pound up the gangway, and police officers round the corner, their eyes searching and catching everything in a millisecond.

"What's going on here?" the lead officer asks.

"I want him arrested." Takemo yanks his arm from mine. "This man has been stalking and harassing us. I want him behind bars."

"Is this true, miz?" the officer asks me.

I nod, too shocked to open my mouth.

"He's been harassing you?"

Snap out of it, Skylar.

"Yes," I blurt out. I point at the Amagi. "This is my ship. He's been coming here almost every day, harassing my crew and me. I'm sure your security footage will back it up."

He nods a few times while looking at us. "I see. Sir, come with me," he says, reaching out for Dominic.

Dominic steps away. "Don't touch me."

The officer jerks his head at the other officers he brought with him, and they descend on Dominic like dogs on a fresh meal. He struggles, punches, and kicks, and the lead officer holds out his arms to push us away from the fray.

A zap rips through the air, and Dominic goes limp. I yelp and leap back against Kalvin. He wraps his arms around me.

"Sorry, sir," one officer says. "I know you don't like us to use the stun guns, but..."

The others haul Dominic off, his limp legs dragging on the gangway.

"I guess we'll add 'Resisting Arrest' to the charges," the lead officer says. "Sorry about that, miz. We'll put him in lock up, and then we'll place an AI tracker on him. He won't bother you again."

Of course, he'll bother me again. And next time, he'll be even more pissed and violent. It won't end well for me.

"Thanks," I croak out, my throat dry and scratchy.

I watch the officers haul him through the doors to the inside.

That doubt flower sits in my head, mocking me.

I could make this all go away right now, but it doesn't seem right. If I give the ship to Mom and Dominic, I'm admitting that I don't believe my own memories of what happened. I'll never be trusted again. I won't even trust myself. I can't do that.

There's no turning back. Dominic has crossed a line, and now I have no choice anymore. This is about to get public and very, very nasty. Sweat beads along my top lip as I imagine what I'm in for, what my network is in for.

But I have to fight him with everything I have because he's only going to keep coming back and coming back and coming back. I need the money from India Dellis. I need the lawyers. And I need my network most of all... if they don't leave me because of this.

It's time to get back to work.

25

BACK INTO THE JUNGLE. I need to return to work and drown myself in tasks that have nothing to do with my actual life. I had a routine going before this brief trip to the city, and it would be a shame to lose that momentum.

Right now, every part of my life is stressful. There is no relaxing. Life on the Amagi is strained, with talk of it being repossessed and Carlos digging through my dirty laundry. The time in the jungle is aggravating with the plants, animals, and military incursions. My love life is bound to give me an ulcer. Saif's family wants to do business with me and make me one of theirs. Kalvin's mother is sick and he's worried about her. And now Takemo is trying to butt in where he doesn't belong, and I can't get rid of him.

As the shuttle circles the landing field, I stare out the window and go over my options to make this easier. There aren't many. Sigh. I wish I had called Vivian or Amira while I was on the ship and had a reliable duonet connection. They would have had advice for me.

Regardless of what they would say, I need to keep going. India Dellis's initial deposit is sitting in my bank account, ready to be spent. If I want to invest in my future, I need another few months of employment under my belt. Hopefully, this new network mate Marcelo is working on will work out for me, though I dread having to do this whole first-date song-and-dance again, especially when I'm worried about the others leaving. Everything is a lot more complicated when my heart gets involved.

My head is not in the game. I'm way too wrapped up in my own drama to concentrate on anything else. I adjust the bag at my feet and think about the next steps. Next steps, Skylar. Just put one foot in front of the other and keep moving.

"We'll be landing soon, and then we're heading straight into the jungle," Luca says, leaning across the aisle to speak to me. "We had to abandon our use of the gem mine. Unfortunately, the military caught on and started setting up camp around the perimeter. People flying in and out and staying on the mine's property are fine. The minute they step out of the fence?" He slices across his neck with his hand.

"Really?"

"Oh yeah. If they aren't killed, they're picked up and thrown in prison for treason." He sits back in his chair. "That's what they're calling it nowadays, treason. As if they run everything in the Duo Systems."

"Don't they?" I ask with a snort. "The military has always been a bunch of assholes with delusions of grandeur. They think they own us." I flex my fist. "They stole my ship a few years ago. Stripped it to almost nothing. It took over two years to put it back together."

"So you're not friends, then."

"Understatement of the year. I'd be happy to see them erased from the timeline." I rest my head back in the chair as the shuttle makes a quick descent. "Something needs to be done about them, but like ten years ago. It's too late now."

"Yeah," Luca agrees. "The upper ranks are full of Reformer

sympathizers now. Absolute egomaniacs. And getting rid of them would take a miracle."

The shuttle lands with a soft thump, and the engines power down.

Luca slaps his legs and stands up in the aisle.

"Okay, here's what we're going to do. You all will get changed into the camouflage gear, just like usual. When the shuttle door opens, my men will be out first at point. They'll sweep the grass to the forest, and we'll follow. It's a four-kilometer hike from here to the new camp."

I groan and close my eyes.

"Sorry." Luca shrugs. "I know you've been on the run a lot lately, but this was the closest we could get."

"On the run is another understatement."

Now I understand the constant pressure Vivian was under when she was dealing with the stress of buying back the family farm land. I'm locked in an eternal dance of earning money, wooing potential network mates, and saving my ship from being repossessed. And that's just this week. Who knows what other shit the universe will dump on me next week?

I inhale and straighten my shoulders.

"No matter," I say, standing up. "We've gotta do what needs to be done."

Luca grimaces. "That's the kind of thing I hear from people who are at their wit's end."

"Yeah, well, comment on it again, and we'll have words about it," I grumble.

"Message received." He turns to hide a slight smile on his face, but I see it.

Sigh. I wasn't trying to be cute. I'm just exhausted.

At the front of the shuttle, the guys crowd around an open duffle bag of clothes. Takemo already has a camouflage shirt and pants on. Saif and Kalvin are looking through and trying to find their sizes.

"How you feeling?" Saif asks, holding out a shirt and sizing me up. He frowns and puts that one in the bag. "You look tired." He finds a better shirt for me and hands it over.

I slip into the shirt, layering it over my t-shirt.

"Um, I'm okay. But yeah, tired. I spent several hours staring at the ceiling, going over everything. I should have slept more." After buttoning the shirt, I tuck it into my pants. "But it's a proud Kawabata trait to forgo sleep in favor of worrying." I tap my fist to my chest twice and raise it. "Power to the eternal gods of worry."

Saif chuckles. "It sounds like we had similar nights."

"Same," Kalvin says, pulling on the camouflage pants. "Though I was thinking about the Amagi and how to safeguard it against Dominic."

"I was thinking about my sister and this business proposal she has for us, how we could make it all work." Saif hands me pants.

I hold the pants for a moment and swallow, my throat dry. "You all were worried about me?"

"Yeah," Kalvin says, running his hand through his hair. "Of course."

"You, the network..." Saif nods as he watches me get into my pants. "Our future."

I turn to Takemo. He raises his hands. "I slept like a baby last night."

I roll my eyes. Of course, he did.

"Let's get going, everyone!" Luca calls from the shuttle's door. "I want to get to the camp before dark."

Me too. There's no way I want to spend an evening camping in the jungles of Rio.

We line up behind Luca and his men at the door, and I psych myself up for this jaunt back into the jungle.

The doors will open, and it's going to be hot. Just warning you, Skylar.

Of course, I'm already sweating. But I would rather be hot any day than cold. I'd sooner be here than on frosty Neve. I've been there before, and it was not fun. Not by any definition of the word. I take a last sip of water from my bottle before storing it away.

The doors will open, and Rio will be out there. Just warning you again, Skylar.

There could be squid in the bushes, monkeys in the trees, green snakes in the grass. There could be so many things out there ready to eat me, ready to chase me. Remember, this is why Luca and his team are with us. They'll know what to do.

I breathe in and out, one, two, three times, while the shuttle door opens and the gangway descends to the ground. The shuttle immediately becomes hot and sticky, and my face sweats.

Here we go.

Three of Luca's men sweep out ahead of us. They kick at the long grass and keep their eyes trained either straight forward or on the ground in front of them. Takemo is next, and Luca and I walk out behind him. Kalvin and Saif bring up the rear with more of Luca's men.

"This area is rich in flora and fauna." Luca's eyes scan the tree line. "It's the main reason why we're here, why the military is here. Did you know that other continents on Rio don't have as much biodiversity as this one?" He points at the ground as we get closer to the tree line. "This is the holy grail of Rio plants and animals and why Renata and India won't give up this camp."

"Yeah, I did know. Have you been to all the Rio continents?"

Rio has eleven continents, and most of the ten floating cities of Rio are over the shoreline of each of them. The continent at the south pole is the only one lacking a city. Instead, there's a space elevator there for hauling heavy cargo to orbit and down.

"No, but I have been to five. None of them are like this one."

We call this continent Primeiro, just like the city above and to the south of here. Primeiro was the first continent ever explored and built upon. From space, inside the rings of Rio, the diversity of flora is plainly evident. I can imagine the first explorers pulling up in orbit, waiting and watching, and then the looks of awe as the continent came into view. Lush green jungles, clear pools of lake water, several river systems, mountains and grassland, and a long sandy shore. They probably said, "Ooooh! What's that?," pointed, and landed lickety-split.

Who could blame them?

I think those people set one foot out of their ship and died when sea snakes snuck up on them. The colonization of Rio took a long time to figure out.

The hair on the back of my neck stands up as we reach the tree line.

"Something's not right," I say, keeping my voice low. "I can't put my finger on it."

"Yeah." Luca lays his hand on my arm and looks up at the trees. "It's... quiet."

"Too quiet?" My heart races, and my mouth dries.

"No birds," he says, his eyes scanning the surrounding trees.

I follow his eyes and trace ahead and behind his sweep.

Fuck.

I spot movement in the forest back and to our right rear. What kind of animal is hunting us now?

Wait. The long barrel of a gun and camouflage gear reveal themselves between the leaves.

It's not an animal.

"Shit. It's the military," I whisper at Luca. "Behind us to the right."

"Yeah. I don't think we're surrounded. We got lucky and

chose the correct direction. Unless they have a spot to ambush us farther in. You know, push us into a trap."

"What should we do?" My voice shakes as adrenaline flows through me.

"Split up. Scatter. You have the GPS beacon, right?"

I nod. We all have them in our bags. There's no way I'd be on Rio without one.

"Okay. We evade our tail and get to safety. Then turn on the beacon and be sure to key it to Athens channels only. No general broadcasts, or it will lead them right to us."

"Got it." I tighten my bag on my shoulders.

"Ready?"

I nod. "Let's do it," I say, raising my voice.

"Do what?" Sait asks.

Luca raises his voice over the sound of the grass. "Military behind us and to the right. Possible contacts ahead. Scatter and meet at the alternate location in two hours. Go."

My legs take off before the rest of my body knows what's going on.

I aim left and hope for the best as the report of gunfire echoes through the trees.

"Go, go, go!" Kalvin calls out from behind me.

I keep going and don't look back.

26

A BULLET ZIPS past my head and blows a tree trunk to itty bitty pieces. I dodge out of the way, duck under a downed tree, and leap over a protruding root system. Crashing footsteps and grunts follow me, but I'm too scared to look back and see who it is. Friend or foe — I'm not sure. I'm not slowing down to find out.

A shout of pain comes from behind me when a gun fires, but all the people in my group are still running. So whoever they hurt was an enemy. Good. Another round of gunfire and someone curses.

"Go! Follow them!" someone else yells.

Panic races through my chest like an unchecked flight descending into a strong gravity well. I'm not much of a crier, but I would give anything to sink into a bed and burst into tears right about now. Instead, I'm running for my life.

I hope everyone else is okay. I hope I don't have to tell Saif's family that he died in the jungle and it was my fault. I hope I don't have to go to Kalvin's mother and explain the death of her beloved son. I hope I don't have to face Takemo's family, either. When I researched him, I knew they were tight with each other, but I never thought I'd ever meet them.

Someone ends up right next to me and grabs my hand.

"To the right," Kalvin says, panting through labored breaths. He tugs me over, and my legs jerk with the change of direction. Up ahead, a clearing yawns out between two trees, and three-meter tall grass occupies the open space.

The grass sways in the wind, and I panic even more. Who the fuck knows what's in there?

"Keep going, Skylar. Don't stop," Saif says, coming up behind us.

I throw a glance over my shoulder. Saif, Takemo, Luca, and one of his men are behind me. Thank God I'm not alone. The sheer panic and terror coursing through my body turns to energy now that I have allies.

I leap into the long grass, my arms forward to keep it out of my face. The edges of the grass are sharp and slice at my skin. I hiss at the pain and the lines of blood that erupt along my sleeves.

"Ouch! Shit." Kalvin whispers behind me.

"I don't know which way to go!" I can't see over the grass. I can't even see a meter in front of me.

The guy bringing up the rear turns and fires into the jungle. "Got another one," he says, turning and following us into the grass.

"Slow down, Sky," Saif calls ahead. "Angle left. The less we make the grass move, the harder it will be to find us. Break off. Give them several paths to follow."

"No. Stay together. Strength in numbers," I respond. I don't want to lose them now.

"Step through the grass, not on it," Luca directs, "and watch out for water horses. They like the long grass."

My feet squish through mud as the ground softens. We must be near the middle of the field. Is there a water hole near here? I part the grass, push it aside, and step between the clumps instead of on them. I'm sure an excellent tracker could figure out which way we went, though. The military is out to get us, and they will spare no expense to track us down.

"Why the fuck am I even here?" I grumble, parting more grass and gingerly stepping into the cleared space. "I should be flying through space."

"I know what I'd rather be doing." Kalvin reaches out to grab my ass. I laugh as I leap forward and swat at the empty space behind me.

"Is there ever a time when you aren't thinking of sex?"

"Nope," he responds.

"Me neither." Saif is now on my right. "And tonight is my turn on the rotation." He raises his eyebrows twice.

"You people have a calendar for fucking?" Takemo asks, his voice dropping to a whisper. I shoot him a deadly glare. "No, really. Is that how it works?"

"That's how it works in my network," I say, speeding up.

"It's actually not a bad idea when your men aren't into each other," Takemo mumbles. "I never thought of it that way."

"I'm not sleeping with Saif," Kalvin says, mock disgust in his voice.

"And I'm not sleeping with you, either," Saif counters.

"See?" I say, turning around.

Big mistake.

I stumble to my left and straight into a water hole. Damn it. I splash into the water, getting my boots, socks, and pants wet up to my knees. An eel slithers through my legs and bolts away, but not before trying to shock me. I squeak a half scream as the electrical current singes my leg.

"Shit, Skylar. You almost fell in."

Kalvin holds out his hand to pull me out when my eyes focus on the creatures on the opposite side of the hole.

"What the fuck is that?" I point, and Kalvin, Saif, and Takemo look.

They're lizards of some kind, but they resemble horses with long legs and drawn-out faces. Black scales shine a rainbow of light over their bodies. A tongue shoots out to sample the air, and it's forked like a snake. Their eyes are yellow and slitted too. After a few more moments, they all lift their heads from the water and stare in our direction. They look at me, and I look at them, but nothing more happens.

"Shit. They saw us?" Luca asks, coming up next to the guys.

I turn to face him slowly.

"Aw, fuck." Disappointment is evident in his sigh. "That's only going to make things harder. They're standing between us and our exit from this place." He looks left and right.

"What... What do they do?" I'm almost afraid to ask this question.

"Once they catch a scent, it's hard to avoid them. They usually chase and grab their prey, then shake them until they can drown them in the water."

Great. Now my boots are going to squish while I run for my life.

"No stopping," Luca insists. "We have to get into the jungle on the other side and find a place to hide out."

His last man comes running up to us. "Good news. We've lost all of them but two. Those two are coming this way."

No time to dump out my boots and wring out my socks. Time to get moving. I slip away from the water hole, and the water horses watch me go, their yellow eyes tracking my movements. That can't be good.

I fall into step behind Luca, thank the heavens. I prefer to be following a professional rather than just winging it, even at the speed he's walking. The long grass cuts me over and over. I'm dripping blood everywhere.

Luca accesses his side pack as he goes. "That's going to be a problem." He hands me a roll of gauze. "Wrap up and pull down your sleeves. Water horses can smell blood almost a klick away."

Ugh. This keeps getting better and better.

I do as I'm told, just barely stopping the blood from flowing down my arms. I'm going to come out of this job looking like I went through a war. I'll need full-body makeup if I'm going to be seen in public at restaurants or anything fancy. Most of these cuts will scar.

Sigh. So much for this incredible body I've been cultivating all these years.

"When we get to the tree line, I want you to run out ahead. If the water horses follow, we can shoot them, but only if they pursue."

I nod my head and keep my mouth closed, so I don't puke all over everything. My stomach is in knots, and my body is thinking about giving up — just giving up, lying down, and wishing for death.

"But who knows what she'll find in the jungle," Kalvin reminds Luca.

"I'm beginning to wish I had taken Skylar up on her offer of staying home," Saif says.

"Yeah, I'm not a fan," Takemo chimes in.

"You all are my favorite people right now," Luca says, sarcasm coating every word. "Go," he urges me as we reach the tree line.

Adrenaline surges, and I run out ahead of everyone else, with Saif and Kalvin on my tail. This time, it's easier to keep a steady pace without gunshots whizzing by my head. But behind me, the rumble of the water horses is abundantly clear. Most reptiles are not fast, especially big ones. But Rio has never been one for details. The animals here are exceptions to every rule. My bet is that these water horses don't have to be fast. They just have to be persistent. And if their prey has nowhere to go, they'll catch them, eventually.

My lungs are burning with the heat and humidity. Running is like swimming through soup, and my legs just can't go any faster. They only get slower, slower, slower. I'm sucking in air, but it's not helping. Whatever I'm bringing in, it's not enough to purge my muscles of the acid they're building up.

"I can't... go... anymore," I say, slowing down.

I don't stop. I can't stop.

My enemies are right behind me.

I expect to turn and find Dominic running after me, too. I mean, why not, right? Everyone is out to get me. It would only make sense that he would be here, too. Him and the ghosts of everyone I've ever wronged or screwed over. Boy, oh boy, Skylar. You really know how to fuck things up.

Launching myself over a downed log, I lose my balance and come crashing to the ground. My feet are so waterlogged they're not working correctly anymore. I roll through two bushes and stop at the base of a giant nest.

I register the eggs first before I see the bird's legs. My eyes scan upward over the large barrel-round body to the tiny head and long curving beak. She looks like a rolled-up gray wool blanket with a katana sword for a head. Her eyes blink, and she tilts her head to the side to look at me. Holy shit, the thing must be at least two meters tall.

I freeze as footsteps run up to me. Kalvin wasn't that far behind, but I don't think he witnessed me tumble into the bushes. Those water horses will find us soon enough. I'm still bleeding, and my arms and sleeves are soaked red.

The bird leans down, and I'm too mesmerized to move. I hold my breath, squeeze my eyes shut, and prepare for the worst. Will she pluck my eyes out? Beat me to death with her wings? What holy hell can I expect now?

Her beak touches along my jaw, and a jolt of current rushes through me. In the split second it takes for me to jerk back, my brain races through a memory from my childhood.

I sat in my room and played a duonet game with Vivian. I was supposed to be asleep, but I missed her so much. So I would stay up, keep the lights low, lock my door, and play the games under my covers so no one could hear anything. I was so lonely, and Vivian's laughter and smiles were the only things that got me through the dark days.

Her beak grazes my chin again, and this time she fills my mind with the desert — long, unbroken dunes, so much sand, a blistering sun above.

Not Rio.

I open my eyes, and the giant bird is staring at me. We lock gazes for a long moment, and oh no, I feel like I'm seeing my past invade my future. What the hell is going on?

The thundering of legs is approaching. I need to get up.

Now.

I pull myself to my knees and ready myself to run. The giant bird backs up, opens her wings to a massive three meter wingspan, and screeches loud enough for everything to halt — my heart, my lungs, and the water horses too.

When I look up, Sejal waves away my concern like it's nothing.

"You're the perfect match for my brother. Trust me," she says, leaning in and stressing the words. She shakes her head in annoyance. "You're worrying for no reason. Everything that happened before *right now* is irrelevant. You are a phoenix rising from the ashes." She lifts her hand into the air. "Women in the Bhaat family do not take this sort of thing lying down. We gather up all our resources and fight back."

"Excuse me, but... Women in the Bhaat family? That's awesome, but I'm not —"

She reaches over and smacks my leg. "My mother fed you six courses and couldn't keep her eyes off of you. You're in. Now we'll go downstairs and have a drink to celebrate our new partnership."

She rises from the sofa, but I stare at her in confusion.

What just happened?

"Come, come," she says, waving me forward. "As much as I want to hang out all evening, I have pajamas calling my name in an hour. Early day tomorrow."

I feel like I've just been bamboozled, and I kinda liked it.

I follow her out as she sweeps from the room and down the stairs. We sidestep the sleeping dogs in the front hall and approach the open doors to the back deck. Voices filter in, and I recognize my name. Grasping Sejal's arm, I pull her to a stop.

"What?" she asks, but I hold up my finger to my lips and close my eyes.

"She was just so skinny, and her brown eyes were like two big shining discs, you know?" Saif pauses, and the fire crackles. "I used to sneak cookies out of the cafeteria for her after they were closed because she was always hungry."

"Do you think they starved her on purpose? Or was it..." Kalvin's voice quiets.

"Oh, it wasn't her fault, like an eating disorder or anything.

"So, we'd put together a contract and everything?"

"Yes," she says with a nod. "I would make it all official."

I sigh. "This is all assuming Saif sticks around, though."

Sejal's eyes widen. Oops, what are you doing, Skylar? I panic, wanting to reel back the statement.

"Well, I... Hmmm, Saif is great," I assure her. "I doubt anything will go wrong."

Her demeanor cools. "No. That obviously slipped out for a reason. Why wouldn't he stick around?"

I press my lips together and scoot away from her a bit. "I don't think you realize the kind of mess my family is. The kind of mess *I am*."

I examine her and decide instantly that she's a trustworthy soul. And if Saif leaves me, I won't have to see her again anyway.

"I'm not good at relationships. In fact, I've never been in a committed relationship. Before Saif, I only had one-night stands. And when I decided those weren't a good idea anymore, I visited sexbots for three years."

If she's horrified, she doesn't show it. Her face is neutral.

"I wasn't the model of a perfect first daughter, though I'm trying to be better now. Still, my mom's third consort wants me dead and his daughter in my place. My mother is starting legal action to repossess my ship, and she's disowning me. I have a dangerous job in the jungles of Rio, and I don't know if I'll survive long enough to even take advantage of your kind offer."

I clasp my hands together and squeeze enough for my knuckles to whiten.

"Saif is amazing, but he wants so much from me. I don't know if I can give him the life he wants." I laugh, and it comes out bitter. "I'm barely a degree above frigid, and he's so warm and kind. I wonder if it's a good match for him."

I groan and rest my face in my hand.

"I'm stupid for even saying anything to you."

27

KALVIN COMES SKIDDING up next to me, his eyes wide and staring at the gigantic bird.

"What happened?" he asks, grabbing my hand and pulling me back. I stop him from going too far. "Are you hurt?" he yells over the screeching.

I shake my head, but I can't tear my eyes from the bird. She flaps her wings steadily, longer and longer swoops through the air, gathering up the surrounding wind. My hair whips around my head. Kalvin and I turn into each other, both shielding our faces from the onslaught.

I crack open an eye and hold my breath. The oncoming water horses are still as stone except for their flicking tails. The bird lifts off the ground a few centimeters and lunges forward. The water horses shift back, their tongues snapping out and heads bobbing side to side. Once more, the bird gathers up the air and lurches at them again. They turn and run away this time, crashing through the underbrush and disappearing from view.

The bird doesn't stop once the water horses are gone. She must identify Kalvin and me as a threat because she turns on us next. I squeak and leap away with Kalvin. The column of wind the bird is creating funnels around her body. The mini tornado picks up leaves and twigs and adds them to the crazy whirlwind.

Movement on the other side catches my eye. Saif, Takemo, Luca, and his other man are all watching the display of power with their mouths wide open. The whirlwind howls and the bird screeches, and the two sounds together send goosebumps down my back.

Kalvin wraps his arms around me. His eyebrows pull together, puzzled.

"I've heard this before," he whispers.

"Yeah, in the desert."

When Kalvin and I had been marooned in the desert together, we were helped and guided by what I thought was sentient sand. I had stuck my hand in the sand and communicated with it, much like this bird and I just did. An electrical current passed through me, and the sand entity had accessed my memories and learned about me, all in a flash. It helped me, though I'm not sure why.

We move away from the bird, step by step. I have to wonder if this bird and that sand entity are related somehow. They can both create a column of air and communicate with shocks and memories. How is this even possible?

Wait. There was an electric eel in that watering hole too. Didn't the lab tech at India's compound say that they had gotten a bunch of plants from a nearby wetland?

"In the desert." His eyes widen. "What... How?"

My sentiments exactly.

"Let's get out of here. She's protecting her nest," I say, pulling him away. I wave to the others and shield my face from the dirt rising in the air. The bird lunges for us again, but we're quicker on the retreat.

Kalvin and I jump over a log and pick up our pace. The bird screeches, but we're gone. I have no idea what she'll do once we're gone, but I have a feeling that won't be the last I see of her. She saw the desert too. At least, that's what I think she was trying to communicate with me. Maybe that's where she wants to go? Or maybe... Fuck. I don't know. There are too many loose ends, and I don't know how to weave them into a cohesive history.

We set a quick pace through the woods. I haven't seen a military shooter since before the waterhole, so maybe we've lost them. The rest of our party is behind us, bringing up the rear, and Luca is not telling us to stop or slow down, so we must be doing the right thing.

And fuck, I just realized I've lost my bag. I don't have it anymore. The GPS tracker is in it! Along with my water. Damn. I'm thirsty.

"I don't... know where... to go," I huff out between labored breaths.

"Straight... for now." Kalvin is at my side, his arms shooting out to clear away tree branches and underbrush as we crash through them.

We run for what feels like ages but may only be five minutes. I don't know. I'm not a runner, and I despise this kind of high-cardio exercise, so anything longer than a minute feels like an eternity. But if I'm going to be running through the jungle on a regular basis, I should maybe consider working out more.

Maybe.

I must be hallucinating if I'm even thinking this.

With my breathing strained and my legs aching, I can only blame the endorphins and adrenaline pumping through my body at an increased rate for my addled brain.

Sweat pours down my back, and my boots continue to squish with every step I take. Even my feet are sweating in my water-soaked socks, and they slip around, making the running more difficult.

Kalvin and I crash through a bank of bushes, and on the

other side, we pull up short. A group of monkeys sits in a grassy space devoid of trees. They shriek and run, galloping off. A scream comes from behind. Uh oh. Bigger monkeys are running straight at us.

"Run," Kalvin urges, pushing me towards a long stretch of grass.

I watch where I'm going, dodging in and out of pockets of dirt and water. The grass seems to lead to a small hill, so I aim for that.

Kalvin calls out from behind me, and I hear him hit the ground.

Shit. I come to a halt and reverse course to grab him.

"Skylar, careful!" he shouts, rolling over to get his feet under him again.

A monkey comes flying towards me. I lash out with a kick that strikes it in the belly. I immediately hate myself for the mewling noises it makes when it hits the grass. But it rolls over and runs off, screaming as it goes. Other monkeys stare at me, fear replacing their rage. I drop into a ready position. I don't want to hurt innocent creatures, but I will not let us become their afternoon snack.

I whip out with a kick to the air, and the monkeys back off even more.

"Hey, look what I can do with my boots, you little shits. Go on! Find something better to do!" I lunge at them, and they all take off, the grass swaying in their hurried wake.

"Shit. I can't believe that worked," I say, bouncing on my toes.

I help Kalvin up, and he looks at me wide-eyed. "You're full of surprises."

I laugh — one big "ha" — before I take his sleeve and tug him to a run.

But after three long strides, the world bottoms out. I'm running one moment, falling the next. My legs and arms whirl around in the open air as I drop, drop, drop. Oof. Something nails me in the back. I bounce down a wall and hit the ground with a crunch.

Am I still moving? I think I've stopped. My chest is on fire, and I can barely breathe between the exertion and all the air being knocked out of me.

"Ow!" Oh shit, my chest hurts. I think I broke a rib. I did hear a crunching sound. Was that my rib?

I open my eyes and look up. I fell down some sinkhole? Testing out my limbs, I gently roll my wrists and ankles. Those feel okay. My arms and legs seem to work at the elbows and knees. I sit forward and wince. Yeah, a broken rib for sure. Maybe two. I try to take a deep breath, and the pain is so blinding it knocks me back.

"Skylar!" Kalvin's voice reaches me. "Are you okay?" he calls.

I blink and try to breathe, but I can only pull in a small gulp of air.

"I'm here," I say at a normal volume.

"What?" he yells.

"I'm here," I say a little louder, though the pain makes me nauseous. "I broke a rib. Can't talk." I swallow a few times, hoping to not puke, but nope. My stomach turns over, and I roll to my uninjured side to lose what's in my stomach.

Puking only makes things worse. The pain is intense, and it just gets worse with every heave. I hate throwing up, but it seems to be the way my body deals with any kind of real stress in my life. I threw up a lot as a kid. It's a wonder that I never developed an eating disorder, but it's probably because I hate puking. Hate it.

I roll away from the sick and stare up at the top of the hole I fell into. I must be at least five meters down. The walls of this sinkhole are dirt and rocks, slicked wet with the ever-present Rio humidity. I don't detect any other animals down here, and that's good. I would have nowhere to run.

For a moment, I close my eyes. How did this day go so wrong? Oh yeah, the fucking military decided I was a prime target.

You know what? After they stole my ship and gutted it, I was ready to burn their entire organization to the ground. But stronger heads prevailed, and they talked me out of it. Now, I want nothing more than to be fucking done with them for good. There has to be something I can do to tear down their little playground. They're like children running around with guns, and they don't understand the consequences of their actions. Well, guess what? Skylar Kawabata will bring them those consequences, and it will not be pretty.

I'm contemplating my next move when something brushes my cheek. I jerk back, sure it's some snake or lizard or other unholy animal, when I catch the fuzzy green plant... staring at me? No. It has no eyes. But I swear it's watching me.

"Hi," I say, and the plant shivers.

Okay, that's weird.

A new plant of the same kind pops up next to it. Like, literally thrusts up through the soil, spreads its leaves, and... waves to me.

I must be losing my damned mind.

"Help?" I say, totally unsure of what's going on. I'm either hallucinating and on a terrible trip, or this is real.

But this *is* Rio, and I've seen stranger shit here. This has to be real.

More of the fuzzy green plants pop out of the surrounding soil. They wave in a steady rhythm like the wind has blown them, but the air is calm down here. The oscillations are soothing, mesmerizing. My heart rate slows, and my body relaxes watching them.

The nearest plant reaches out and touches my hand, and that instinct to pull away doesn't surface. They draw me in, my fingers between their leaves and stalks. A sense of calm pleasure pushes aside the pain of my broken rib. Energy returns to my body where there was nothing but fatigue a moment ago.

I smile. "That's nice. Thank you," I say, keeping my voice even and low. I take short gulps of air to keep the pain in my ribs at a minimum as I watch the plants sway across the floor.

Wait. Is this *my* plant?

Rio has plant pairs for many humans. It's something Vivian figured out when she was on the Amagi with me. Sure, many plants give people superhuman powers, but not all of them. And still, some plants have a human pair, and those powers are enhanced. Ken, Vivian's second consort, has a plant pair that gives him heightened empathy. They figured out it was *his* plant when it moved towards him. It interacted with him. The heightened empathy plant is a good match for someone like Ken. His plant never makes him sick, and the symbiotic nature of their relationship is pretty unique.

Out of all the plants I've been around on Rio, this is the only one that has interacted with me. It reaches out, and I'm tempted to pluck it from the ground and pop it into my mouth. My hand hovers over them as they extend their fuzzy tendrils up to my fingers. It would be the height of stupidity to ingest one of these right now. I have no idea what they do or how they would affect me, and my life is still in danger from the fucking military. I'm broken and bruised and tired and down a fucking sinkhole.

I'm up there for India Dellis's Employee of the Month.

I drive my hand farther into the plants, close my eyes, and the weirdest thing happens. Well, weirder than any of the other stuff that's happened lately.

I see myself move backwards, time rewinding. Ew. I puke backwards and shoot up and out of the hole.

My eyes fly open, and I pull my hand from the plants.

What the hell was that?

"Sky?" Kalvin's voice comes from almost right over my head. "Are you okay? I think I see you."

"I'm here," I say, trying not to raise my voice. "I'm not okay, but I'm not close to death either."

"I'm looking for a way down," he says, his voice moving.

"What about the military? Or anyone else?"

"Coast is clear so far. Even the monkeys are gone."

He moves off, and my plant beckons to me like the wind across a grassy plain. Okay, they want me to move.

I rise to my feet gingerly, just in case I busted something I wasn't aware of on first inspection. My head swims from the pain and nausea, but I can stand upright. Somewhat. The walls of the sinkhole keep my head bowed.

More of my fuzzy green plants pop out of the ground, leading away from my landing spot. I walk to the side of them, carefully, one squishy foot in front of another. Each step I take is solid. I don't want to slip, fall, and hurt myself again.

"Where are we going, little ones?"

They shiver, and the motion feels like excitement.

"Okay, okay. I'm coming."

The sinkhole is a lot bigger than I thought it was. It's almost a straight path forward, through a three-meter-wide channel cut through the land. Is this natural? The uniformity of the walls makes me think this is manmade somehow.

I push aside a giant root system, duck under, and come out into a wider portion of the sinkhole.

Well, that explains a lot.

"Kalvin?" I call out, wincing at the pain in my chest. "Kalvin, you have to come down here!"

I look up and see his head poke over the edge. "What's wrong? I found a downed tree up here that I think I can maneuver into the hole, and we can use it to climb."

"I'm not leaving just yet, and you need to come down here. Now."

"What? Why?"

I gesture to the dirty metal of the space probe buried in the dirt in front of me. It looks like it's aged a thousand years, but I recognize the design. This design is current to now. The plants at my feet wave back and forth in front of the probe, practically singing about its existence.

There's something here I'm supposed to see.

"I have a mystery to solve," I tell him, "and I could use your help."

28

I'm not going near that thing until Kalvin can come down here and help me with it.

"Just a second!" he calls down to me. "I've almost got it. It's big and probably weighs a billion pounds. But I'm using a rock and another branch as a lever."

"Don't throw out your back, old man." I smile at him as he gives me a dirty look and disappears from view. After a few grunts, the end of the trunk appears over the edge of the hole. I move off to the side. Kalvin levers the other end, and the tree trunk slips into the sinkhole, standing up on the edge. He peeks over the side again and closes his eyes.

"Yes," he says, pumping his fist. "That actually fucking worked. See? I'm not so helpless in the jungle."

"You're a regular Indiana Jones."

He throws his legs over the side and climbs down the trunk to me.

"Who?"

I roll my eyes. "Some days, it really shows that I was a locked-in kid with no friends but the movies I could watch and the books I could read."

"Well, if this Indiana Jones is a daring, ne'er-do-well jungle adventurer, then I'll take that as a compliment."

He smiles, and I shake my head. He's close enough.

"Are you okay? Take off your shirt and let me see your ribs."

I smack his hand away from the hem of my shirt with a huff. "If you think you're getting lucky down here, you are mistaken."

His smile softens. "Thought you could use some humor. This has been a shit day."

I sigh. "It has." I lift the hem of my shirt, and he winces at my mid-section.

"That does not look good. And we both lost our bags about a kilometer ago, so I have nothing that can help you." He pulls my shirt down. "Just go easy on it. Anyway, what did you want to show me?"

I grab him by both arms and turn him around to face the space probe. His mouth falls open.

"What the fuck is that?" He takes a tentative step forward, but I stop him from stepping on my plant.

"Wait. First, avoid this plant." I wave to the fuzzy green carpet undulating at Kalvin's feet. "This is *my* plant, and I don't want anything to happen to it."

"What do you mean, your plant?"

I hold up a finger and squat down. Relaxing my hand, I bring my fingers out over the sea of plants in front of us. They all sway towards me, reaching out to get as close to my hand as possible. Several stretch far enough to touch my skin, and the calming effect is instantaneous. I let out a slow breath, close my eyes, and the tension leaks from my overworked body. Once again, I see myself move backwards in time, talking to Kalvin, and watching him come down the tree in reverse.

"Whoa." Kalvin pulls me away from the plants. They slip from my fingers and curl back on each other, sad that I'm gone.

I lift my eyebrows at him, almost in a drunken state from that small amount of contact.

"You look high," Kalvin says, leaning away from me.

I sink back on my heels. "I feel great whenever I touch them. It's amazing. Not high, but more like peaceful, content. And then, I don't know. I relive everything that's happened to me?" I shake my head. "They show me everything that just happened, in reverse." I shrug.

Kalvin hovers his hand over the plants, and they don't move. They don't acknowledge him. He pulls his hand back, disappointment twisting his lips.

"Hmmm, so they move and engage with you if they're 'yours?' What else will they do?"

"I don't know what these particular ones will do once I ingest them, but generally, when a plant is yours, it becomes a symbiotic kind of relationship. They don't make you sick, and their powers are enhanced with you and you only."

He looks around at the ground of the sinkhole and stretches his neck side to side. "Shit. There is so much I don't know about Rio."

"Well, now you know more than most people do, so don't feel like you need to catch up or anything." I pat his arm. "Let's walk around it to the left."

Kalvin and I skirt to the side of the plants and approach the space probe. I squat down next to it and pull some moss from its top. Looking back at the sinkhole, an idea pops.

I point to the path of the hole, and Kalvin nods.

"What do you think?" He tips his head and stares at the sky. "It was launched from orbit." He points. "Probably skipped across the land once or twice and came to rest here." He pushes his hand forward, indicating the earth the pod has shoved up behind it. He rests his hands on his hips. "But this looks like it's been here for decades."

"Longer," I say, tapping my foot. "This is, what, a rho or sigma class probe?"

"From Alpha Core? No." He shakes his head. "Wait." He

narrows his eyes and approaches the probe. "Maybe? My last ship didn't have any probes."

"I've never had them on the Amagi either. But I've seen them on the Lee home ship."

He smiles briefly. "Remember when I gave you shit for going to the Lees on your weekends?" He rolls his eyes. "I didn't realize how close you were with your cousin and her network. Not until she saved our asses in the desert."

"We got lucky," I remind him.

"No," he says, facing me. "Never forget it was your smarts and determination that got us out of that situation. A situation I helped put us in. I would not be alive and here with you if it weren't for your quick thinking. I owe you my life, Skylar."

My chest warms with gratitude. So few people ever thank me for the hard work I do. Often, I put my brain to work out a problem for someone, and it surprises them I can even help. I'm treated as an abnormality, 'too smart for my own good.'

I step to Kalvin and lightly wrap my arms around his waist. "You owe me nothing." I rise to my tip-toes and lay a kiss on his cheek.

"Skylar..." He purrs my name as his arms come down to pull me into an embrace.

Ow! I draw in a hissing breath, and he lets go swiftly. I had almost forgotten about the broken rib. Sharp, stabbing pain radiates through my chest. I fall to my knees and shove my hand into my plants. They eagerly wrap around my fingers, palm, and wrist, and the pain fades away. I sink and let my muscles relax.

"Yikes," Kalvin says, dropping to his knees next to me. "Sorry. I forgot about the rib."

"So did I. The plants take away most of the pain." I breathe in and out and stand up. "Let's get back to work here. I don't want to think about what Rio is like after dark."

"Right. Absolutely."

He clears more dirt, rocks, and moss from the probe, enough to access the control panel. He struggles with opening it before grabbing a rock and smashing it on the stubborn latch. It pops free after three hits.

"You're right. Sigma class. Those came out two years ago."

Chills climb up my spine as I approach to stand next to him. Yeah. The stamp inside says it was manufactured last year. But...

"I don't get it." My brain takes this information and folds it back and forth, one layer on top of another, like preparing pastry dough. When did the universe stop making sense?

"Look," Kalvin says, pointing to the rear end of the panel. A stick drive is plugged in, secure in its socket. Hmmm, that could be anything.

He grabs it and pulls it out before I can stop him. I gasp and lean away. We both freeze and wait for something while my heart hammers in my chest. Will it make noise? Or blow up? Or...

Nothing happens. We let out a simultaneous breath.

My heartbeat returns to normal, and I punch Kalvin in the shoulder. "You're going to give me a fucking heart attack. Can you stop with the impulsive shit?"

"Sorry," he says, irritation edging into his voice. "I just... I figured we should take it."

No comment.

"Stuff it in your pocket," I tell him, circling to the rear of the craft. This part of the probe is wedged into the dirt and stone. I don't think anything but a jackhammer could get it loose.

I crouch down to look at the underbelly of the probe and find the rear doors torn off. Were they open? Tearing the doors off would be hard if they were closed.

"Hello down there!"

I jump forward and knock my head on the probe at the voice bellowing down from above.

"Ouch! Motherfucker," I say, rubbing my head.

"Yep. It's Skylar." Saif's face appears over the edge of the sinkhole. "Hey, gorgeous. Fancy seeing you around here."

"How did you find us?" I call back, smiling at his eager face. But I wince at the pain in my ribs. I should not be raising my voice to anyone.

"Retraced your steps. We found your bags, and then one of Luca's men tracked you to here." His smile falls. "Are you in pain? Are you hurt?"

"Yes and yes. Broken rib. Maybe two." I rest my hand on the side of my chest, and I can tell it's hot. "I'll probably need to see the doctor soon. Hey, is Takemo up there?"

"Yeah, we're all here. Luca's men are getting a climbing rope set up. They came prepared."

Takemo's head shows up next to Saif's. "Ah, you found them."

I wave at him. "Hey, can you come down here? I have something to show you." I point to the space probe, and his eyes widen.

"Is that what I think it is?"

"Maybe?" I beckon him over to the tree log. "Shimmy down this and come see."

"I'm coming down too," Saif says, queueing up behind Takemo.

"Sure. Why not? It's a regular party down here."

They each climb down, I have them step around my plant and inspect the space probe.

Takemo stands next to me with his arms crossed. "I don't get it."

"That's what I said. What is a probe that was manufactured only in the last two years doing in a giant hole on Rio when it looks like it's been here a thousand years?"

"Longer," he says. He throws up his hands. "Well, I think there's only one explanation for this. It's time travel. Obviously." And then he laughs. "I mean, why not?" His wide eyes tell me he's full of shit. "Right? Because Rio isn't strange enough. Someone sent this probe back in time to make it even more incomprehensible. It's the only explanation."

He throws his head back with a laugh again but stops at my stern glare.

"What, Sky? That's ridiculous, of course." He waves at it. "It must be some kind of... I don't know, movie set prop? I think I remember an action flick that takes place on Rio." He rubs at his shadow of a beard. "Not that I've seen a movie in the last two years. I work too much." He stops with a sigh.

But looking at both Saif and Kalvin and their blank stares, I can't help but think Takemo is correct about the time travel.

There really is only one explanation for the whole thing, and I already know about the possibility of time travel through the jump gates.

This was one hell of a fortunate accident.

But really, are there ever any accidents? Do I believe in fate? Or was it planned?

I snap out of my deep thoughts. "Let's get out of here. I need water, food, and a shower." If I stop to think about how dirty and sweaty and gross I am, I may puke again.

Luca peers over the edge of the hole. "We're going to throw down a harness and a line. You can each use it and this tree to climb out. We're less than a kilometer from the new camp, so if we leave now, we'll arrive before sunset."

This is my chance.

I kneel down at the plants and put my hand out to them. Saif and Takemo watch in fascination as they twist about my fingers and pop out of the soil close to me.

"I'm going to take some of you with me," I whisper, and they shiver. I hope that's an agreement, but I feel a tremendous amount of guilt ripping them from the soil. Taking several handfuls, I stuff them into my jacket pocket and zip it up. If they're upset about the whole situation, they don't show it.

I'm the second to last person up out of the hole with Kalvin right behind me. Luca saves the location to his GPS tracker in case we need to return and leads us in the direction of camp. I follow at the rear, turning to watch the spot disappear from view as we head into the jungle once more.

29

WE REACH the camp without incident, something I'm grateful for. My ribs are killing me, and I'm sure my feet are covered in blisters. I feel like shit on a stick, and I probably look it too. This is definitely starting to feel like punishment for the crappy person I am, and my spirits sink lower and lower with every step I take.

I limp through the gate, and the amount of activity on the other side gives me pause. People run from one building to the next, and only half the usual buildings have been erected. The large armored vehicles sit inside the fence, open and awaiting passengers.

Something tells me we're not sticking around for long.

"I'm going to escort Skylar to the infirmary," Saif says, taking my arm as the limp starts to slow me down. "You two figure out where we're going to sleep tonight."

"It's your night tonight," Kalvin reminds him, shouldering our bags.

"Huh? Oh." Saif looks at me. "Okay, well, we'll see about that."

I squeeze his arm. "You can sleep in the same bed with me.

I'd like the company."

I don't want to be alone with my thoughts about everything that happened today. I'd like someone to be there for the eventual nightmares.

Saif doesn't respond. He smiles and ushers me forward.

The infirmary is blessedly quiet despite the activity in the main camp. Dr. Emily is both glad I'm alive and annoyed that I'm so injured. She takes me to the bathroom in the back, and I strip down for her so she can assess my injuries before I shower.

"Just don't do anything with my clothes. There's a plant in the jacket pocket I want to save." I turn on the water and wait for it to get hot.

"Are you sure?" she asks, holding the clothes away from her. "Maybe we should burn them."

"Don't you dare," I say, no malice in my voice. "Not until after I go through the pockets, please."

Showering is so painful I cry the entire way through it. Lifting my arms to wash my hair causes my ribs to smart, and the hot water coursing over my fresh blisters is like having needles stabbed into my feet.

My mood is low through the entire process. I escaped death at the hands of the military, and I found the weird space probe and my plant in the wilds of Rio. But I didn't do anything valuable for the mission. In fact, I made it harder to get to camp sooner. We were late getting to Luca because of dealing with Dominic, and I'm sure that caused issues, too. I've been called worthless before, and now I actually feel it, deep in my bones. Ever since I came aboard on this operation, things have spiraled out of control.

Same for the Amagi.

Same for Saif's and Kalvin's lives.

I am nothing but trouble.

Once I'm clean, I'm given random fresh clothes and a shot of nanos that Emily programs to heal my broken ribs. Both of them. I was right; I broke two. She deals with the blisters on my feet, sprays them with painkillers and antibiotics, and bandages them up. She delivers my boots clean with new socks. My dirty clothes are stuffed into a bag and handed to me.

I grab my datapad and glance at the universal clock. Shit. It's my birthday. I'm now twenty-nine years old. Fuck. How did that happen? Twenty-nine years old, no real network, no business, nothing to show for all of my life's work except for a Class Three pilots license.

I really am worthless.

I exit from the infirmary tent and run right into Saif.

"Oh, hi," I say, aiming my eyes at the ground. "Were you waiting for me?"

"Of course." Saif's returning smile is kind. "I got some sandwiches and a room for us for the night. Let's go relax and try to get some sleep." He pulls me close to him with his arm over my shoulder.

"We don't have to." How can I get out of this? If I stick around, I'm just going to be the cancer that grows and eats everything good in this relationship. Tears sit in the back of my eyes and beg to be shed. My throat burns as I hold them back.

"We will. Come on," he urges me, directing me to our room.

I eat the sandwich in silence, assuring Saif I'm just tired.

I *am* tired. Tired of everything.

Now I know what Vivian went through when she was fighting to win back her farm. This really sucks. It's a constant stream of stressful, horrible things with no rest. That doubt flower in the back of my head has bloomed, and it's having little baby flowers.

There's no end in sight to this madness.

I want to give up.

I can't get into bed fast enough. My body is like lead, and my chest is hollow and cold.

I let Saif kiss me good night, then I roll over and close my eyes.

Sleep comes swiftly.

"Oh, come on, Skylar. You're going to sleep with me to get what you want," Eamon said to me. "It's what you're best at." He was going to rip off my clothes if I didn't do it myself. He liked to play with dominance in bed, and I was never sure if he would hurt me or not. I took my clothes off myself to try to take control.

I had no control.

Dominic gestures to Eamon on the bed. "Don't you see? Everyone already knows you're trash. You could have been better. You could have made better choices. You chose this. It's your fault." He leans into me. "You're nothing. Nothing."

I inhale sharply and sit up in bed.

"No."

Dominic is right. I'm wrong, and he's right. I press my fingers to my lips as cold shivers run down my back. Why didn't I listen to him? He's always told me how worthless I am, that I can never do anything right, that I'm a sham of a daughter, that I will never be anybody special. And shit, yes. I did sleep with Eamon to get what I wanted, a ship's AI I couldn't afford. I've slept with countless men for favors or just because I was bored or angry.

Oh fuck, there is something fundamentally wrong with me.

I look around the dark room, and my eyes fall on the bedside clock. Four-thirteen in the morning.

"You do nothing but cause pain and suffering to your mom and all the dads. You should be ashamed of yourself," Dominic had said to me when I was sixteen.

Tears fill my eyes, and I cover my face with my hands.

He was right. He was one-hundred percent right about me. The reversal of fortune is a betrayal I should have seen coming. I should have seen what Dominic saw, an unfaithful and unreliable daughter who preferred her own happiness over her family's wants and needs.

Sobs bubble up from my belly.

"Sky... Skylar." Saif sits up next to me, and his warm hand rests on my mid-back. "Are you okay? What's wrong?"

"I'm a horrible person," I say, my tone matter-of-fact. I bark out another sob. "My mom and Dominic have always known it. I should have seen it years ago, but I was too vain, too full of myself to care about what they needed. And here I am, defying them, turning my back on them. I could end this madness if I just stop fighting and hand everything over to them."

I'm a horrible, terrible, evil person. I think I've always known and just never wanted to accept it. But the events of the last few days have worn me down, taken away all my self-control and self-esteem. These past few days have shown me what I was incapable of seeing before.

"No," Saif stresses, rubbing my back in smooth circles. "No. That's not true. You are not a horrible person."

I nod my head and let the tears fly off my nose. "I am. I need to give up. I need to stop all of this. Stop this job. Stop this fighting. Let you go. You don't need to be saddled with someone like me. It's over. It's done."

I throw my legs over the side of the bed, and Saif scrambles in panic. He grabs his wristlet and makes a few gestures as I get up and pace, thinking of what to do next.

"It's a good idea to end this now before your sister gets pulled into my problems, too. I'll pack up my bags, and I'll get out of here as soon as the sun's up." I walk back and forth, back and forth. "India is going to quit this, anyway. I've got my plant. I'll figure out what it does. I'll end this."

I inhale and look at the room. There's an hour until sunrise. I can pack up and be ready to go once the sky lightens. It's not like I unpacked much, just enough to find some pajamas and my toothpaste.

Saif jumps into his pants and pulls them up with swift precision. He approaches me with his hands out.

"Skylar, you're tired. I think you were having some kind of nightmare. Why don't you come back to bed?"

"No." I cross the room to the bathroom. "It's time I ended this hellish life of mine. I don't need to drag you and Kalvin down with me. Or India or your sister," I repeat. Did he not hear me the first time? "I'm nothing but a burden. Didn't you hear Dominic? I'm just a liar, and I conned you into believing everything. You're better off without me."

My head whips around at the sound of the doors opening on my suite. The inner door opens, and Kalvin comes through, his hair a mess. Takemo stands behind him, his back against the outer door.

"I'm here," Kalvin says, dropping his shoes in the vestibule.

Sait turns to me. "You don't mean that. Don't say that about yourself. I don't care how tired you are. You do not tell lies about yourself."

"Why not?" I lash out, snapping my arm out into the air. "No one is ever going to believe me. They will all believe him, believe my mother. I can already see the doubt on everyone's faces. Hell, I doubt my own memories of the whole situation."

Tears pour down my face, and I turn to hide them from the guys.

"No one will believe me because I already have this awful reputation that I gave to myself of the flying, fuck-em-and-leave-em, drinking whore who can't settle down. Why would *anyone* believe someone like me?" I smear the tears from my face. "Why do *you* believe me, huh? Why? I never told you, back then, about what happened to me. I never said a word because Dominic told me I wouldn't be believed, and he was right then, and he's right now." I laugh through my tears. "Fucking bastard. He knew what he was doing right from the beginning, and I fucking played right into it."

I storm into the bathroom, and grabbing everything I left out from the counter, I shove it all in my bag.

Saif stands in my way when I return to the room.

"I didn't need to hear from your lips what happened to you. I saw it with my own eyes," he says, sighing. "You were so skinny, yet you ate like you had never eaten before at every meal. And then you were obsessed with the self-defense courses and anything having to do with survival in the wilderness. I could see the desire to run away written on your face every time we ended up at far-school together."

He hangs his head for a brief moment.

"When you left far-school, the time we were thirteen, Dominic came to get you. You couldn't make eye contact with him. You were smaller like you were trying to draw into yourself. I saw him grab you and practically wrestle you onto the train, even though you didn't struggle. You were like a limp doll, and he just tossed you around." He pokes himself in the chest. "I hate myself for not having spoken up for you then. I should have."

I stand still with my bag in my hand. No one has ever told me they saw the way I was back then. So many people either didn't notice or turned a blind eye to it, and it wasn't like I saw many individuals in the flesh, anyway.

"Don't do this to yourself, Sky." Saif reaches out and takes the bag from my hands.

Kalvin's been silent, but he now steps forward. "Don't doubt your own memories. That's what Dominic and your mother want. They want to drive you crazy until you can't tell red from blue. Then really, no one will believe you if you can't believe in yourself. It's a tactic. Don't let them win."

"They've already won," I say, turning my bleary eyes on him. "They took my future, sold off my business to him." I wave at Takemo, still standing in the doorway. His face is like stone.

"We're going to build a new future," Kalvin says. "Right? We already talked about this."

"That was before."

"Before what?" Saif asks.

"Before we got Dominic arrested. It'll be all over the news. There'll be no hiding from it. It's better to end this now before you both get dragged into it, too. Publicly. I remember what happened to Vivian. I can't let that happen to you. Me? I already know what they say about me. But you can move on and have a great life with someone else without being sullied by this."

Saif and Kalvin look at each other. Kalvin nods.

"The arrest changes nothing. We're in this for the long haul." Saif approaches me with his hands out. I let him touch me, touch my face, push my hair behind my ears, lay his hand on my shoulder. He knows I don't like to be held, and I don't even know what a hug would do to me at this point.

"You should go back to bed. Sleep. Those nanobots are still healing your ribs." Kalvin walks to the bed and lifts the covers, pulling them back and tucking them in.

I turn in time to see Takemo cross the room from the door in long strides. He opens his arms and pulls me into a hug that makes me squeak with shock. He's careful to squeeze only my upper body across my shoulders, and only just long enough for the hug to register before he pulls away.

Saif and Kalvin stand frozen, too stunned to move.

"She needs hugs," he says, pointing to me. My cheeks burn. "I know she doesn't want to be held, but for fuck's sake, she needs them. Don't leave her without them."

I draw in a ragged breath as he strides from the room, slips on his shoes, and exits.

We all stand still for a long moment.

Kalvin huffs. "So he hates you, huh?"

He turns around and lifts his eyebrows.

That was so unexpected that I struggle to pull in a breath. "Maybe not?"

Okay, yeah, I'm ready to go back to bed.

30

I step out from the suite, hoping for a meal from the cafeteria, only to bump straight into India Dellis.

"Skylar!" She grabs my upper arms. "There you are. I was hoping to see you this morning, but I must have missed you."

She didn't miss me. After my freakout, I went to sleep, and when Saif got out of bed, I rolled over and slept again. I have slept the whole morning away, yet I could go back to bed right now. I could sleep for a hundred years, and it would not be enough.

"How do you feel?" She looks me up and down. "You look better than I imagined."

I look her up and down too, and besides the slight sheen of sweat on her brow, she looks like she's had her feet up all day. Her shirt is still pressed and crisp, and her straight-leg khakis are fresh from the closet.

"You look like you belong in an office."

She smirks at this.

"I'm exhausted, I feel like shit, and I'm hungry. Food?"

She twists her lips as she looks left and right at the continued chaos of the camp. "We can grab some sandwiches and coffee. We scaled down the cafeteria because I think we'll be leaving again tomorrow."

"Again?" It comes out as a whine, and I'm too tired to hide it. "What the fuck, India?"

"Come on," she says, easing me along. "Let's chat over food."

The covered kitchen tent is quiet. An egg salad sandwich is just what I need, so I grab two of them, a plate of fried potatoes, and a hunk of chocolate cake because I fucking deserve it after the day I had yesterday. India sips on a protein shake while I stuff my face with food.

"We're at a breaking point. Somehow, the military is on my tail at every turn, and I can't shake them." She leans back in her chair. "I don't know how they are tracking us so easily. There have been no drones. I've had every piece of machinery checked for trackers. I've vetted every employee for the third time. I adjusted down to a smaller team." She throws her free hand up. "At this point, we may have to quit and do something else."

I swallow a mouthful of egg salad and wash it down with a sip of coffee. It won't matter how much caffeine I have because I'm going to pass out for an afternoon nap, and there'll be no stopping me.

"Well, it's not a bad idea to move this out of the jungle. You could have a small strike team who does the plant gathering and then bring everything back to the city like Takemo suggested."

She shakes her head. "We're thinking of quitting this continent entirely."

"What? Why bother when most of Rio's environmental diversity is here? I mean, Vivian found other plants elsewhere, but this is supposed to be the center of... it... all."

My mouth slows down.

The space probe. The center of it all. Time travel.

Everything comes back to time travel.

Maybe the universe is trying to tell me something.

I suck down more coffee and quiet the anxious butterflies zooming around my chest. Pieces of the puzzle click together in my head.

Click, click, click.

Boom. A picture of what's happened focuses in my mind.

"Hey, so... how's that whole jump ring thing going?" I ask her.

"Jump ring thing?" India asks, her eyebrows climbing.

"Sorry. I'm tired." I glance around, but we're alone except for the man washing dishes. "Have you spoken with Renata about the jump ring the military had on Neve? Because, you know, when we were there, Vivian suspected that the ring we found wasn't the only one the military had up and running."

She sets her protein shake down. "And?" Her voice is as hard as stone. "Yes, remember, I did speak with Renata."

I close my eyes and rewind through my memories. "Right. I remember. But back on Neve, we heard from Nina Correa that the gate was unstable. That they had a hard time keeping it on one destination."

She nods. "Right. Even with a massive amount of power, they can't keep the focus of the sending gate on a location without a receiving gate."

"So," I say, raising my finger in the air, "what if they decided that time was an easier destination, especially if they keep the gate in one place?"

India holds still for a long moment. "Motherfucker," she breathes out.

"Exactly." I open the box of chocolate cake. "So they set up a gate here on Rio, and they use it to go back and scout. Your people haven't been betraying you. You're being spied on by time travelers."

When I look up from the chocolate cake, India's mouth is open in awe.

"How do you do that?"

"What?" I ask, my mouth full of cake. I hold my hand over my mouth as I chew.

"You come into my life right when I need you, and you're always able to draw the right conclusions from so little evidence. If this is all true..."

I shrug. "I could be wrong. But I don't think I am. It's what I would do in their place."

My chewing slows down as I remember my time in the sinkhole. It can't be a coincidence that the space probe is here on this continent, that it looks thousands of years old but was only manufactured two years ago, and my plant was waiting for me there.

It was one hell of a fortunate accident, but my instincts tell me it was no accident.

The bag with my clothes is resting at my feet.

"Hey, so, there's another thing," I say, leaning down to grab the bag.

India rubs her face with both of her hands. "What now?"

I pull the jacket from my bag and unzip the pocket. Setting the green plants on the table, the giddy butterflies in my chest reappear.

"I found my plant."

"What? No." Her eyes widen as she leans forward to examine the green fuzzy tendrils on the table.

Guilt sits in my stomach like a giant rock, knowing I pulled them from the dirt. I ended their leafy lives. But I have to believe that's what they would want. They exist for me, as selfish as that sounds.

"What does it do?"

"I'm not sure, but I have a feeling." I pick one up between my fingers and stare at it. "You know, I've always had a tenuous relationship with time. When I was younger and taking care of my entire family, I would wish for more time so I could finish all the tasks assigned to me before they punished me for being 'lazy.' Or I would want time to go by faster so I could get through the punishment quicker."

India's face is the still countenance of a master card player. This happens to every person I open up to about my childhood, so I ignore it.

"Before I pass out from exhaustion, let's figure out what it does."

I pop it in my mouth as India leans across the table to stop me.

Too late.

"Jesus, Skylar. We shouldn't be doing this here. We should be in the lab." She stands up and looks around, maybe hoping to find the doctor or one of her lab techs.

Doesn't matter. I chew the plant and hold it under my tongue for a long moment before shoving another bite of chocolate cake into my mouth and swallowing.

"We should always test plants with chocolate cake chasers," I say with a laugh. I clap my hands together and lean back, waiting... Waiting...

I push the fried potatoes across the table to India. "Share while we wait?"

She eyes the plate warily.

"Come on. Live a little. Starch is good for you."

She picks up a potato between her fingers like it's a dirty diaper and sighs before nibbling on it. I swear she lives on alcohol, protein shakes, and air.

"You ate your dinner out of sequence," she says, pointing to the cake. "It's no wonder I never see you at any of the high society balls."

I wave my hand. "Pshaw. I'm not high society, and I never will be. I'm a backwater pilot from a shitty family who just happens to know some big wigs. You are slumming with the best." She nibbles at the potato again. "Whoa there. Slow down. You don't want to get a stomach ache from eating too quickly."

I laugh at my joke, but it lands quietly.

India doesn't move, and at first, I think she's ready to dress me down for being so self-deprecating. Not that I've said anything that's untrue. I accepted who I am a long time ago. I continue with my life by making lemonade from lemons, per usual.

Hmmm, I tilt my head to the side and realize that sound has been sucked from the world. That's strange. The plant must be working. The last plant gave me superhuman hearing. This one is going to leave me deaf? No. Wait. I'm not deaf. Sound comes to me in longer, lower waves.

Hmmm. I lean forward across the table and get a better look at India. She's not frozen. She's moving... very... slowly. Her blink is taking an age, and her chest rises at a tortoise's pace for one breath.

Everything is going at the same glacial speed. But I'm moving and breathing and alive with no issues. I wonder what direction time is flowing in now — forward or reverse?

Reaching out my hand to India, I inhale as she moves backwards.

What the fuck is happening?

Wait. I thought 'reverse,' and that's what happened.

Wow. I told India to slow down eating the potatoes, and that happened, quite literally. This is amazing.

My chest buzzes as I consider my next move.

Let's turn back time, shall we?

As I think it, as I imagine what came before, it happens in reverse. India sets down the fried potato, and the plate pulls back to me without touching it.

Faster.

Everything moves faster. I sit still while I watch India have a conversation with me backwards. Sound comes, but it's distorted and weird. It's familiar, though. Have I heard this before?

She gets up and leaves, walking in reverse. And as I stand in the cafeteria tent, I watch the chefs in the kitchen unmake my sandwich and un-fry my potatoes and on and on, possibly an hour or two previous to when I was here.

Stop.

Everything slows down until it stops moving. I move my legs, and they still work, so I tiptoe over to the unmoving chefs making egg salad, and I get an idea. Swiping their bread off the table, I take it and stash it away in someone's personal bag on the other side of the tent.

How easy is it to alter time, to change things? And what happens when something small is changed?

Forward again. I step out of the way as a chef rushes past me to chop the potatoes. I don't want to be in the way, so I hide on the other side of the tent where I can watch. Another works his way through the egg salad, and then he searches for the bread. He looks all over the temporary kitchen but comes up empty-handed.

"Where's the fucking bread?" he calls out at a rate three times faster than normal speech. Everyone breaks to search for the bread, and I hold my breath. But I guess I hid it someplace no one would bother to look because they give up, and the chef moves to the cupboard instead. He pulls out packages of crackers, makes individual bowls of egg salad, little packages of crackers, and puts those out instead.

Now what? I'm supposed to walk in with India here in a moment, get egg salad sandwiches, and talk with her.

Will I see myself?

The tent flap opens, and India and I walk in. Chills run down my back as I watch myself grab a bowl of egg salad with crackers, a plate of fried potatoes, and the chocolate cake and sit down at a table with India. She grabs our drinks and joins me.

I eat everything with gusto, picking up gobs of egg salad with crackers and shoving them in my mouth. For crying out loud, Skylar, I need to eat prettier. Am I really this much of a heathen?

I probably am.

I get to the point where I take out the plants and eat one of them.

I blink, and I'm gone. India jumps out of her chair and stares at me, the time traveler me, standing on the other side of the tent.

"What the fuck? How did you do that?" she asks, pointing at me.

"I caught up to myself," I whisper, looking around and thinking through everything that happened.

The memories of the previous timeline begin to slip from my head.

"Wait, wait," I say, holding out my hands to India. "I ate egg salad sandwiches the first time through, not egg salad with crackers."

The chef overheard me. "We couldn't find the bread. Sorry, miz." He glances at my empty plate, probably wondering why I'm complaining.

I point. "The bread is in that bag over there."

He laughs, but one of his employees opens the bag and finds the bread there.

"Huh," he says, taking it from his employee.

Once I have the story straight, the two timelines live in my head, side by side. That's really strange, and keeping them separate will be a problem.

"Let's talk outside," I say, approaching India and ushering her out of the tent.

Once I have her away from prying ears, I pull her close. "I

just time traveled. That's what my plant does. That's why it looked like I moved without you seeing me move." I close my eyes and cement the two timelines in my head. "I hid the bread just to make a minor change and see what happened. Do you remember me eating egg salad sandwiches?"

"Skylar..." Her voice is weary.

"Do you?" I insist.

"No." She shakes her head, and I release her arms. "You ate the egg salad with crackers."

I press my fingers to my lips to stop a laugh.

"This is it. This is what's been missing."

"What?" she asks.

I press my lips together, determined to make this work.

"The military has been playing with time travel." I poke myself in the chest. "Now, it's our turn."

31

It's our turn to infiltrate the enemy camp and see what we can learn.

Once the sun has set, Luca leads us all to the outskirts of the nearest military camp. Yes, we keep tabs on them, too. The difference is that we watch them so we can avoid them. They watch us so they can hound us, steal what we've learned, and kill a few people along the way. We're decidedly more pacifist.

Even though the sun has set, Belem, Rio's moon, and the glittering rings fill the sky, making everything glow. We assembled a small team for this — Luca and two of his men, two of our lab techs who will spy on the labs on the other side of the compound, and Saif and Kalvin, who wouldn't let me go without them. Takemo and India are helping our location pack up and move while we do this.

What are we doing? Hell, if I know.

My idea was to just get here and figure it out as we go.

"Did I say I love danger?" Kalvin whispers as we approach the fence on the outskirts of the base. He stops and pulls back his boot as a snake slithers across our path. I grab his shirt and hide behind him. "Oh, holy fucking shit, that was close."

I squeeze him and bury my face in the back of his shirt. "I hate snakes."

"You and me both."

"Get down, you two," Saif warns, "or I'll be the only one left in this network by the end of the night."

"Sorry," I mouth to him.

We crouch down and peer through the fence at the back of the compound.

"What do you see?" I whisper to Luca.

Luca gets on all fours and leans forward, his head practically at the fence.

"Hmmm, mess tent. Maybe some storage? Hard to tell since the bastards don't have to move as much as we do." He sits back on his heels. "Let's go right and circle around. Our other team is on the opposite side."

We move right, skirting around the outside edge until we reach a point with a guard and have to stop. I lie on my belly and peer through the underbrush, hoping I won't encounter anything poisonous along the way.

Five minutes later, the guard moves on to a spot much farther down. I let out a long-held breath.

"What about now? Any ideas?" I ask Luca.

His grimace shines in the wan light. "I don't know. Nothing's really sparking anything. If only I had a clue about what to do. Are we supposed to break in? Or gather intelligence or what? We made it out of that scrape the other morning by the skin of our teeth. I don't want to get caught again. I'm surprised we weren't caught before."

Ding, ding, ding!

We have a winner.

"Hey, what happened on our trek the other day?" I whisper. "I figured we were done for. They had guns trained on us, and we had nothing to defend ourselves except to run."

"I...," he begins and trails off. "You're right. None of us got hurt. What happened?"

He sits and thinks for a long moment. I say nothing because I don't want to bother his thought process. Something is sparking a memory here. I'm not sure what it is, though.

He turns to his man and rests a hand on his arm.

"Did it sound like their guns jammed when we were running away?" he asks.

The guy perks up. "Yeah. Yeah, boss. I heard cursing, and the shooting stopped."

"Right, right." Luca nods, his eyes focused far off. "And that one guy who ran after us? He stopped after a bit. I wonder if maybe he had gotten sick or something." He turns to me. "That happens a lot on Rio — random sicknesses. Usually puking or diarrhea. The plants here get in everything, including the water supply."

A plan starts to form — bullets and water.

"Okay, then. We need to find their armory and their water supply."

Kalvin gasps. "Good idea, Skylar. I like where you're going with this."

"Jam the guns and poison the water?" Saif asks. "You think that will work?"

"It already has," I say, smiling at him.

We traverse the side of the military's camp, under bushes, crawling past downed tree trunks, and avoiding every guard we can. A dog barks; we hide again. But the dog moves farther into camp.

"Seems quiet," Luca says, his eyes narrowing at the expanse of the camp in front of us.

"Maybe everyone turned in early?" I whisper.

A door flies open on a nearby building, and a man flies across the lawn like his pants are on fire. He opens a door and slams it behind him. The dog barks again. I catch the scent of onions. Hmmm.

Luca taps me on the shoulder.

"There," he says, pointing to the building to the right of where the man just entered. "That's their water supply. It backs up to the mess tent. Potable water will all be in one place." He points to each of the buildings. "There are tanks at each private building for non-potable water for washing. It's boiled and filtered, but only the drinking water is processed further."

"Okay." I commit the location to memory.

We circle even more to the left, and Luca stops us again.

"That's the armory."

My stomach sinks. Two men stand on either side of the door with their giant guns at the ready. A vehicle, armed to the teeth, sits right next door. I bet it's guarded night and day.

I sit down on my knees and face away with my eyes closed. This is a challenging task, but it's not impossible.

And what do I have to lose here? Honestly, if I died tomorrow, it would affect no one. Dominic would be happy he wouldn't have to deal with me. My mother? I'm not sure how grief-stricken she'd be. Vivian would definitely miss me. Marcelo might shed a tear, but he'd go on to help Lia build her network. Carlos would miss me, but Vivian would take care of him. Kalvin and Saif? Well, I know they care, and they want to stick around. But I haven't committed them to a contract, and they're both young enough. They'd move on. Everyone else would just continue to exist without me. Even my brothers and sisters.

I have nothing to lose.

"How far is it back to camp?" I ask.

"Uh, about two kilometers?" Luca says. "Give or take."

I shake my head. "That's too far. I'll never make it there and back in the time it takes for the plant to wear off. Hmmm. Wait. Which way should I go?"

He points back. "You should be able to pick up the trail."

I tip my head up and gaze at the rings of Rio while I think. I need to trust my gut and do something. Whether I live or die today, this place means something to me now.

"You don't have to do this," Saif says, sitting across from me.

"I've already done this."

I pull the plant from my pocket and pop it into my mouth.

* * *

Okay, so time is not an issue, right? Because I can control it. I need to divorce myself from time and think instead about distance and my own abilities. I can walk two kilometers safely, especially if time is standing still and I won't be attacked by animals. And I have enough of the plant to last me a lengthy time. So I'll continue to ingest it and keep myself in this state as long as I can.

I stand up, and they all look at me.

Stop.

The world is sucked free of noise, all in a blink. Everyone and everything stops — the trees, the camp, the universe. I step out of the way and off to the side before changing things.

Reverse, reverse, reverse.

My team disappears, walking backwards into the bushes we just came from.

Faster. Dammit. I want to see the sun.

The sky lightens after a few breaths, and the sun climbs back up overhead. I wait until it's midday, and then slow time to a stop again.

Okay. Time to hike. Now that I can see where I'm going, and nothing is moving, I should be okay. I remember how we got here, and our camp is not that far. I just need to put one foot in front of the other.

It's super strange traversing the jungle when it's still. I pass birds in mid-flight, insects hovering in the air, and a snake on its way up a tree. Eek. I don't even want to think of them in the trees at all.

As long as I have the plant in me, I have all the time in the world. To keep its magic in my bloodstream, I eat another as I draw closer to camp. As I suspected, I feel pretty good while eating the plant. It gives me energy and removes any leftover pain from my previous jaunt through the jungle.

Luca and his men are doing their usual thing when I arrive. They have their own operations tent so I head straight there. Glancing at the clock on the wall, it's a little after lunchtime.

Start time again.

"Ah!" Luca cries out and jumps away from me. "Jesus, Skylar. Are you part ninja or something? I didn't see you there."

"I wasn't here," I say and shake my head with a smile. "We're going on a mission later to fix a few things. I'm going to need to jam their guns."

"Whose?"

"The military."

Luca pauses. "I don't get it."

"Try not to think too hard." Holding back a laugh is tough. "I need something that I can put in their guns so they jam. Sorry. I know little about weapons, so I'm not sure what to ask for."

They all stare at me for a long moment. Hello! Snap out of it!

"The training rounds, sir," one guy says. "We can load up some magazines with a few of them. That'll jam them, assuming you remember what they were carrying."

"Sure. Yeah. I do." Luca scratches his head. He's definitely thinking too hard.

"Great. Perfect. You go do that." I clap my hands at them. "Chop, chop. I haven't got all day."

I actually do, come to think of it.

"Boss?" the one guy asks, but Luca waves them off, so they leave.

"Are you...? Um, what?" Luca asks, rubbing at his chin's stubble.

"Like I said. Don't ask and don't think about it. It'll all make sense in a few hours. I promise. I'm going to wait outside."

With me out of eyesight, I speed up time by twenty minutes when I notice the men returning. They drop several magazines into my hands.

"Just swap these out for whatever they're using. That should do the trick."

"Thanks. I'll see you guys later."

"Uh, sure. See you then, Ms. Skylar." They wave as they walk off. I put the magazines in my pockets, my bra, my waistband, wherever I can fit them, eat some more of my plant, slow down time again, and head back to the military camp.

Returning is much easier now that I've walked the same way twice. I keep a brisk pace and my eyes on the path. With nothing but me moving in time, though, I'm better able to hear my own thoughts and relive my past errors. I'm already sick of my mistakes lately. Ugh. They tumble in my head, over and over.

I really lost it last night, and the shame of my breakdown in front of the guys coats me from head to toe. I'm not supposed to doubt my own memories, and every time I do, it will introduce more doubts into my relationships, too. It's so hard to stay strong and resilient when it's me against the universe. I'm the only one who experienced these things. A few others witnessed them, but they're not coming to my rescue. It's only me.

How can I possibly win?

My mind is wandering all over the place — from my breakdown to the space probe to sex — by the time I return to the military camp.

Okay, time to get back to work. I eat more of the plant

again, in case my increased activity caused it to metabolize faster, and I find the armory. Picking a spot behind a tree on the outside of the fence, I reverse time and speed it up to see what happens.

I shield my eyes as I go through night and day again. I'm starting to get a headache, so I hope that's normal. My stomach hollows out, so hungry it could eat itself. I watch the armory become a hive of activity for a short while, then soldiers leave it in reverse. While they're gone, people come and go from the labs and the mess tent and the infirmary. Everything looks like an ordinary day in military land.

I have to go farther back. Reverse, reverse… and here! It's morning, and the men return to the armory, leave behind their guns, and then retreat to the mess tent.

Pause.

I test out the jungle; nothing is moving. I walk over in front of the guard standing next to the gate. He's frozen still. Good. I sneak past him and inside, heading right for the armory. The soldiers are standing guard as I enter the building.

I gasp. Oh shit.

It's Nina Correa, Gus's mom. She's sitting at a desk, her eyes trained on her datapad. She was the one who got the Amagi hijacked a few years ago, and it ended up a skeleton on Neve. My blood boils for a brief moment before I examine her closely. She's hardly the person she was years ago. She's gaunt, her skin pale and gray. Her blond hair is in a limp ponytail, and she's lost a lot of weight. The military put her in prison for a few years after the stunt she pulled on Neve, helping us out on the military base. What's she doing out? She doesn't look happy.

I ignore her for a moment and hide behind a nearby cargo carrier. Speeding up time, I watch to see where the men get their guns and ammunition. The door opens, and the men come in. Nina stands up.

"Is everything set?" one man asks Nina.

She nods. "We sent someone back and got intel on when the blockade runner will return with the Kawabata woman."

I blink my eyes a few times at 'Kawabata woman.' Obviously, that's me, and she knows who I am. Why won't she call me by my first name? Too informal?

"Remember, this is a snatch and grab. Do not, under any circumstances, shoot to kill or even wound them. You need to take her into custody and bring her back here."

The man nods. "Yes, Ms. Correa."

I wince. Ouch. The military stripped Nina of her rank. No more Commander Correa. I edge to the side, and, yeah, she's wearing civilian clothes. What the hell is going on? She must have made some kind of bargain with the military to get out of jail. What was it?

The men grab guns and ammo from a locker on the far wall, so I stop time again, run it backwards and freeze once they're outside. Nina has her feet propped up at the desk, reading from her datapad, like before.

I cross to the armory closet and open the doors. I take out all the magazines and replace them with the ones I'm carrying in my pockets, my bra, and my waistband. Carefully, I arrange everything like it was before and close the closet door, making sure it looks exactly the same. I grab an empty bag, place the military's magazines in it, cinch it up tight, and leave it in a different locker.

But when I turn to face Nina, I get an idea. I need to leave her a note. She looks unhappy, and if she's working for the military out of spite, then maybe we can convince her to become an ally. There is a stack of paper on the desk and pens, and it makes me chuckle. Only the military uses paper anymore because they like the impermanence of it. Once something is on the duonet, it's there forever.

I grab a piece of paper and a pen, and I write, "Meet me on Laguna in five days. You know where. Skylar." I fold it up in little squares and slip it into the pocket on the shirt she's wearing.

I turn to leave, and once my back is turned, my skin prickles.

"Skylar."

I jump and whirl around. The voice was definitely Nina's, but she's still frozen in time where I left her. What the fuck? I stare at her for a long few breaths, but nothing happens.

Maybe I imagined it. Move on, Skylar.

Get going!

Leaving the armory, I stride across the grass, find an interesting looking bush on the outskirts of the military compound and strip its leaves until I have an armful of them. Getting them into the water supply is a pain, and I'm sweating buckets by the time it's over. I've lived three days in the last several hours. I hope there's a nap in my future.

Outside of the camp, I find a sheltered place close to where I left everyone, and speed time back up again until my team enters the area. Watching myself gives me the chills, and then I blink out.

"Shhh, it's me," I say, approaching them crouched down. "It worked."

"But..." Saif points to where I just was. "How...?"

"It's a mind-trip. Don't ask."

"Shit. That's weird," Luca says, shaking his head. "I now remember you asking for the ammunition. I... I..." He stumbles, looking for the right words, but it's impossible.

"Once the timeline changes, it's hard to remember it like it was before," I tell him. I look at the fence and notice it's not being watched anymore. "Where's the guard?"

"Ran for the bathroom about five minutes ago, remember?" Kalvin asks.

I close my eyes and see the two timelines. The newest one includes the intestinal distress of the guards. Sorry, not sorry.

"I do now." My stomach growls, and hunger surges up. I'm suddenly starving.

"Wow, time travel really works?" Saif's eyes are eager.

"Yeah. Can we leave now? I just walked back and forth from here, and I'm dying to eat."

"Dinner's on me," Luca says with a smile.

I leave while keeping the camp in my sights. Time travel, Nina Correa, the end of the military, and now a promise to meet on Laguna in five days — there's too much here to ignore.

But, oh, so much here to take advantage of.

32

"I COULD GET USED TO THIS," I say, sipping a glass of champagne and leaning back into Saif's arms. I prop my feet up on Kalvin's lap, and he rests his hands on my ankles. I'd love a foot massage, but my feet are still pretty banged up from the last few days in the jungle.

It's nice being back on my ship, in my home. Now that India knows we're being spied on and she can't stop it, her wilderness operation is toast. She'll follow Takemo's suggestion of a guarded lab in the city and just send strike teams into the jungle.

"I think you *should* get used to this," Saif says, leaning down to kiss me on the cheek. "It looks like your days in the jungle are over."

I shake my head, sip, and set the glass down. "No. I have a feeling the Rio jungles are a permanent fixture in my life. I'll be back there before long. You'll see."

I lean forward and look at the spread that Lia put together for us. It's downright luxurious, with smoked meats and printed proteins (always for Saif), decadent cheese, nuts, crusty bread, and bean spreads. I think I'll start with a giant tower of crackers, meat, and cheese.

Marcelo ambles his way into the common room, and I compose myself a little, pulling my feet off Kalvin's lap and sitting up straight.

"Hello, everyone. Well, look at this beautiful spread. Lia?"

"Yep."

Marcelo nods, impressed. He must be gathering data for when he matches Lia to her network. "May I?"

"Of course," I say, waving to the seat across from us. "You should have some champagne, too."

"Absolutely," Saif says, pouring Marcelo a glass.

He tops up all the glasses, and we raise them in a toast.

"To new beginnings," Marcelo says.

"I like it." I bring my glass in to match the rest and sip. "And speaking of, I set our departure time for three hours from now. First, we're going to hit Ossun to talk to Vivian and Renata. Then we're off to Laguna for a little relaxation."

"I'm glad the plans are set," Marcelo says, crossing his legs and leaning back. "The potential match I have for you, the one I've been talking to, will be on Laguna for the next month. We have fortuitous timing."

I raise my eyebrows at him, but he demurs. "You know, I have learned quite a lot about you, Ms. Skylar, in the last few years, and one thing I know for certain. You like surprises."

"Well..." I start, but he cuts me off with an open hand.

"You like fun and exciting but not life-threatening surprises," he amends.

"Okay, I will agree with that." I look left and right at Saif and Kalvin on either side of me. "Another network mate to vet. How do we feel about that?"

"Sky, this is *your* decision. Not ours," Saif reminds me. I shake my head.

"No. It's both mine and ours." I poke myself in the chest. "I determine whether I'm compatible with him, on a platonic or romantic level, and then, if I like him, he'll need to pass your muster."

"We get to muster?" Kalvin asks, leaning back. "I'm not sure if I know how to muster."

I laugh and smack him on the arm.

"You're ridiculous." I turn to Saif. "What do you think?"

He shrugs. "I like it if you like it. Shall we take this man out for drinks? Make him run naked through the streets? Have him serve you on his hands and knees?"

I turn to Marcelo. "I have added two of the strangest men to my network."

"They are unique." He raises his glass.

"Look, we will not haze anyone new," I say like I'm scolding children. "But you know, if you want to take him out for drinks and get to know him, that would be great."

"We'll see if you like him first," Kalvin says, and Saif nods in agreement.

"Okay then. I'm looking forward to meeting this new man."

Marcelo's smile is small and devious. He's up to something, but I'm not sure what.

I pluck a tiny orange off the fruit bowl and wiggle it at Kalvin.

"Want to share?"

He scoots in next to me, pressing his hip to mine.

"You mean, you're actually going to share your orange with me this time instead of just eating it seductively and then walking away?" His eyes travel down my body. "Though I do like watching you walk away."

Saif laughs. "Something tells me there's a story here."

I peel off the rind and hand a section to Kalvin.

"Thank you, gorgeous. Don't mind if I do." He pops the section into his mouth and hums. "Oh yes, there's a story here. But first, let me tell you all about our flight school rivalry."

I settle back into the couch and prepare for a harrowing story, but Nanci chimes to interrupt us.

"Skylar, I regret to inform you that your mother is at the port side airlock."

All of my good cheer evaporates away, and my shoulders sink. Funny how she couched the statement with, "I regret to inform you..."

Kalvin touches my knee, and I jump.

"Ah, shit," he says, closing his eyes. "We just got you all unwound, and now you're ready to jump out of your skin again." He stands up and growls under his voice. "This woman. I'm going to tell her to leave."

"No," I say, reaching out to grab his hand. Saif and Marcelo are now on their feet. "This is my problem. I'll deal with it."

Kalvin flips my hand around and pulls me to him. "This is us, right? We're going to be a real network now?" His lips hover over my palm while he looks me in the eye. I feel my face heating under Marcelo's gaze, but I can't stop it.

"Yes. For real."

He kisses my palm. "Then we'll handle it as a team." He jerks his head at Saif. "Come on. Let's back her up."

Saif's hand rests on my lower back as he ushers me from the common room, through the cargo bay, to the port side airlock. Marcelo follows at a distance, and I wish he wouldn't. He's a father figure to me now, and he is going to witness something extremely unflattering and shameful, I know it.

I sigh, and it's so bone-weary and tired that I have the intense desire to turn around, go to my room, and hide under the covers. And that is very un-Skylar-like. Usually, I come at problems head-on, sometimes too aggressively.

But this? I just want to hide.

The door cycles and swings open. I hold my breath until Mom steps into the bay.

Her eyes fall on me, and they're hard, maybe just as weary as I am.

"Skylar," she says, coming to stand opposite us. "Can I have a word with you in private?"

"Nope," Kalvin says before I can open my mouth.

"Who are you?" Mom's voice turns cold, and I already regret letting her inside.

"Kalvin Vidal, ma'am." He touches his chest. "And this is Saif Bhaat. We're Skylar's network mates."

Mom's eyebrows climb.

"So if you have something to say to her, you'll say it with us here as well, and then you will leave."

My heart lifts with pride at hearing Kalvin speak like this. At flight school, his good looks and charming smile always got him his way. But seeing his more serious side is a pleasure too. I had no idea he was so multi-faceted.

"Listen here, young man. You will not tell me what to do in my own home."

"This is not your home," Saif reminds her.

"Like hell it is." She huffs and throws her hands out. "Skylar, the Amagi was always going to be a temporary loan."

"You never said as much, and you signed the title over to me right away." I lift my chin. Show no fear, Skylar.

She smiles and waves the statement away. "A technicality. If we hadn't, then we would have been on the hook for the insurance and taxes."

"Which I paid as if this ship was my own, which it is. You can't take it back from me because I own it."

"Yes, but you were a part of the family business when it was given to you, so it was still mine."

Ah, that's the angle they're going with?

I point my finger up. "That's irrelevant. I also spent my own money and called in my own favors to put this ship back together when the military tore it apart. You stopped by during rehab, what? Once? Twice? Oh wait, you *never* stopped by. You may have followed the written reports but that was it."

Mom folds her arms over her chest. "You know, I just spent five thousand credits bailing out Dominic from jail, only to find out there's now a restraining order against him."

Thank you, Ai.

"The media practically assaulted us on our way out of the courthouse. Now everyone is going to know that our family is fighting. I'm sure you don't want that."

I press my lips together, willing myself not to comment.

"So, I have a suggestion for a compromise."

Mom smiles, and my knees shake. She sounds way too reasonable, too calculated.

"Takemo Diaz informed me this morning that I've been let go from Diaz Waste Management. They have given me severance and cut me loose." She shrugs. "It happens. I didn't like Diaz, and I figured he would fire me, eventually. But I hear that you and he are... close. So here's what I want. I'll drop this suit to get the Amagi back if you tell Takemo to return the Mikasa. We'll call it quits, fair and square."

Kalvin glances at me. He remembers overhearing my discussion with Takemo. His eyes narrow as my body heats to blinding levels.

I take a step forward, my chest heaving with heated breaths. "I told Takemo to fire you and sell the Mikasa. Your severance comes from that sale. That was *my* decision based on the treatment I have received from you and Dominic and Dad and fucking everyone who has ever abused me."

"Wait a second now —" Mom starts, but Saif steps in front of me with his hand out.

"Don't try to deny it. I saw it for myself almost twenty years ago."

This stops Mom quickly, and her face pales.

That's it. I'm done.

"You will take the severance package and figure out what to do with your life and your network. I'm no longer your daughter, period. End of story. You will not get the Amagi. You will not get the Mikasa. You will leave my ship and never speak to me again."

I point at her as my anger rushes me towards the inevitable.

"And if you drag this into a court of law, I will lay waste to you and your reputation in the court of public opinion. If you think those doctored videos Dominic has been giving to you for the last twenty years will absolve you of guilt and prove that I'm a liar, then you are mistaken. Think very hard about this before you move forward."

Silence falls on the cargo bay with only my heartbeat ringing in my ears.

"I see," Mom says, stepping back. "I was hoping you'd change your mind. Okay then. We will file the lawsuit tomorrow in Sakata City. You better get a good lawyer." She turns to walk out but stops at the door. "Dominic did what he had to do because you were out of control as a kid. I saw the videos. I know I wasn't there, that I failed you by being so absent. But Dom did not. He kept you cared for so you could grow up to betray him. I hope you live with that guilt for the rest of your life."

"If you call starving your first daughter 'caring,' I'd hate to see what punishment you held back," Kalvin says, his voice cold with hatred. Mom's eyes widen. He sweeps out his hand. "Leave now and don't come back."

"Don't call, and don't contact us," Saif fills in. "You're not welcome here ever again."

I keep my eyes trained forward as the airlock door swings closed. Once she's gone, the tears begin — hot, blistering, angry tears. No. Fuck you. Fuck this. Fuck it all.

Crossing the bay to the empty storage boxes, I growl, grab a box, and throw it at the wall. Fuck you. I kick the box, and it bounces off the wall. This inanimate object doesn't deserve my anger, but that's what it's going to get. Kick, kick, throw. I scream and rage at it, kick it again and again, until *crack!* It splits along its side. A sob bubbles up from my belly as I press the heel of my hand to my lips.

I throw my hands out to the side and scream "Fuck you!" at the ceiling before turning around to face the men.

All the anger evaporates from my body in a rush, and it leaves behind unbearable sadness. "Oh no. What have I done?" I whisper.

The guys approach me, all looking just as sad as I am. Saif grasps my upper arms.

"You did what you had to do. I'm proud of you. That wasn't easy." He pulls me forward and kisses my forehead. "We'll get by without her, and we'll figure out how to keep the Amagi. It will be okay." He looks into my face, wet with tears. "Hear me?" When I nod, he nods. "Believe it. Nothing is going to stop us now."

He hugs me, holds my head to his chest, and wraps me tight. Kalvin's arms come around from the other side, and he rests his head on my shoulder. I fight off a moment of panic, but the calm comes quicker than it ever has.

Takemo was right. I do need hugs.

"Come on now. Off to bed with you. Kalvin will fly us out of here, and we'll go back to the farm and figure this out with your actual family and friends."

Kalvin nods and kisses me on the forehead. "I promise not to crash her into the spaceport."

When I turn around to head to my room with Saif, I catch sight of Marcelo, and he has the same haunted look he had on his face when we were at Saif's parents' house.

His voice starts slowly. "I have tried to be diplomatic about this, weighing both sides of the story and giving your mother and her network the benefit of the doubt. But that?" He points at the door. "That was a bridge too far."

His chest rises and falls in heaving breaths. "You know what this means?" he asks, and a cascade of shivers drops down my back.

I shake my head, afraid of what he'll say. Marcelo has always been a gentle presence in my life. Seeing his steely expression cools me from the inside out.

"This means I get involved in a significant way. This means I call in favors and turn over every rock to find the people we need to get this taken care of."

He backs away and holds his hands out to the side.

"I'm angry, and I won't back down."

He turns back to his shuttle.

"Skylar, this means war."

* * *

Check out my website for more books like this...
http://www.spajonas.com/books

Visit via your phone, tablet, or laptop!
Use the QR code below for quick access.

THANK YOU!

Thank you for reading *A Fortunate Accident*. Skylar just barely made it out of the jungle alive. Now she's off to Laguna! We'll have to hang in there to see what happens next...

If you want the next book in the series... You can check for availability on my Books page. https://www.spajonas.com/jump/books-amagi/

Please leave a review! I would love it if you left a review of *An Unexpected Debt*. Please return to the store you bought this book from and leave your review there.

To get my email alerts about new books and other content, sign up at http://www.spajonas.com/newsletter/

You can check for more books on my website at http://www.spajonas.com/books/

BONUS CONTENT

Be sure to check my website for bonus content from this book and other books I have written. Bonus content can include deleted scenes, scenes written from other points of view, or essays about the books.

All bonus content can be found at
https://www.spajonas.com/bonus-content/

ACKNOWLEDGMENTS

Big thanks goes out to all the people who helped or inspired me with this book including...

Tracy Krimmer,
Charity Vandehey,
Germaine Fletcher,
Lola Verroen,
My mom, Claire,
My brother, Brendan,
My husband, Keith,
And my two girls, C and D.

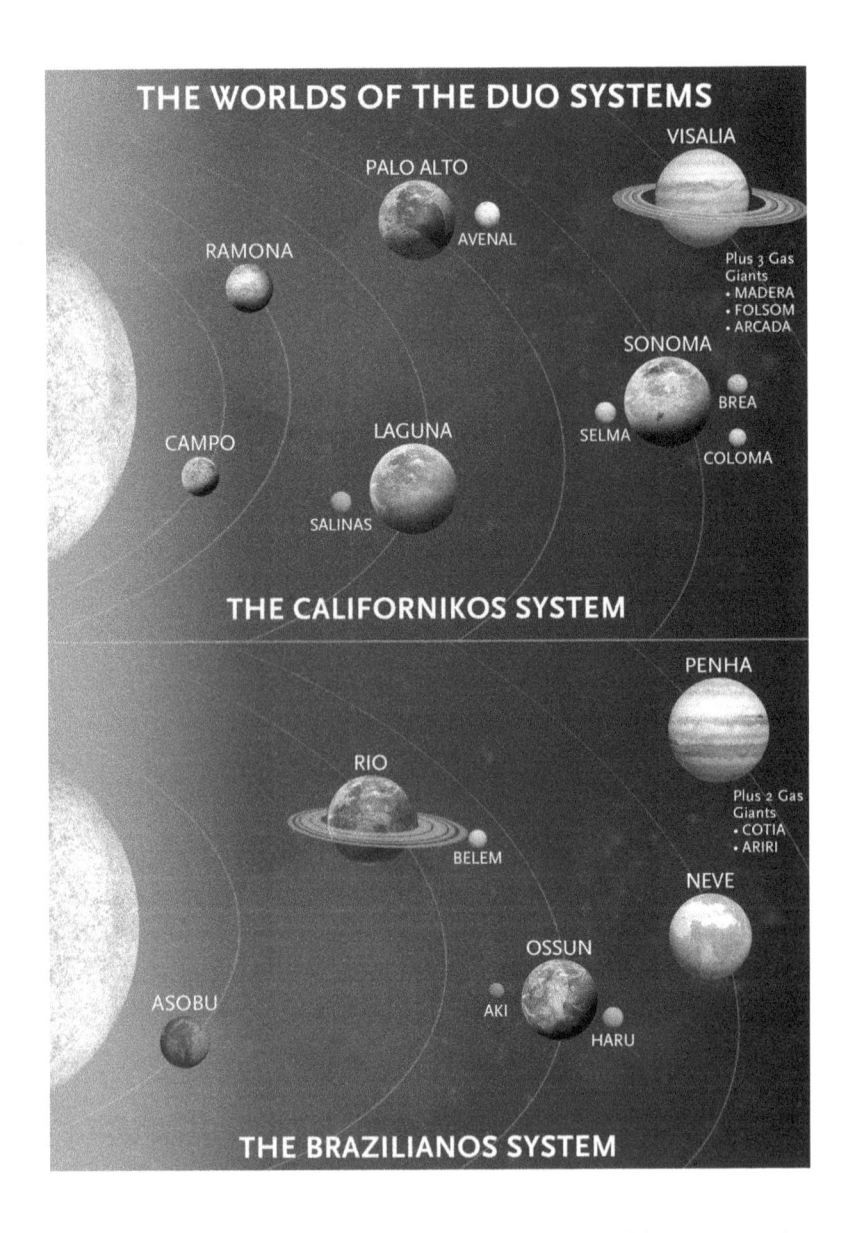

See this map bigger at https://www.spajonas.com/duo-systems/

ABOUT THE AUTHOR

Stephanie (S. J.) is a writer, knitter, Capricorn, Japanophile, and USA Today Best Selling author. She loves summer, downtempo beats, yoga pants, foxes, owls, dogs, sushi, pasta, and black tea. She lives outside NYC with her husband, two great kids, and her dog who always wants to play. When it comes to her work, she writes about everyday women and uncommon worlds.

Find her online at...
www.spajonas.com

faccbook.com/SJPajonas
instagram.com/spajonas
bookbub.com/authors/s-j-pajonas